BILL JAMES is a pseudonym. In addition to the Detective Chief Superintendent Colin Harpur series, the author has written numerous espionage and crime novels as David Craig. One of these, *Whose Little Girl Are You?*, was filmed by Warner Brothers as "The Squeeze." Under his own name, James Tucker, he is also the author of a critical study of the novelist, Anthony Powell.

Mr. James was a reporter with the *Daily Mirror* in London after serving as a Flying Officer in the R.A.F. He has subsequently written for *The Spectator*, *Punch*, *The New Statesman*, and other publications. He is married, with four children, and lives in South Wales.

Take

Bill James

Take

A Foul Play Press Book

The Countryman Press
Woodstock, Vermont

This edition published in 1994 by Foul Play Press, an imprint of
The Countryman Press, Inc., Woodstock, Vermont 05091

Library of Congress Cataloging-in-Publication Data
James, Bill, 1929
Take / Bill james.
P. cm. — (Detective chief superintendent Colin Harpur novels)
"Foul play press book."
ISBN 0-88150-294-4: $20.00
1. Harpur, Colin (Fictitious character)—Fiction.
2. Police—England—Fiction.
I. Title.   II. Series: James, Bill, 1929—
Detective chief superintendent Colin Harpur novels.
PR6070.U23T34   1994
823'.914—dc20   94-1299   CIP

10 9 8 7 6 5 4 3 2 1

Printed in the United States of America
by Quebecor Printing Book Press, Inc.

I have been young
Book of Common Prayer

Chapter 1

'Keep driving, not too fast. No stopping. Well, I'm recognisable, aren't I? Someone like Harpur get the word I been around here once or twice lately and we're . . . So keep driving. Just around the block, Tyrone, and then around again, etcetera.' Preston sat as low as he could in the back of the car.

On the third circuit they were able to watch the money van pull up and check in at the gatehouse, then go on to the pay office. That was where the job had to be done, when the crew opened up the van and started bringing the bags out. There was a gate to go with the gatehouse, but it never seemed closed.

'Always the same driver – must be getting on for sixty, poor old lump,' Preston said. 'Older than me even, and not so fit. Guard changes weekly. Younger. Heroic?'

'Seventy thousand? Never more than that, Ron? Not more noughts on the end?'

Preston laughed: 'Hark at him, will you? You saying that's small-time, Dean?'

They turned the corner. 'Round once more, Tyrone,' Preston told him.

Dean Tait said: 'Ron, I just meant—'

'Most times you're taking stuff not even into double figures. Pensioners' handbags, or some nothing burger stall. So, yes, always about seventy thou. Payroll. What I've learned is there's high-fly dreams and there's availability. This is availability.'

'Seventy split four ways can't sound too great,' Dean Tait said.

'If you like, you can walk away now, Dean. We'll trust you. You'd keep quiet.'

When they came around the block again, the van was past the gatehouse and into the yard.

Preston said: 'So, three weeks today.'

Tait said: 'What I mean—'

'And, look, not a four-way split. I told you. You and Tyrone – Jesus, sorry, Tyrone, but I mean, what a name, where's it come from, off of a disinfectant bottle, or what? – you and Tyrone, you're new yet. You come in at seven grand each—'

'There should be negotiations, Ron,' Dean declared.

'Meaning twenty-eight each for me and Mansel here. That's up on what we thought first, which was five for you and Tyrone.'

'You need to understand, this job, it belongs to me and Ron,' Mansel explained, nice and gently. Often he tried for that style. 'You're just hired, you two.'

'Christ, but Tyrone! That Scottish or something?' Preston asked. 'Manse and me, we got others to maintain, not like you two, sauntering free. Great days, but they change. Now, I got a daughter and a very lovely wife, Doris, who've seen me through I don't know how long, so loyal, and I like to spend on her. And then the other, down Devon, I expect you heard of. A kid there, too. Lovely youngster I can't see enough of. Mansel? He's got a sick mother who needs the best. Responsibilities.'

'Round again, Ron?' Tyrone Gullen said.

'No. Nothing more to see. Home now. These are commitments, Dean. Health insurance, school fees in Devon – the sort she is. Plus myself. Hair transplant? She in Devon's fussy about how I look. Well, she's a lot younger. There's others eyeing her.'

'It all needs thinking about,' Mansel remarked.

Preston said: 'Payrolls in cash are scarce. Most using cheques now. And this one's so easy. That driver, sixty or even more. He move fast, his heart's going to start asking serious questions. The guard? Well, they both got sticks, but I ask you, against what we're going to be carrying? And then the lad in the gatehouse. He'll try and get to his panic button, so we got to be quick, that would be your side of it, Dean, if you're in.'

'Seven grand. You could turn milord for weeks on that, Dean,' Manse Billings said. 'Get down the Mediterranean or have them fucking horrible tattoos cleaned off. So common.'

'I don't take no offence,' Preston said. 'It's youth. Look, we're going to need at least two more meetings before – get the moves exact, timing and that—'

'And taking cars,' Billings said.

'Of course. Then the armament. I'll have to bring that for

sharing out. You thought of that cost? Early next week. I'll be in touch with Mansel. We meet regular. No phoning to us.'

They drove on to the Ernest Bevin estate.

'Put me down a few streets away, Tyrone. I'll walk. Better like that now. Normal, I'd ask you all in for a cuppa, but better like this now. There's eyes.'

The thing was, he did not want that Dean in his place, not just now. Dean was just the sort girls would go big for, no question, but Dean was not the sort he wanted for Grace. Tyrone she would probably say was a yawn, or worse – too quiet and those square-frame glasses and the denim, like some shop boy off duty. But Dean, with the suit and the all-colour, insect, wrist tattoos, and the slip-ons, that might be her language. She was starting to come alive to that sort of thing. What was not wanted now was a tie-up for her with somebody like Dean, because Preston's idea was that Dean would not be around long, one way or the other, and Grace would be no good at all as a sort of widow. She was a kid who felt suffering very deep, too sensitive, really. That would really set her back, if someone she thought a bit about got blasted, and Dean was right in the frame. Preston had seen too many like that before. They didn't look for trouble, but they didn't look to keep out of trouble, either, and it came right on time to find them.

When he reached the house, he went in through the kitchen door and found Grace helping Doris with her hair, getting it into a pony-tail. Doris had on her gear for the *Annie Get Your Gun* show at Troy Hall and the pony-tail was for that as well. Doris was very keen on the dramatics, especially musical. She had a bit of a voice. He wished she wouldn't do it. He didn't like any kind of show. He liked to lie quite, out of the light, until you had to make the move. Then quiet again until next time. But Doris was different and always had been, and no good trying to change her. You didn't get married to make the woman different from the one you picked. Where was the sense? He always went when Doris was on, sometimes twice or three times if the tickets were sticking. It wasn't too bad. She liked to see him there and he always kept awake and kept half a smile on to show he loved it. Once you been inside you knew how to make your face show whatever was suitable. It was not just the people on the stage who knew about acting. Some of these musicals had one or two quite decent songs from way back.

9

'Just seeing how I'm going to look, Ron,' she said.

'Well, great, of course. Real great.'

'Yes, she does, doesn't she, Dad?'

'Starts Saturday week you know,' Doris said.

He laughed and kissed her on the cheek. 'How many times you told me, Dot?'

'Well, I'm edgy.'

'She'll be great, won't she, Dad?'

'Great. Look, they all get nerves, Dot: Marilyn Monroe, Sir Richard Attenborough was it, when he was Gandhi: well, having to wear a loin-cloth in a picture that went on so long.'

He didn't like nerves, either, but found as he grew older they took a harder hold every time.

'Wilf's here,' Doris said.

'Wilf Rudd? Here?'

'In the lounge.'

'He's edgy, too, you ask me,' Grace said.

'Oh, poor thing. He knows he's not supposed to come here, but I think it's important,' Doris said. 'Something up, Ron?'

'Well, something, yes. On the cards.'

'Looks as if he's got a message, then,' Doris told him. 'Now, go easy with Wilf. He wouldn't risk it if it wasn't urgent, would he?' She stood up. 'How do I look, Ron?'

'Great.'

'I'll have some orange make-up on, of course, for the Ohio sun.' She pirouetted slowly.

'Really great. I can't wait,' he said.

She sang a scale up and down. 'It's no great part. A few years younger . . . all right, a good few . . . I could have done Annie.' She began really to belt into a number he knew and liked, 'Doin' What Comes Natur'lly'.

The door from the lounge opened and he saw Wilf Rudd standing there, holding a can of lager and smiling a bit to look as if he was enjoying the singing and the costume but really in a full sweat, you could see. Wilf had never been inside, so he did not know too much about acting. Today, although it was summer and hot, he had on that anorak that went through the siege of Stalingrad and the heavy duty brown trousers. He stared at Preston, trying to signal trouble, and doing it bloody well, too, but Preston had joined in the song at the words about reading the

10

good Book from Fri till Monday and wanted to wait until Doris had finished. Wilf was all right, but you had to give your wife some solidarity, and you couldn't let someone's nerves like Wilf's get to Doris when she was tense already because of the play.

'I like it,' Rudd shouted, when the number ended. 'I'll be there. I've got tickets. Maybe I'll come twice.' He held up the lager can and toasted Doris. It was a pretty good show, when you thought how bad he was.

'You've forgotten this, Mum,' Grace said. She waved a holster with toy pistol in it.

'Oh, yes, we'll all be wearing guns, in keeping,' Doris said. Grace strapped it on.

'Looking frightening,' Preston told her.

Rudd said: 'Ron, could we go into the . . . ?' He swung his eyes towards the lounge.

'What's it about, Wilf? It's all right here. Doris and Grace – they understand about business. You can't run a house any other way.'

'Well, great,' Rudd said, but he didn't sound too sure.

'Yes, it's all right,' Preston told him. 'Have a seat.'

Wilf was small, but healthy-looking, with very fair hair, and good on his feet, like a school kid waiting to be discovered by Manchester United. 'I didn't want to come here, but how else, Ron?' Rudd said. 'The phone – well, that's crazy. And I didn't know if I'd bump into you down the town, not in time.'

'It's all right, Wilf,' Preston told him.

'So, I didn't come in the motor. You don't want that parked anywhere near. Bus and walk. I'm careful, Ron. Who wants to bring trouble to somebody's lovely home, and such matters as family?'

'Thanks, Wilf.'

'He came through the lanes and then in the back door,' Grace said. 'Wilf's a gem.'

Rudd said: 'Well, this street – I mean, no getting away from it, it's known. People like that big cop, that Harpur—'

'Oh, Harpur,' Doris muttered, trying to get the holster to lie more comfortably on her hip, 'Harpur's kids are in *Annie*, as a matter of fact. Girls. People say they're all right.'

'Harpur's kids?' Rudd said. He looked shocked.

'One's called Hazel. I ask you, Hazel. She won't thank him

11

for that when she's a bit older. He comes to pick them up from rehearsals sometimes,' Doris replied. 'Big blond character? Stroppy-looking. Or sometimes his wife comes.'

Rudd said: 'Well, I mean, Ron, is that—'

'We can't live in a vacuum, can we, Wilf? Doris can't do that. She's got her life. We're part of the community. So is Harpur and his lot. How were we to know? What's a couple of kids, anyway? You and me, we won't talk when we're there, and not sit close in the audience, obviously. It will be all right.'

Rudd took a drink. 'Well, yes. Seems funny, that's all.'

'I haven't even talked to them – the kids. No need,' Doris told him. 'Nor the parents, naturally. The wife seems all right. Gushy? Big on the community and participation and litter and such, I should think, by the look and sound. How's that, Grace?' Doris had the gun as she wanted it now. She put on a stetson and tightened the lace under her chin. Then she began to sing the same number again and they all joined in this time. Preston made tea in mugs.

At the end of the song, Rudd said: 'Grand, Doris, I wouldn't be surprised the West End.' He had sat down at the end of the kitchen table, the can in front of him.

Preston gave the teas to the other two and had one himself. 'Why not take your coat off, Wilf?' But maybe it would not stand too much sudden activity. Anyway, he did unzip the anorak. The sweater underneath was just as grim, probably used for cleaning Arnold Palmer's cups until it got too bad.

Then he blurted his piece: 'For some reason, don't ask me, they're putting three men with the van starting as of now, Ron. That's the long and short of it.'

Preston set the mug down with a bang on the table. 'This I don't like.'

'Three men not two?' Doris asked. She was setting up an ironing board near Rudd and began to do some shirts, the Wild West hat hanging behind her head now.

'It's not just three for two,' Preston said. 'It goes beyond. It's what it could signify, isn't it?'

'You mean why do it just at this moment?' Doris asked. 'This is close to the time of a job? You're saying, what do they know, Ron?'

'Well, of course. Yes, very close to the time of a job.'

'I think of you boys,' Rudd said. 'Of course, I got a stake in it, too, but most I'm thinking of you boys, Ron. Mansel, and so on, whoever.'

'It's good of you, Wilf.'

'So, why do they say they're changing to three?' Doris asked. 'What's the story?'

Wilf raised his hands to show he was helpless. 'Look, Doris, I know I work for Safemove, but I don't get told anything, not official. I'm only working in the canteen. It's what I pick up from chat – drivers, people in the office.'

'We understand that, Wilf,' Preston said. God, what sort sat down in a canteen that let Wilf near the grub?

'It could be rumour then,' Doris said.

Rudd nodded. 'Well, it could, yes. But rumour, that's all there is to go on, sometimes. What we call it is "pointers", Doris, or "information". Ron's sort of business depends on that. With us, we don't have official announcements from Number Ten Downing Street.'

'It could change the picture, no question,' Preston said. 'What I've got at present is four of us looking at this, and one of them could be touch and go – arguing about how it's going to be run. You know the sort, Wilf. If he hears there's an extra I don't know where we might be. And you know my rule – I don't move unless we got one to one, at least.'

'I realise that, Ron. Why I came fast,' Rudd said. He shook his head to show the worry.

'Never less than one to one. There's our driver who's out of things, anyway, just waiting in the vehicle, then two of us for the two in the van, and one for the lad in the gatehouse. If they got extra we're right off balance. You start cutting down on manpower and you could be into a situation where you got to use the weaponry, I mean really use it, not just for frighteners, and I keep away from that, if I can. Guns are great, a treat, but only inside limits. Well, it's like NATO. Deterrence.'

'What, you think they've picked up some sort of tip, Dad?' Grace asked.

Preston watched Wilf turn to stare at her. 'What? What you saying, Grace?' Wilf was snarling a bit, like a child given a short ration of rusks. 'What tip? Listen, Grace, they don't learn anything from me, if that's what you're saying. Any information, it flows one way and one way only, that's me to your dad, and not vice versa. This is well established. Ron knows he can trust me.'

Grace was sitting close to him at the table and leaned over and squeezed his arm. She was young but had learned a little bit about managing men. 'You don't have to tell me all that, Wilf. I know it's not from you.'

Rudd said: 'The tone. I just didn't like it, not one bit, Grace.'

'Hey, easy, you scare everyone when you get angry, Wilf,' Preston told him.

'Too right,' Grace said. 'But, no, what I mean, some tip from somewhere. I mean, what else?'

'Are they carrying extra money?' Doris asked.

'Nobody said that,' Rudd replied.

'I mean, maybe suddenly doing two or three calls instead of one – payroll for several firms?'

'Not that I heard,' Rudd said. He went relaxed again, or as near as he ever got, that little bush-baby face trying to look bright now, not angry. 'The drivers would talk about new schedules.'

'If it's some tip, it won't be just an extra guard,' Preston told them. 'That's obvious. The law's going to be there, aplenty, and tooled up if the tip's a real one. I don't know where it would come from.'

'That's what I thought, Ron. Marksmen. Why you ought to know fast,' Rudd said. 'Am I going to leak so the law can set you up for targets in front of their top boys, like that Cotton, for Christ's sake? You thought out what you're suggesting, Grace?'

She ignored him. 'So are you going to call it off, Dad?' she asked. 'Wait for a softer touch?'

'Call it off?' Preston said. 'Well, it's on the cards, got to be. What I like dealing with is—'

'Availability,' Doris said.

'Yes, availability. I'm not ashamed of that. Anything else is crazy. If I was meant to be a kamikaze pilot I'd have been born a Jap. All of a sudden, this job is not availability.'

Doris, finishing the shirts, said: 'Can't you bring in someone else? You've got all sorts on your books, Ron. The point is, it could be extra money, maybe even double money or triple, explaining the extra security. Not certain, but it could be. It could still be something they're handling themselves, no police. In which case, it could be a very big chance, Ron.'

'Double? Triple?' Preston replied. 'I don't like fat dreams – these big-time tickles. We've got an objective here, and we know what it is, the size, the timing, the whole thing. Changes make me nervous.'

Doris said: 'Yes, but if you had a bit of extra help . . .'

Rudd sucked at the empty can while he got his words together. 'Pity, but I can't take any part in it myself. I'm working for the delivery firm. First thing the police will be looking for anyway is an inside link. I've got to stay right out. Coming here's bad enough. Harpur – he's got eyes, that one.'

Preston replied straight off: 'We appreciate that, Wilf. You've done your whack – the intelligence. That's what we live by.' God, imagine taking Wilf on an outing. 'Well, yes, there are other boys who could be available. But not much time. Anybody new's got to be put in the picture, and properly, or you're asking for crack-up mistakes again. People with guns, you got to know how they'll behave.'

'Postpone, then,' Doris said. 'We need the cash so badly?'

'Postpone it to bring in somebody new and you can lose some of the people you already got,' Preston explained. 'I said, it's already dodgy with one, a good one. He might say, Well bugger it, and move off where he wants to go anyway, you ask me, that's London, and look for bigger things. Boys like him, they think it's a sort of come-down to work here. Noddyland. They're costing it out continuous – time, overheads, cash-flow.'

Wilf said: 'In any case, if the law's involved—'

'Oh, if the law's involved, if there's been a tip, well it's off, that's obvious.' Preston said. 'I'm not taking on Harpur and a string of snipers in a trap. Pick us up off the ground after and tear along the dotted line. Okay, throaty outcries from MPs and what have you about the shoot-out, but I wouldn't be able to pay attention, would I, cut in half?'

Doris argued: 'All the same, Ron, a multiplication by three is—'

Preston said: 'Mansel does quite good for whispers from inside the law when they got something juicy on the menu, ambush, anything like that, lined up, and we haven't heard a murmur from that direction yet about this. I'll put out a feeler now you've told me, Wilf, but I think his source would have got

15

to him already if he knew something. I mean, this is flesh and blood – bodies in the street.'

'Why I came myself,' Rudd commented.

Wilf liked to keep on and make sure you understood what he was getting at, just like a kid. He expected to get paid something whether it happened or not. Ten per cent of sod all was sod all, and he thought he should do better, in view of all the communication. You could understand, what with his tailor's bill.

'I've been working on this an age,' Preston said. 'It would hurt if I had to chuck it now.'

Doris said: 'Yes, Ron, but don't let pressure get to you.'

'A minute ago you were saying give it a try.'

'Of course. If it looks good. Only if.' She was putting the ironing board away. 'We're not up against it for cash. Decide in a nice cool, careful style. Well, like always.' She kissed him on the cheek.

'Never been chatted up by a cow-girl before,' he replied, grinning. 'Come on, Wilf. We'll go in the other room now. Leave them to their rehearsals and so on.' In the lounge, he gave Rudd another can from the sideboard.

'Doris is so great. And Grace,' Rudd said. 'In a way, it's amazing, the way you can talk in front of them.'

'It's been a long time, Wilf. A long time with Doris. You can't live in the same house as a woman all that time and keep her out of big parts of your life, can you? Would that be decent? Taking it around the other way, think of Mr Thatcher. He's got to be in on things, hasn't he? To some extent. And, then, Grace – I don't know, it just seemed natural for her to hear things.'

'Well, yes. But you're lucky. They're great, both. You couldn't do it with all women.'

'I know. Not everything, mind. Some things stay private, that's obvious.'

'Of course.'

They sat down in the big armchairs opposite each other, Preston still with his mug of tea. Wilf had that twitchy look saying he did not feel sure there would be cash in this for him now, because of developments. The lager could not bring enough blot-out and comfort yet. 'They can't know the whole picture about the money, Wilf. I was scared you might say something.'

'No, never, Ron. I can see the situation, can't I?'

'They'll do really well out of it, but it's still confidential.'

'Unavoidable.'

'Some of that money will go to Devon.'

'Obvious.'

'I don't want to have to account for every penny, do I, here?'

'Can't.'

'Devon costs me a lot, Wilf. It's worth it over and over: warm and humorous and really loving, but it's a lot of outlay. She deserves it, and the kid. Nice clothes, even down there they cost. Ilfracombe, some nothing boutique with kids serving who talk like scrumpy – but you'd think it was Mayfair for prices.'

'Fashion, it's just not around on the cheap these days. Who wants a woman looking like Oxfam?'

'Right. You're lucky you've only got yourself to think about, Wilf. Well, lucky in a way. But I wouldn't like to be on my own. I couldn't take that. Yes, the money goes: this place – Doris and Grace, I mean, a girl that age still a student, it costs.'

'You're good to them, Ron.'

'And then Devon on top. What it adds up to is I got to multiply everything by two.'

'It's a problem.'

'And Doris and Grace don't know all the other details, either, not timing or exactly where. It could worry, couldn't it? Or, again, one day some of Harpur's heavies could start leaning on them.'

'Exactly.'

Preston said: 'Not even all the boys in the team know all the money details, as a matter of fact. It's difficult. I tell them seventy, seventy-two.'

Rudd giggled. 'More like eighty-odd.'

'But we got to get your percentage out, Wilf, haven't we? This one, the one I'm thinking about, called Dean, he could turn difficult about that – if I'm taking a big slice out before the cut. These are London people. They heard about the bottom line.'

'He's a cheeky bastard this one, then? I mean, Ron, this job, it can't even start without me.' Wilf went into a fighting mood, that little voice very sharp and hurt. 'Is he saying I don't have rights?'

'He doesn't know about you, Wilf. He knows there's infor-mation, sure, but not about how or where. And he won't, don't worry. Well, of course you earned your share. It's just they're boys from outside. Big expectations.'

'So it could be dicey when you make the cut? They're watching the count. I know guys like that. Eyes like casino inspectors.'

'Don't worry. Ten grand comes out before they even get a sight of it. Not just you. There could be this police contact of Mansel's now as well to be taken care of. He's an investment, too. All sorts of costs.'

'Of course. But I still say you better be careful, Ron. Some of these kids – well, they're wild, they're not like the old days. Savages. In made-to-measure suits, but they're savages.'

'Don't worry. I can handle this one.'

'So you think you'll do it, I mean, regardless – the extra guard?'

'We'll ask some questions, but discreet. See if there's any feedback. And you, Wilf – you listen out, especially about whether this is the law working with them. What we're talking about is a possible dead-eye ambush, simple as that. They mutter "Armed police" into their flak jackets a couple of times, and then it's like the end of *Bonnie and Clyde*. Blitz. It's immediate, you said, when they start increasing the guard? But we're not due to move for three weeks. So maybe it doesn't mean anything. Just coincidence. But maybe, too, that's what they want us to think.'

'Yes. Why I came here right away, Ron.'

'What you've got is judgment, Wilf.'

'Not much call for that in canteen work.'

Chapter 2

Preston found that the officer Mansel knew was into high-class cookery. Two nights a week he moonlighted as chef at a smart restaurant in a rough street behind Valencia Esplanade, the kind of place people liked to drive to from decent areas because it was an adventure, and they thought the food had to be more Continental because of all the whores and pimps and stereo thieves hanging about outside. The place's name was The Calaboose, jokey, meaning jail, but most locals called it Wankers, after the clients. The policeman, Barry Leckwith, had a desk job, not shifts, so he could take the same nights for cookery every week and Mansel said the easiest way to reach him was to go and wait in a service lane at the back of Wankers until he came out for a break and a smoke when the big gut-stuffing rush was over. Leckwith obliged now and then with a disclosure about what his bosses were thinking and doing, but he was definitely not somebody who could be rung up at work in the nick or at the restaurant – nor even at home, because he lived with his old mother who became very agitated if the phone went off deep into the night, say after eight-thirty p.m., and might swallow her false teeth. Mansel had an old mother, too, so he felt sympathetic, though his mother was in a residential home now. He could get touchy about that.

They hung about in the dark near some big waste bins that stank the way only the very best scrapings could stink, kicking at cats, and a couple of times pulling high quality fish skeletons and other remains off their shoes. When anybody came out to throw more stuff in they kept back in the shadows. That was not something Leckwith did because, being a chef, he had rank. Mansel said he was out of this world for veal. He had this from real eaters.

Although they were here, Mansel had not wanted to come. You could understand it. He did not mind taking disclosures from the contact when they were offered, but he thought it best not to ask this officer about particular matters, because by asking him something you were telling him something. If this lad talked to Mansel, who knew who else he talked to, including other police? In the world, there were people who talked and people who did not talk, and people who talked could talk all round, and people who did not talk did not talk to anybody, except people they were supposed to talk to. This was the trouble with Wilf. Wilf was a talker. Wilf had rubber lips. You could not be evil about him because it was obvious you depended on people like that, and like this cop-chef, there was no getting away from it. If nobody talked there would be no work. But it was not comfortable. Mansel was right, there. He wanted to leave the arrangements stand just like they were, hope for the best, not bring in the officer, but Preston persuaded him. If you had a contact, use him. The thing about Mansel was he always looked on the bright side, right up to the moment they chalked Billings M. on the board outside his cell again.

'No,' he said, while they waited for the policeman, 'it will be okay, Ron. Cancel? You got to be joking. After all that work? So, a third guy in the van. He's not going to be armed, is he? You really think Wilf's put a word their way? Jesus. But then he comes around your house and tells you. That make sense?'

'Wilf Rudd's variable. He could tell them one day, and be sorry as hell the next. I mean, if he whispered, he'd know we could be dead and under rugs on the street three weeks from now. Wilf could get suddenly upset. He knows my family. Or then again, two payments. He collects for telling them the raid's on, and he collects from us for saying enough to make us call it off.'

'That's playing very dangerous.'

'Rudd's not a thinker. Like undeveloped? Most he can do is count, and if he's counting twice as much as he expected, he's delirious.'

'Yes, a sweetheart.'

'Or I might have it wrong. It could be like he said – a mystery. They increase the guards just because they feel like it. A fluke.'

Mansel's face lit up in the shadows. 'Yes, Ron. That's it. Something like that. Or training someone on the job. I heard somewhere that's how they start them off. Just a learner, no front-line record.'

Round about eleven-thirty Preston saw this prince of veal come out into the lane, have a stretch and light up a cigar. When he noticed Mansel he did not seem too delighted, and a bit less delighted when he saw Preston as well. 'I hear nothing but good about the meals in there, Barry,' Mansel said. 'Congrats.'

'Yes, an achievement,' Preston added.

'What the hell are you doing here, Manse?' the officer asked. 'Look, this is a bad idea, I've told you before. And two of you now.'

'This is Ron Preston, a good friend. No problem.'

'I can see it's Planner Preston, can't I? Customers park up the other end. Headlights. What am I doing talking to Mansel Billings in some dirty back lane in the middle of the night? You don't think enough, Manse.'

'You've been good to us, Barry. Often,' Mansel told him.

'No, once in a while. And when I can be good to you again I'll get in touch. That's how it works. *I* get in touch with *you*. Not coming down here.'

Preston said: 'Come on, Manse. This is getting us nowhere.'

'Right,' Barry said. He had the big white hat on and white trousers and a vest, not a mark anywhere. Hygiene must be another of his strong points, on top of veal. In the few bits of light from the kitchens he glowed like the one on TV using the right washing powder. The big hat made him look cheerful, the way chefs ought to look, but he did not sound it.

'This could be very brief, Barry.'

Barry took a long pull on the cigar, like this was his last and he would be going back in to work. Preston could understand why he did not want to hang about. This had to be very dicey for him. It was a job he should not be doing at all, and he was talking to people he should not know.

Mansel must have seen time was going, too, and just came right out with it: 'We need to know if there's something heavy lined up about three weeks from now, that's all, Barry.'

He did not answer for a while. Then he said: 'What's that supposed to mean, for God's sake? What sort of heavy? Where?'

21

'Well, robbery squad. An interception. Over-the-pavement job.'

'Over the pavement? What's that mean?'

'Armed ambush. What the Yard calls it.'

'I forgot you had day trips to London, Manse. So where, this ambush?'

That was the trouble. If you started something like this you had to tell everything. 'In the town,' Mansel said.

'Where?'

'If there was anything like that, I mean, a big posse and weapons, you'd have heard, wouldn't you, Barry – so many people in on it, and excited?'

It seemed crazy to be talking to Barry about this kind of topic in all that gear, the big hat wagging about on top of his very tall, cop body whenever he turned his bony, hard cop face. 'Three weeks?' he asked.

'Something like that,' Preston said. 'Give or take.'

A woman came out to throw some rubbish into one of the bins, and Billings and Preston turned away and stood against the lane wall, facing it. When she had gone back in, Barry said: 'Three weeks? That's a hell of a long way ahead. They wouldn't make up their party till closer the date – for security.'

Mansel said: 'Yes, but if the big boys knew. Have you had a hint at all? Harpur, Iles, any of those?'

'Harpur and the Assistant Chief don't whisper in my ear, Manse. What is it, wages?'

'Something we've been thinking over for a hell of a long time, Barry,' Preston replied. 'Now there've been some sudden changes.'

'Where in the town? Wages in cash?'

'Whether these changes were something we ought to worry about in a big way,' Preston said. 'Well, a trap.'

'So you haven't heard of any big operation?' Mansel asked.

Barry threw his cigar butt away. 'I can't help you, that's a fact. Manse, I'm never going to be able to help you on this sort of basis. You understand? If I know something, something I think's up your street, I'll get it to you. If you don't hear it's because there isn't anything, and no good coming down here. That was the arrangement, and if you want us to stay friends, stick to it.'

Mansel said: 'Listen, Barry, we've looked after you pretty good. We've got a right—'

'Oh, fuck off, Manse, will you? Looked after me pretty good! What am I doing here, kitchening two nights a week and talking on a tip, if you looked after me pretty good? You think I enjoy dishing it out to a room full of prats and twats?'

Mansel pulled back fast. 'Yes, but this is your creative side, Barry.'

'Arseholes.'

Mansel replied: 'Well, look, Barry, if you do hear—'

'If I hear what? Where's the location? What is it we're talking about?'

'Any big-time hits, Barry.'

He stood for a moment in the kitchen doorway. 'If you don't trust me, how do I look after you, Manse?'

'No, it's not that. Some things not finalised, that's all. You know the picture.'

'I'm not getting pulled into any of your cock-ups. Now, look, I've got to get back to creativity.'

Chapter 3

Preston was driving Grace to the dentist to do with an abscess, poor kid, when he realised someone might be on his tail. That sort of thing, it happened now and then. It was a trial, but something you better get used to. Every so often, somebody down there, some brass like Harpur or Harpur's crazy chieftain, ACC Desmond Iles, would find they had nothing much to do and decide that Ronny Preston was too damn quiet, so send someone up in a plain car to stick with him and see what he was thinking about, map his outings, find who he was talking to and how long it took. That was how they worked, known as policing.

They would try to stay unseen, but they must know it was a poor chance, because he and everybody else with a bit of unhappy background was always expecting something, and usually it was only a couple of kid detectives in the car who still had everything to learn. Sometimes he thought all Harpur or whoever really wanted was to put on some pressure, make him sweat, let him know they still had him on the agenda and took a bright interest in his career now he was out again. Just giving pressure and some harassing were known as policing, also.

That's what he hoped it was, anyway – just routine, nothing to do with anything particular, and especially nothing to do with the van project. A thing about being tensed up for a job was you thought everything you saw was to do with it somehow. Nothing but a kind of panic, really, and something you had to learn to sort out and fight, or you'd be so scared you would never make a move. You could get so you were always looking for signs that the opposition were just waiting for you, like that extra man Wilf Rudd said with the van. And then, if the sign came, or if you thought it did, which was just the same in this state, you would ditch everything because it looked too dicey. Pathetic. Almost always just imagination, and some of it old age.

This car behind him, a Belmont, was not bad at it, and now and then he felt unsure it was really watching him at all – some more of that imagination, maybe. A couple of times he thought it had gone, but then it turned up again in the mirror, taking things nice and easy. It stayed way back, and he could not be certain how many were in it, but he thought only one, which was not the usual. Police liked pairs so if it ever came to evidence there would be two voices doing a sweet chorus for the jury. Anyway, you could never be sure. Some could lie out on the seats and only pop up when they were needed. They loved a joke like that.

He did not recognise this Belmont, but they had all sorts, and he did not think he recognised the driver, either, and definitely not Harpur, not big enough by a yard. He watched it off and on in the mirror but on the sly. He did not want to upset Grace. She was het up enough about her mouth and swollen. She hated needles, that was the trouble. He had told her it was only a little prick and over very quick, but, of course, he knew as soon as he said it it was not the best way to explain things. But she did have a laugh, despite everything. She liked a laugh. 'Speak for yourself,' she said, even if talking hurt.

Preston just kept a steady eye in the mirror. The trouble was, when there were conversationalists like Rudd in this job, and now Mansel's kitchen cop, Barry, you wondered even more who knew what, or half knew and wanted to sniff out the rest. After all, this was about the opportunity to get your head shot off by police experts in a public thoroughfare, so you best give a bit of thought. What police did not like, what Harpur and Iles did not like, were people living on their ground who had a record of armed robbery. How they saw it, you do it once, you could do it again once you're let out. That was understandable. Well, more than understandable. Most times, like this time, it was right. They did not mind if you did it again, as long as they knew the place and time and were ready with the right people, a lot of them. Harpur, Iles, all of them at the top, always hoped to tempt you into a street contest, where you could be legally torn open by fire-power after a couple of those shouted warnings, or maybe not. They liked what they called 'settling up'.

25

The police had it very easy because when they heard a tiny murmur about somebody they knew, just a crumb of rumour, they decided right away they better find out a bit more. That's what it meant, having a record. Don't expect any such item as privacy or the quiet life once you were a dossier. But it was just the same if the police did not hear any little murmurs, because then they started fretting and wondering why the fuck not, and they came up to see what was keeping that tricky swine Planner Preston so quiet all of a sudden, unless he was sick or gone born again.

Near the park the Belmont suddenly accelerated. It still looked like only one man in it, but now the rest might suddenly sit up, grinning that top-dog way only police knew how to grin, and he would have to pull over, and watch them start turning the car inside out while they asked questions and said intimate things to Grace, abscess or not. The Belmont went outside to overtake and then Preston was shocked to see it was Tyrone at the wheel, the driver for the van job. Tyrone, smiling like Happy Snaps, signalled to him to stop and drew in himself. He walked back, that bloody denim swagger they copied from Michael Jackson, came around to Preston's window, then tried the rear door. 'Let me in, Ron, will you?'

Preston unlocked and he climbed into the back, so cool. 'Where's that car come from, Tyrone? This is a main road, for God's sake. We're on stage.'

'Only taken a couple of hours ago. It's probably not even missed yet. Rest easy. I'm going to get rid right away. This family, Ron?'

'My daughter. Grace. You can talk. Tooth trouble.'

'It'll pass, Grace. Don't fret.'

He gave her a good, very helpful smile. Yes, the denim again, and the glasses, but he seemed like somebody different, today – stronger and older and full of himself, with that 'rest easy' and 'don't fret', like some medic. 'I needed to see you, Ron. No phone, so how else?'

'You're supposed to lie low, Tyrone, until the word. That's important. That's agreed. I don't use people who can't do what's agreed. There's no knowing.'

'Tyrone?' Grace said, best she could. She had turned around to talk to him. 'That's Ireland, isn't it. A county?'

26

'This is a name that goes right back,' he said. He made it sound like he had more history than Windsor Castle.

'Talking here,' Preston said, 'I mean, you're a stranger. If I'm being watched and they see me and you, they'll—'

'You're not being watched, Ron. I had a good look around your street, a long time before you came out. That's basic.'

'You didn't say you had somebody from away working with you, Dad.'

'Best not talk, love,' Preston said. 'It's doing you no good.'

'I like it around here,' Tyrone said. 'Plenty of trees, and some space.'

'All our trees are genuine,' Preston said. 'And the space.'

'Are you from London?' Grace asked.

'Wherever there's work,' Tyrone replied.

'I love London,' Grace said. 'You know that Rock café in Piccadilly, open all hours, queuing on the pavement?'

She wanted to be in on the talk with Tyrone, that was obvious, even if today the words did give her trouble.

Tyrone said: 'I've been doing some research on this project, Ron. I need to get a personal grip on a situation.'

Now, he sounded like some big business meeting. Preston knew things could happen like this, but it was still a shock. The ones you thought would give the trouble, like Dean Tait, turned out to be no problem at all, and then somebody who seemed quiet and all nods and spectacles, like Tyrone, started acting admiral of the fleet. 'What research? All that been taken care of a long time before you even arrived.'

'Dad's a real fuss about work, Tyrone. That generation?'

'I need to drive over the actual ground a few times, get the possibilities in my head,' Tyrone said. 'The motoring's my responsibility. Once a job's under way there's not always time to think, Ron.'

'I've got street maps for you. I told you that.'

'I need the feel of the place.'

'Ugh, maps?' Grace said. 'I can never make head or tail. I'm always stopping to ask.'

'Driving around up there,' Preston said, 'it could be noticed, don't you realise? Stolen car. That number could be everywhere by now. They'd put two and two together.'

'The van had a run today,' Tyrone replied.

Preston was dazed for a moment. 'The wages van? Today? This isn't their day, not pay day.'

'It had a run.'

'What run? A delivery?'

'Three blokes up, not two.'

'Three?'

'There've been some changes, Ron. This was just good luck. I didn't know it was having a run. I was charting the roads, that's all.'

It did not matter how much Grace liked talking to Tyrone, Preston knew she would never say Wilf had already told them three. This was a sensitive kid, sensitive not just about abscesses and needles, and she could feel what a situation was and what there was no need to mention. To Tyrone she said: 'Driving's your line. You take a pride in it, anyone can see.'

'What changes?' Preston asked. 'So, three up. But something else?'

'This wasn't a delivery.'

'No. It's not the day.'

'This was a practice run.'

'Practice? Practice for what?'

'Dad, calm down. Shouting. You're the one who didn't want to draw attention.'

'It looks as if they're doing a new route, Ron.'

'Oh, they vary routes. I told you, we don't need research to tell us things we already got itemised. The route makes no difference, because we're not interested until they get to the gates and the pay office.'

'Not just varying. Going to two other factories afterwards. One called Linklater's, the other Pan Products. It looked to me that they were sorting out their best way and timing themselves.'

Astonished, Preston said: 'Two more?'

'They stopped at each place and the old guy introduces the new man to the people at the gates. He's making sure they know his face for the future. This is starting a new procedure, Ron. This is three lots of money in the van when they make their first stop, at Brand's.' He had a big smile on again. 'We're on a bonus, Ron. You've planned it better than you knew. Linklater's and Pan new customers? Or, is this just cost-cutting, running three deliveries together? It doesn't matter which. The important thing is the extra. Maybe three times as much, maybe more.'

Preston felt bad, some nausea and sudden body heat. He said right away: 'This is all guess and maybes.' It was the sort of dream stuff he had already heard from Doris.

'Dad hates it when his plans turn out wrong, Tyrone.' She gave Preston a kiss on the side of his face, gently so as not to bump her mouth. 'But don't let it upset you, Dad. Tyrone will help, won't you, Tyrone?'

'Not wrong, Ron. A bigger catch, that's all. Well, and an extra man to deal with, yes. We've got time to adjust. It's still your project, Ron, still a great operation to have spotted and worked out. Just a bit more beautiful, that's all.'

'That's all, Dad,' Grace said. 'It's still yours.'

'No, I don't like it,' Preston said. 'Not what we thought when we started. Not the operation we're ready for. I can't work blind.'

'Some extra cash, Ron. What's wrong? It won't make a transport problem. It could be how much? Say it's three times what we were expecting. That's—'

'We don't discuss finance except at proper meetings,' Preston said. 'Not in some rush thing, like this, parked any old how, and Grace with a bad gum, for God's sake.'

'Oh sorry, Ron, but I thought you said we could talk in front of—'

'Not these circumstances.'

'But roughly how much, Dad? It could be great, couldn't it?'

'That kind of talk is stupid,' he replied. 'We have to know for sure, not stupid dreams. This is work, not Ali Baba. Just get moving now, Tyrone. And stay in cover. I don't want you up around my house again.'

'He's really funny when it's to do with the house, Tyrone. The sacred ground.'

'If it's on, I'll call you,' Preston told him.

'If it's on? Of course it's got to be on.'

'No of course. There's a case building up against this job,' Preston said. 'Not only what you just said, Tyrone. Quite a few factors. I can't work when I'm uneasy. What we've got here is what's known as imponderables. You can recognise them straight off if you been around a while.'

When Tyrone had gone, they drove on to the dentist. Grace

said: 'Boys like that, I mean, smart and young, Dad, and from London way, they still know you're the boss, don't they? I think it's great.'

'People have heard of me. Not just local. They know I don't miss imponderables. It's leadership. Leadership's not something that grows on trees.'

'Tyrone, he seems—'

'He's no good to you. All right, no wrist tattoos and he can put a couple of words together, but he'll be moving on, Grace. Too much talk. Trees and space. Who's he supposed to be, Prince Charles?'

'He just seemed— I don't mean like that, Dad. He just seemed . . . straight.'

'Straight? He'll do.'

'He thinks a lot of you, that's obvious.'

'Here we are, Grace. Now just relax, girl.'

'You're going to come in with me, aren't you?'

'Of course. I'll be right there.'

Chapter 4

Mansel decided he ought to go down and see the boys, Dean and Tyrone, just a social call, he had no information from Ron yet. They were comfortable enough, he had made sure of that, but this was a couple of youngsters hanging about in a flat, just waiting for some time the week after the week after next, and there could be difficulties and stress. Kids like that put on the consequence and talked almighty but tension got to them. This was the kind of thing Ron would not think about. He did not understand welfare, couldn't give a fish's tit about it, anyway, except when it came to Doris and Grace or Devon.

In a lot of ways, Ron was a holy gem. He knew better than almost anyone how to run an operation, as long as it did not get too big, and as long as he had everything tidy in his head, all the problems catered for and what he called 'fall-back plans' for any unexpected disasters that came. 'Contingencies' was another word he had bought ready-made somewhere and loved to bring out, which was fair enough. But he did not always understand people too well and he did not see that boys like Dean and Tyrone might need a lot of taking care of and jollying up in these long, loitering days. For Ron, a job was time-tabling and scheming. These were the whole picture. He could not be bothered wondering how his lads were thinking or how they coped with pressure. The way he saw it, that was their problem and if they could not handle it they should go in for hairdressing.

He would never admit it, but this attitude had sunk him once, years before Mansel's time. Ron, being Ron, always said that arrest was down to some late switch in guards' rotas or something similar, which put everything haywire, and ever since, because of that, he hated any alteration. A change could throw him. It was like a superstition. But, really, as Mansel heard it from others, the trouble with this job in the deep past was that he had not looked after his boys properly, and they were all nerves on the day, their brains useless, their bottle shattered. Mansel knew Ron considered him a bit of a joker and a wishful-thinker, but what Ron did not realise was that you had to have morale as well as information and morale did not just come out of nowhere. Welfare paid. And it needed work and it needed talent.

Dean Tait opened the door, looking full of joy. He had the sort of face that if you glanced at it quickly and he was smiling at the time, like now, you might think this was somebody who could be trusted, and who was going home afterwards to a very genuine, murderous mortgage and a warm family, a face that could sell you time-share or the new way to stop your roof slates slipping. The tattoos would make you wonder, but kids of that age, even quite decent kids, did all kinds of crazy things when wanting creativity.

'Manse. Glad you came,' he said.

'What's the good news? You look right on top.'

'Too right. Listen, I had a dream last night, Manse. You'll love it. We're running, all of us, loaded with money – in plastic bags, pockets, even in my mouth, yes, I'm holding fifties in my teeth, would you believe, like a dog with the *Daily Mail*?'

That really pink glow you could get in a kid's face when something happy happened, such as having a bag of Easter eggs, that was there, all over Dean, and the blue eyes gleaming and signalling, as if they wished they could talk. 'This is a real insight, Dean, a revelation.'

'There's police behind and they're running, likewise, but they stay far back. They're shooting, shooting a real barrage, but we're all right, and then out of somewhere suddenly comes Nelson's Column. Nelson's Column! It's standing there in the street. Don't ask me how it's supposed to have come from Trafalgar Square to here. You know how it goes with dreams. Anyway, these bullets from the police are all banging into Nelson, not us – you can see big stone bits flying off him, his hat and the funny arm. So, it gets so bad that the column starts to shake and sway about and then, crash, bang, down the whole lot comes and he's flat on his back in the road, old Nelson, his hat still on, most of it, and he's laughing such as you've never seen, Manse. It's a right mess – the statue and all the column in bits, dust all over the place, and there's so much wreckage the police can't get past. They've got to climb over all this débris. They're struggling and sliding back. And, at the end of the street, there's a ship, but an old ship, like the *Victory*, Nelson's – see, Manse, victory? – with sails and rigging and all that. And we get aboard her, and the ship pulls away into the harbour, going to sea, and the police are there on the dockside in their peaked caps waving their arms about and yelling stuff about the Queen's Peace, but they can't do a thing.'

Mansel said: 'Were they still firing?'

'What?'

'Were they shooting?'

'The police?'

'This is only a dream, and I'm not bothered, of course not, but what kind of armament, Dean? Is this handguns or rifles? Flakjacket people? The bloody special squad?'

'Shooting? No, they've given up, Manse. We're all right. They know it's useless.'

'Yes?' Mansel nodded, and gave one of his best grins. It had been so feeble to panic like that at a dream. Who was the kid here, himself or Dean? 'This is valuable.' Mansel gripped Dean's arm for a minute. 'A good omen.'

'I thought so. Look, old Nelson on our side. And he can see the joke of it – us getting clear with so much cash.'

'Dean, this is wonderful, you telling me this, because I have good dreams myself like that before a job sometimes. And it's always a sign things will go just right.'

They were talking in the little hallway of the flat. It looked obvious that Dean felt so excited he wanted to say it all straight away, while it was still alive and brilliant in his head. It reminded you of the thrills of just a kid, yes, but it did not matter. What mattered more was that this would keep him hopeful. The stuff about the money in Dean's mouth could be important, because it seemed to show he was right into this job. He was going to eat it.

Nelson? Mansel could not sort that out properly yet, but it must have a bright meaning, too. Dean could be right about the laughing. Or, because of Trafalgar Square, it might be to do with the London side of things – Dean and Tyrone coming from that way, the big scene, and showing a nowhere town like this how to do a job. Mansel never dreamed much himself, and it was total balls what he had told Dean, but he did believe something like that could bring a good message.

'And not only this dream,' Dean said. 'You didn't hear? Developments, Manse. Three times the take, maybe more. Two later drops after Brand's. The van's going to be stuffed with it. That's why I had to use my mouth in the dream, I reckon. Nowhere else to put it all.' He was yelling and laughing, like a boy at the fair.

'Who says? Where does it come from this information?' Mansel felt fogged, suddenly. One minute this kid was talking dream money and dream police and dream guns, and the next they were into something that sounded real. They went into the living-room of the flat. It was a bit of a mess with empty food packets and clothes, but Mansel had seen worse. No women, anyway, or women's things. Ron had told them a definite, super-ban on pussy in here because girls could talk after, and girls could get hysterical right now. Tyrone was lying out on a settee, shoes off, reading a book that was open on the carpet, so relaxed this one.

'It looks like Ron's really smart,' Dean said. 'He must have had a tip this change was coming. Why else are we waiting three weeks?'

Tyrone looked up from the book. 'Ron hasn't told you about these extra calls, Manse?'

'Not yet.'

'I talked to him about this the day before yesterday.'

'He'll let me know when he's ready.'

'He's a mate of yours, but I do worry about him, Manse,' Tyrone said.

'Worry how?'

'Just the usual way. This change seemed to trouble him,' Tyrone said.

'He'll take a while to adjust.'

'If he adjusts.'

Laughing again, Dean said: 'Listen, Manse. Tyrone thinks Ron might call it off – the whole thing. Call it off because it's become so much better. I told him that's crazy.'

'Of course,' Mansel said.

'How old is Ron, anyway?' Tyrone asked. 'What I'm saying

is he looks so great, so fit, you can't really guess. But he's got to be into the half century, Manse, yes? All credit to him. His own teeth?'

'He'll be fine,' Mansel replied. 'Just give him time to re-do his plans. Nothing can shake Ron, when his mind is made up.' He spoke as quietly as he could. Shouting did not make things any more believable.

'That's what I hoped, Manse,' Tyrone said. 'But you're sure to be right, aren't you? You're his friend from way back.'

'I know his ways.'

Tyrone rolled off the settee and stood up. 'Yes, we're going to accept that. Ron's got quality. You feel everything's going to come out fine because he's there. And he's clued up on which police we've got to cope with, this Harpur, was it, and Iles? Know your enemy.'

'Right,' Dean said.

Tyrone had a laugh now. 'Did he tell you about his dream, Manse?'

'Great.'

'Yes. I wish I could sleep like that.'

'You having trouble, Tyrone?' Mansel asked.

'The run-in to a job, I'm always like this, wide-awake most of the time, wondering about possibilities.'

'Possibilities? That's Ron's side,' Mansel said. 'Known also as contingencies. No need for you to bother. Get your sleep. Look, I can bring you pills. Knock you out instantly.'

'Tyrone won't touch any drug – I mean, nothing of any sort,' Dean said. 'Not even medical.'

'It's a thing with me. I like to keep my head all right, clear.'

'Sure,' Mansel said. 'But these pills I'm talking about—'

Tyrone spoke very gently. 'Suppose Ron did want to drop it.'

This kid, Tyrone, he might have a name like a day at the races, but anybody could see he was a thinker. He had his eyes open behind those nice-guy glasses, and he did not miss much. His face might be round and cheerful-looking, except for the adam's apple, but he was still a fierce analyst.

'I'm going to tell Ron about the dream,' Dean said, beaming away. 'Sure to put everything right.'

'That's it, Dean,' Mansel replied.

'What's obvious about Ron is that he's got commitments,'

Tyrone continued. 'I met his daughter, Grace. Smart girl. And then the Devon thing. Well, sure, all this could mean he needs income, and this would be in favour of the job going ahead. But the other side is that he might not be eager when it comes to any extra risk. There are dependants to think about. Nobody's saying his nerve's gone, Manse. He wouldn't have that sort of buzz going for him nationwide if he had started to worry too much. This is just someone considering the people who need him and deciding he shouldn't go against the odds.'

Mansel was no great drinker but he could have done with one now. Looking urgently about he saw nothing, though, not even a can. These days a lot of bloody kids did without it altogether. How they kept their skin so young, maybe. If Tyrone was scared of pills he probably did not do alcohol, either.

'You're right on one thing, Tyrone: Ron needs steady income,' Mansel said. 'He likes something decent coming in every so often, something not huge and liable to frighten all the law in Britain, but something pretty regular – a nice, manageable job, with a fair return, and then another one of the same when things have gone quiet again after a few months. This could be somewhere else altogether, somewhere he's not even been heard of. Ron gets information from all over. This job, the van, happens to be home patch, obviously. But it's quite a while since he's done anything around here, so he's not bothered. Oh, yes, he thinks the world of Doris and Grace, and the world of Devon, too, but don't worry, Tyrone, that won't stop him. The opposite. Like you said, he's got to see them right, hasn't he? This van is going to be fine, believe me.'

'I do believe you, Manse,' Tyrone replied. 'I've said that. Nobody knows him like you, so we're bound to believe you.'

'If only we could speed it up,' Dean said. 'I'd like to be out of here.'

'On the *Victory*, I suppose,' Mansel cried, laughing. An inspiration hit him then, the way it did sometimes, thank God, the kind that was really special to him, or even unique, and he began to do a bit of a hornpipe dance in the middle of the room.

He had learned it ages ago, as a party piece, and used it now and then to produce a smile. His heart banged away very fast, but he kept at it, because the other two were smiling and clapping, and the activity might give a real relief and turn the talk by Tyrone away from doubts and the rough questions. All credit to him, Tyrone began to dance with him, shooting his feet and legs out in the style old-time sailors used for it, and occasionally taking Mansel's hand and pulling him towards him, then pushing him back. Tyrone's glasses slipped down his nose and he pulled them off and stuck them into the pocket of his shirt. Without them he did not look so fucking superior and difficult. This fooling had been a good idea – a method of breaking tension, the kind of tactic Ron would never think of. No question he would consider it poor discipline.

At the end, Tyrone sat down, gasping a bit and grinning, but Mansel forced himself to stay on his feet, and did what he could to keep his breathing reasonably quiet. Sweat made his shirt stick to his shoulder blades and he did not let that bother him, either.

Tyrone put his glasses back on: 'Manse, think about this for a minute, will you: if Ron decided – just say, despite what you tell us – just say he decided not to go ahead, what chances do you reckon of the three of us handling it without him? The three of us as the core. Maybe recruit one or two more. I don't know it's necessary, as long as we're tooled up. There's time to find some reinforcements, anyway, and I've got contacts: good people, one with no form whatsoever, like Dean and myself, a real charmed life so far.'

Now, it was all right to sit down – not like a collapse – and Mansel took a chair, almost opposite Tyrone, but a bit sideways on, because he wanted to avoid anything that looked like confrontation.

'Only an idea,' Dean said. He was still standing near the window, hands together in front of him, like saying grace, from when he had been clapping the hornpipe.

'Just for discussion,' Tyrone said.

'I can't help you on this,' Mansel told them. 'It's not something I've ever thought about.'

'It's sensitive, I see that,' Tyrone replied. 'But we get on pretty well, the three of us?'

'I like to see how people are making out, and show some companionship,' Mansel said. 'Just my way.'

'And it's appreciated, believe me,' Tyrone told him. 'You're damn fit – that dancing, and no shortage of breath.'

'Never smoked a cigarette in my life,' Mansel replied. 'My first words as a kid were "Smoking can damage your health." That's where the government got the idea.'

'I like it, I like it,' Dean cried.

'We value you, Manse,' Tyrone said, 'and we'd certainly want you on any job we tried.'

'I'll be there – and so will Ron,' Mansel said. 'Out in front.'

'It's great, the loyalty and team spirit,' Tyrone replied. 'We're lucky to be made a party of it, I know that. I see you as being a different generation from Ron, though.'

'Ron's older, but we've been through a lot together, that's all.'

'To be respected. The age factor, it needn't matter one iota,' Tyrone replied. 'Now and then, though, it makes a difference. I'm not talking about fitness or strength. I'm more interested in mental attitude. Edge and drive. Age can be crucial there, even a couple of years.'

Dean said: 'I can't afford to put three or four weeks into a job, and then find it's scrapped. This is not a holiday spot.'

'Manse, this is our problem. I agree with every one of the great things you say about Ron, but he's made me anxious. It brings tears to my eyes if I think of that van trundling up to Brand's as ever, down on its axles with extra cash, and us doing nothing about it but wave because Ron's turned twitchy.'

'Best not to talk of him like that,' Mansel said.

'Why? Are you going to tell him?' Dean asked. Suddenly, he was not laughing but very cold, like some sort of menace.

'Now don't get het up, Dean,' Tyrone said. 'What I'm saying to Manse, I'd say to Ron to his face, I hope. Why not? All I'd tell him is that if he doesn't want to take on the van, leave it to some people who do.'

'This is his operation,' Mansel replied.

'No question,' Tyrone said. 'But if he kills the operation?'

Mansel said: 'Even if he did call things off now, it wouldn't be permanent. We could come back to it when things are easier. That would be his thinking. It's a question of time, that's all.'

'Exactly how we see it, too,' Dean replied. 'Stuck here what we're wasting is time.' He still sounded pretty evil. Dean was the one who went from mood to mood and let it all show. He did not care too much, and spoke his mind straight out, what there was of it. Tyrone supplied the mentality and he came at things round about. It could get so that this outfit had two leaders, him and Ron, and nothing ever went right when that sort of thing happened.

'You say, "we could come back to it", Manse, but who's we?' Tyrone asked. 'How long's the postponement? Where will I be when Ron decides it's the okay moment? Anything could have happened. Who says Ron will want me next time?'

'Or me?' Dean said.

'Yes, or him.' Tyrone said it in a way that made you think nobody sane was going to ask for Dean twice, and also made you think there were a thousand people just as good to be found for this job, most without tattoos. 'And what about you, Manse – your personal view?' Tyrone asked, in a nice, quiet voice. 'I know you support Ron but, when you look at the situation for yourself, do you think we ought to call it off?'

Oh, yes, he had a brain and good eyes behind those goggles. And cheek. It was a nerve to ask these things, and to behave as if he did not care if Mansel told Ron what had been said today. Mansel replied: 'Well, I haven't got the facts yet, have I? All I hear is what you tell me. I don't know Ron's information and thinking.'

'You sound like a politician on the news,' Dean said. 'An answer which isn't.'

Tyrone jumped up suddenly and started the hornpipe again. In a minute or two, Mansel joined him. They kept it going just as long this time. At the end, when they were resting once more, Tyrone said: 'That's what I mean, you see, Manse. You're like someone as young as me and Dean. I don't think of you as past it at all.'

Chapter 5

Once in a while on a decent summer's day Harpur and Ruth Cotton would drive to a beach up the coast a few miles and swim and laze for a couple of hours. Arranging this outing was never easy. She needed to be back when her sons arrived home from school, and Harpur had to be able to steal the time from police duties and justify dropping out of sight for an afternoon. It was riskier than the privacy of a hotel room because, although they chose a secluded bay, there were always a few other people around, with little else to do but stare.

It was the kind of excursion Ruth and Harpur both loved, though, because it seemed to proclaim their relationship went beyond the hotel and bed. At the beach, they were almost like an established couple, and 'not just a couple coupling', as Ruth said once. For a short while they could feel as if honestly entitled to each other's company, and not simply two marrieds burning each other up in an affair. Rot, and they knew it: the sea did not wash away adultery. They could kid themselves for a while, though, and did.

Today, they lay in the shade of the cliff on two big flat rocks, like ancient sacrifices, the sound of the breakers far enough off to be soothing and hypnotic. He held her hand. As contact went this fell very short, especially when she was almost naked, but he accepted it as the limit on this trip.

As happened sometimes, she wanted to talk about Robert, her husband: 'He's very keen to stay with firearms, despite everything, Col.'

'Well, why not?'

'I think it would really knock him if he lost that. I don't understand, but it's true.'

'Ruth, we're desperately short of people willing to carry a gun. Nobody's going to stop him.'

'Even though he's—'

'He's fine. He's had counselling and he's fine.' Whenever they came here they seemed to talk about their spouses. He could have done without this, but understood why it happened: because they were pretending for a little while that their relationship was open and respectable they would discuss Sergeant Robert Cotton and Harpur's wife, Megan, as if they were outsiders, friends common to both of them, and not more than that. In Cotton's case, he was a colleague, too: a cop, like Harpur.

'He's killed someone, Col.'

'It was necessary.'

'We get hate calls.'

'He fired to protect himself and his mates. Ditto Repeato, the man Rob shot, was armed and about to fire in a bank raid. All the warnings were given. They shouted "Armed police" so often one of them lost his voice. Rob's over it, completely over it.'

'Maybe.'

'I'd trust him in any firearms situation.'

She was silent for a while. 'Anyway, whether he's through the trauma or not, he's still determined to stay with guns. I suppose it's classic. And corny, is it? Like advertisements. The gun equals manhood. If he suspects his wife's having it off with one of his superiors—'

'No, we're not sure he does, Ruth.'

She lay silent for a while. 'I don't mean he wants a pistol to use on you one day, Col. Well, obviously. That's not Rob, I mean, no matter what stress does to him. I don't believe he could ever change that much. He's a good man, Col. Jesus, listen to me praise him while I'm lying here with you. But, anyway, he needs all the macho things that are supposed to go with guns. It's compensation. Do I sound like a shrink?'

He was chilled by what she had said, despite her denial of any threat. Stretched out on the rock, he suddenly felt vulnerable and sat up and gazed across the almost deserted beach. It was the beginning of June, very warm, but still too early in the year for most trippers.

She said: 'There's nothing on the books, is there? I shouldn't

41

ask, I know, but he seems so tense. Why I brought this up, really.'

'On the books?'

'Something where there could be shooting, with Rob out in front again?'

'Ruth, operations like that come suddenly, from nowhere. We don't get advance notice, love.'

'I know. But sometimes – ambushes after tip-offs. Think of last time. And those police traps in London.'

'Nothing like that at present. All our known gunplay merchants are lying low. Perhaps they've turned law-abiding. Perhaps the London shoot-outs have done the trick and scared them. I hope so.'

She sat up with him. 'You don't mind if I quiz you sometimes about work?'

'Bound to happen, love.' He was not keen on it.

She looked at her watch. 'God.'

They began to dress hurriedly.

'It's crazy, isn't it, Col?' she said, on one leg and with a towel around her. 'I'm asking you to take care of him. I'm actually asking my lover to take care of my husband.'

'He's very good at taking care of himself, Ruth. Nobody better.'

'But you'll do what you can, Col?'

'Of course, love.' Yes, crazy: provide a gun recommendation for a man who might crack up and come looking for you one day with it.

Chapter 6

On the next wages day, Ron Preston decided to go up alone to Brand's and check Tyrone had it right about the van's extra calls. That niggling bloody voice and the management glasses meant Tyrone was the sort who *would* have it right, but Preston wanted to see for himself. This was leadership. Napoleon, Kennedy, they might think something else, but always he wanted to see for himself. Delegation? Stuff it. Try delegating the ten years if they caught you through not doing your homework. The difference from being Kennedy was that J. F. had a sign over his desk saying 'The buck stops here', but with this sort of work the buck started here, as well.

Despite everything, this job remained a possible, and more. There were still two weeks to get it all sorted out. But today, he wanted no advice or pressure from the two new kids, and none of that sloppy, fingers-crossed stuff from Mansel, either. Mansel saved a hell of a lot on booze because he was like happy drunk when sober. In any case, a carload of them hanging about again up there meant more chance of being spotted. Police might have surveillance if they had been tipped something was in the wind. And, if their information was only general, no date, they could be here in full force every wages day until it happened. You had to think yourself into their mind. Even going alone was a risk, especially after Tyrone had been lurking the route in that shiny stolen vehicle, the thinking twat, but one thing Preston had learned over and over was, Don't cut costs on reconnaissance. His own car would be a give-away, so he hired a Polo for the afternoon.

If he spotted any police vehicle within a mile of Brand's today, anything, even only a recovery trailer, it meant the whole thing was a come-on, and that would be the end, wrap-up, no argument from Tyrone or anybody else. And, of course, the same if he saw any police face, such as Harpur or Garland or that uniformed hotshot and killer, Sergeant Cotton, or Erogynous Jones, or even the high-flying, low-down, rough-house lout, Assistant Chief Iles. Well, as a matter of fact, especially Iles. Any contact with that bastard was too much. A few times Preston had said to Doris it was unbelievable and a disgrace such a savage could reach high rank. No wonder public respect for police was falling when devils like that took charge.

He went up half an hour before the van was due and drove past the turn-off to Acre Street, where Brand's was, without stopping, and staring about really hard for any sign of a reception. It looked clear, but these were crafty operators and they had handled this sort of situation often before. They could have taken over rooms in a couple of houses or offices near the gates and have their vehicles out of sight behind buildings in Brand's yard. Plus, a team might be hidden in the back of the wages van itself.

Coming around again, he went into Acre Street and pulled up a decent distance from the gatehouse with the Polo facing away, and watched through the rear window. It was one of the oldest tricks. People expected anyone doing a watch to have the car pointed towards the target. So, if you observed from the back, you might stay unseen. Of course, police knew the ploy – probably invented it – so you could never bet they would be fooled.

Even from the start he had not liked the location of Brand's. He liked it less now there were real fears of an ambush. Brand's was in The Pill district, a mixture of old houses and bits of industry dating right back, and the whole area a dirty, run-down mess. The factory yard's entrance lay between two terraces of ropey houses and some offices and other works, and Acre Street was a cul-de-sac, closed off by a high railway embankment at the end where Preston had parked.

As he looked at the situation now, he thought of the last big shoot-out laid on by Harpur and his people. That had been against 'Tenderness' Mellick's bank-raid crew a long way from here at the centre of the city, but also in a street with only one means of escape. What the police did there was let the raiders in after a tip, then blocked the exit with JCBs.

This was when Sergeant Robert Cotton very neatly put two

bullets into the head of a long-time nobody villain, Ditto Repeato, as the gang tried to get out on foot. The story went, two bullets but only one and a half holes in the chest, and Ditto had been running and dodging and weaving at the time. This was some shooting. They had very talented boys these days, the police. You still heard talk around now and then that Cotton or some of his family would pay because Ditto could have been taken alive, but that's what it was so far, talk. And then, did anybody really care enough about Ditto?

There was another story, too, to do with Cotton, or, at least, his wife. This tale said Harpur was doing a bit in that direction, a matter that had lasted years and was under way even when Ruth Cotton had been married to her first husband, another cop. These rumours were hard to turn into real information, though. Anyway, Cotton was not the only clever one they had these days, and a few marksmen on that embankment could knock over everything they did not like around Brand's entrance, especially if the way back on to the main road was shut off.

The wages van turned into the street and approached Brand's. Yes, three men in the front now, like Wilf had said, but no way of knowing how many might be in the back. He gazed about again, looking for any signs that people in the houses or offices or concealed in Brand's yard were tensing up now the van had arrived. There was a big metal waste bin near the entrance that could conceal a few. He still saw nothing, though. The van stopped as always at the gatehouse and, also as always, was let through almost at once, on its way to the pay office. In a quarter of an hour it came out and turned up towards the main road again.

Preston was now at his most obvious, he knew that. He had to turn the Polo and follow, to see if the van really did make more drops. He waited two minutes, then went after it. Maybe Tyrone had done the same the other day, and even somebody as past it as the old van driver might have noticed in his mirror first the Belmont and now the VW tracking him. Somewhere there could be a nice, neat leather-bound book recording every move they made preparing this job, like the log of the *Bounty*.

The van kept going, anyway, and half an hour later Preston knew that Tyrone did have it right, and the two extra calls were part of a new routine. Also, when you thought about the size of

Linklater's and Pan, Tyrone most likely had it just as right about the load the van carried now. Yes, it could have suddenly multiplied by three. Maybe more. The take had moved up to around a quarter of a million, and although this was old news, the idea still made him sweat and shake for a moment. He did not like it any better now than before. This was funny money.

You had to know your league. That was another thing about leadership. Stay in your element. You could move up slowly, which was all right, and safe. That was just improving yourself, say a few thousand at a time, say even ten, like a kid in school going up from class to class, when he was ready. But what Preston dreaded was the craziness and carelessness that could suddenly hit people who thought they were on to 'the biggie' as they called it, soft sods, the dream package supposed to put things right for ever, or a year or two, anyway, which was the same as for ever in their daft minds. Always he kept on guard in case this brainlessness hit him, too, one day. It had been something similar with Tenderness and Ditto, something that stripped away sense and made them volunteer for a trap.

Preston left as soon as he had seen the wages delivered to Pan Products, returned the Polo, then walked home. As he walked, he made his decision, and with no trouble. The job was off. O-F-F. Dead. Although he had seen no sign the raid was expected, and nothing to show the police were involved, it all felt so bloody wrong, and you listened to what your feelings told you. There was that dead-end street and the echoes of Ditto, and the three men in the van so busy not noticing they had company, and above all, that perilous extra money, the untold extra money. That was the word, 'untold'. He remembered it from stories. People searched for 'untold wealth'. Well, he did not like wealth untold. He wanted to be told just how much. He could not believe in it until he had a figure, and also knew it was a tidy amount, but not more than tidy, not something fairy-tale.

These things had to be put together and weighed up, and they came out very bad. He could have still shut his eyes to the message his feelings gave him, but that was not his way. People depended on him, people who did not let their minds do much, such as Mansel and Dean, and someone like Tyrone who could think but had not grown up. All foresight matters Preston had to handle for them. That rôle you just got used to and accepted.

Then there were others who depended on him, in a different way – Doris and Grace and Devon.

Once he had made his mind up, he felt better. This thing had been dragging at him from the beginning, he could see that now. He would tell Mansel when he saw him in a couple of days and he could pass it on. The other two would be ratty about losing the chance and about the time wasted. Tough. If they wanted regular wages, get down the Job Centre.

When he reached home there were some women friends of Doris there from *Annie Get Your Gun* drinking tea and chattering and giggling and saying how nervy they were about the first night, really full of it, like opening on Broadway. One of them called Carol, who was going to be a squaw, he had noticed before, a real dark-haired treasure with legs, and young, but not queening it, not being girly among the older pieces. He told them over and over they would be great. 'Triumphal,' he said. Well, they needed that, a bit of a boost at the right time from someone they respected, and it did the trick. He could see them starting to believe they were on top. Sometimes you had to make people feel more sure of themselves, sometimes you had to knock the cockiness out of them, it was all part of the same thing – getting the best from those around you. A couple of the girls wanted to know now why he didn't join the dramatics himself, and said they could tell he had a great voice and would look grand in a stetson, yes, really full of it. Carol, the squaw, was asking as much as the others, and it could be she really meant it. He said perhaps he would one day, when he had more time, but he could see Doris did not believe it, and neither did he, really. Spotlights he dreaded.

He left them to it. In the other room he found Grace at the mirror, putting the last touches to her hair for something special tonight. Her mouth trouble had cleared up, and she was looking really great now and he told her. 'What's the big deal?'

'I'm going out with that Tyrone.'

'Oh?'

'What's that supposed to mean, Dad?'

'How?'

'How what?'

'How did you get in touch?'

'He got in touch. I don't ask men to go out, do I?'

'How did he get in touch?'

'Oh, that? You're cross about the phone?'

'He rang here?'

'Daddy, it's all right. Don't go all white-lipped and controlled.'

'Did he ring here?'

'Well, obviously. Where else? But he asked for *me*. If anyone's tapping, this was just a man ringing a girl for a date. Nothing else was mentioned. He could have been anyone.'

'Do you think he sounds local?'

'Dad, it doesn't matter. He's a boy asking for me, that's all.'

'Harpur or someone else listening in says to himself, This is a stranger. Planner's getting a team together.'

'Nothing to do with Planner. There are other people in the world. The call was for Grace. He could be someone I met anywhere – at the college, say. There's plenty there from away. They ring me.'

'Yes, but he's Tyrone. Why do you want to go out with someone like that? Didn't I tell you?'

'I felt sorry for him, hanging about. Look, nothing heavy, Dad. It's a foursome. There's a second boy, isn't there? Dean?'

'Four? Another girl? Where from?'

'Oh, Dad, please, I don't know.'

He tried to keep his rage down. Always he found it hard to get angry with Grace, and he knew she made the most of that. Well, she was sickly when a youngster, and it had not helped much when they took him away. She was better now and accepted things how they were, but he still liked to treat her very gentle.

She was sitting opposite him in her blue and gold dress and looking great, not too much make-up and wearing some big circular earrings he had brought her from somewhere, paid for. 'Never give a present that's not above board,' his father had always said. 'Presents must be clean.'

Grace would have been a picture wherever, in any company, nice, fresh skin, a little, pretty nose, and her eyes big and brown and kind. So he could not understand why she wanted to go out with this Tyrone. It hurt, he would admit it. Somebody you thought about a lot because you thought she needed you, somebody whose future you really had in your mind when you were making decisions, someone like that turns around on you and tells you, Thanks very much, I'll do it my way.

'Grace, love,' he said, 'this is two men in a strange town. What sort of a girl are they going to meet. You see what I mean?'

'One of them met me. I'm a girl.'

'Now, come on, that's through business, isn't it? That's different.'

'This other girl, Debbie Something, is a slag, that what you're saying?'

'Of course a slag.'

'I don't know. If he met her at a dance?'

'He's not supposed to go to dances, for God's sake. He's working.'

'Not supposed. Oh, Dad. But he might have. These are grown-up men. They run their own lives, whatever you tell them. Debbie could be just a perfectly decent person he bumped into in a dance or a club.'

She had begun to grow agitated and he hated to see her upset. 'I wouldn't hurt you or spoil your evening, but I've got to say I don't want you out with two men like these, and this girl. You know nicer people than this, surely to God. And your mother wouldn't like it, either.'

The party in the other room began to belt out a chorus from *Annie*, with lots of Indian whoops and cowboy calls as back-up. This was the kind of nice, harmless, fun thing he liked for women, not talking about going out with a couple of loud, smart, boy villains and their diseased floozy. Carol, the squaw, wouldn't want to be seen dead with people like Tyrone and Dean. She would spot what they were right off. Why was Grace different? He had thought she might fall for Dean and the tattoos and kept him away, but now, here she was, making herself look great for this so-called Tyrone, although he had glasses. It was a smack in the eye when you realised you did not even know your own daughter. Of course, by now she probably realised she did wrong agreeing to go out with Tyrone, and she realised he did wrong telephoning, but she could not admit it because it would be all about the fucking rights of the young to have their own life. They thought they were a different kind of human being, the first ones who had ever been on this earth, and making all

49

their own rules. That was half the trouble. Well, Tyrone would be disappearing from the area pretty soon, once he had the decision from Manse, so that might solve it all.

'I don't know why you're so nasty about them,' Grace said. 'It's only an outing – one evening. I don't want to marry him.'

'Just it's a mistake, that's all.'

'Oh, mistake. Your point of view.'

'Mine's the only one I've got, Grace.'

'Why? You say that as if you're so proud of it. Why not try to see things from someone else's angle for once?'

Oh, Jesus. For a second he thought she was going to talk about an item called empathy. He had heard her mention that a couple of times lately, which he had thought was some sort of women's illness until she explained. She got it from the college, probably. 'Tyrone's angle, for instance?' he said quickly. 'Do me a favour.' But he was not shouting. He never sounded off at Grace, and there were the people in the other room. You did not let a family row reach guests, like some public bar.

She stood up and smoothed out her dress. He saw that she meant to go, whatever he said. There were not many arguments he won with her these days. 'Something like this happens and suddenly—' she said. 'Oh, look, Dad, the thing is I always believed it was great you could still work with people as young as Tyrone and Dean, and that they thought so much of you. Not just those two. There've been others. It used to make me really proud.' She gave a big frown, like when she was a child, and waited a second. 'That sounds funny, I suppose. What I mean – the sort of work we're talking about. I mean, I wish it was something else. Well, of course I do, or I did, anyway. But it isn't, and I'm used to it now. Too late for change, isn't it? Too late for getting regretful. It's part of you, and part of all of us.'

'Why I don't try to pretend with you, love.' He did not want to go into all that. It was pointless. 'Anyway, I'm not so old.'

'No, I know, but it's grand, all the same, that you're not left behind by these youngsters. Or you didn't used to be. Till these last few days. And then something like this comes, this row, the bad feeling, about nothing at all – really, now isn't it, Dad, absolutely sod all? – and it seems to put a big age gap between them and you, and between me and you, too. I hate that. It didn't seem to be there only a little while ago, and now it is. Yes, I hate it.'

'Because I'm showing a bit of sense?'

'What you call it. To me, it just seems narrow, not like you. It's like when we were in the car that day with Tyrone, you saying this job, whatever it is, might have to be off because there was something new come up. I could see Tyrone was shocked and he didn't understand it, not a bit. Something new? So what? And I could see he was thinking, suddenly, that – well, I'm sorry about this, Dad, but thinking that you might be past it, never mind what great things about you he had heard from others. I didn't believe it then. That didn't fit in with my idea of you at all. But, honestly, after something like this stupid row about a night out – I begin to wonder. I'm sorry, but I do.'

'Past it?' He could hardly get his voice going he felt so angry and desperate, her using just those sad words he had been thinking about the age-old van driver. 'What do you know about past it? Nobody ever said that to me. Nobody. Grace, you shouldn't say things like that. I've looked after myself.'

'Oh, I don't mean your body. You look great. Always will. But up here, and in here.' She touched her head and a spot over her heart. 'Fight.'

'Thanks a lot.'

'Perhaps they're wrong. Perhaps I'm wrong. I hope so. Really, I do, Dad.'

The singing in the other room came to an end and there was more chatter and laughing and then, through the open door, they could see the women beginning to leave. A few of them, including the pretty squaw, looked in from the hall to say goodbye.

'I know you'll be great,' he said to her.

'You really ought to think about joining. I mean, really,' she replied. This girl, Carol, was not much older than Grace. 'It's *West Side Story* soon. Do have a go, Ron.' Then she went into a little pose and began to sing a line – 'Hold my hand and I'll take you there' – nice and slow and warm. 'That's from "Somewhere", Ron.'

'Well, who knows? I might join,' he replied.

When they had gone, Grace said: 'She fancy you, then?'

'I tell them all they're great. It helps.'

'She was coming on strong.'

51

'Rubbish,' he said, trying hard to keep the pleasure out of his voice. This was a lovely kid around twenty, with such legs, making a fuss of him.

'Anyway, I've promised I'd see them, so I have to now,' but she moved nearer to him. 'Perhaps I shouldn't have said some of those things, Dad. I went over the top. You're not past it, not at all. That chick certainly didn't think so, anyway.' She put her arms around his neck and pulled his face down gently so she could kiss him on the forehead, obviously not sure if he was too offended to allow it. But he did not sulk. 'They've got it wrong, Dad, haven't they, Tyrone and his mate? Please say they have. We're the ones who are right about you – me and that leching girl.'

Dean and Tyrone are poncy out-of-town kids, he wanted to reply. 'I have to think more than them, that's all, love. I have to use what's up here, as you call it.' He pointed to his head. 'I have to make decisions.'

'I know. I do understand, Dad.'

'I don't leap into things.'

'But you don't chicken out, either, do you? I mean, when things look right. That's the main thing. You haven't turned feeble and yellow because you're – because you're not a lad any longer?'

He had a very big laugh, a laugh he was able to put plenty of confidence into. The squaw had done a lot for him tonight. 'A chick', as Grace called her. Chick. Chicken. You had to choose. 'You know me better than that, Grace. I'm like I always was. No, I don't chicken. This job, for instance. It's on. Of course it's bloody on – whatever clever-Dick Tyrone thought, or thinks. O-N On. Got it? All right, there were doubts, there's always two sides, but I looked at all the factors and made my decision. Today. On balance, it's right. Points against, but more in favour. That's how I form my view, you see. I make my two lists and compare. Never any real doubt it would go ahead, as a matter of fact. You're the first one I've told.'

She grinned and clapped her hands once in front of her face. 'First one to know? It's a privilege.' She kissed him again, on the cheek this time. 'Dad, you're great. I always knew it, really.'

'Oh, of course. Of course. One thing, though, Grace—'

'I won't tell Tyrone. That what you were going to say?'

'There's a way of doing these things.'

'I do understand, Dad. This mustn't come from me. Honestly, I wouldn't tell Tyrone.'

'There's what's known as procedures. So, please.'

'I promise.'

'Things like this go to Mansel Billings first. For consideration. Confirmation. He'll be all right, but it's got to be done. And I don't see him until the day after tomorrow.'

'Proper channels?'

'Right. You smile, but it's important. I might have to work with Mansel some other time. Stupid to upset him now. He seems carefree, but he's sensitive, too.'

He did not want it looking to every bugger as if he suddenly changed his mind because his daughter said he had begun to sound and think old. Especially he did not want it looking like that if it was true. You could not run an outfit that way. Grace could even have picked up that the squaw had done things to him, also. Jesus, was this how most of life's big decisions happened? Fluke? You could be a planner and then, wham, something came out of nowhere and knocked it all stupid. Frightening, that, and enough to make your soul feel very dark.

Grace was going from the room, obviously eager to get to bloody Tyrone, but then turned back: 'You'll take care? You're still going to take care, aren't you? We chat away here in a nice, safe, comfy lounge, and we don't say a word about the, well, the danger.'

'Oh, danger. You'll never hear me talk like that.'

'Danger, risk, odds, hairiness – what you like. Just it's there. You've really got it worked out, have you? It is all right, Dad? I mean, this Cotton, and other one I heard of. Sinbad?'

'Not the sailor, no. Constable Sid Synott.' A bit posthumous to start worrying about that, but just like a woman. Who was she bothered might finish up on the end of Sergeant Cotton's or Synott's cheeky Smith and Wesson, himself or Tyrone? He disliked thinking about that too much. 'All right? Of course it is, Grace,' he said.

She frowned again. 'You won't like this, but wouldn't it be great, an end to all the fret, if one day you could do a job, some big, super job, where you really cleaned up, I mean really, so there would be no more need to ever—'

'No, you're right, I don't like it. Baby talk. Not professional.'

53

Chapter 7

When Mansel Billings came out to his car from visiting at the old people's residential home he found a capital letter note, like a ransom demand, under the windscreen wiper. It said, 'DON'T MOVE'. Trying to smile, he gazed about with the piece of paper in his hand, half convinced it was a joke from somebody who knew he loved a laugh, but not moving, all the same. Ron Preston used to tell him he ought to vary his visiting times, but Ron took more precautions than the ambassador to Iran. Billings could not be bothered with all that. After a while, a car door slammed somewhere behind him and he heard what sounded like a man approach quickly on foot. He was scared to look immediately, but when he forced himself to turn he saw, walking swiftly towards him, Barry Leckwith, the tall, slab-faced police source, and part-time veal expert from Wankers. Leckwith gave no greeting, did not even glance at him, but passed and kept going. After a minute, Mansel followed. Leckwith turned into a service lane at the back of the residential home and Mansel found him waiting there. He had on an olive green bush suit that had cost something, but the colour was wrong for his complexion, too close.

'Always the loveliest places, Barry. I'm fond of lanes.' This time, instead of the restaurant's waste bins, they stood near a heap of black plastic refuse bags from the home. The smells seemed about equal, even if the menus weren't. 'I miss the chef's hat.'

'How's your dear mother, then, Manse? Every Thursday evening. You're a saint. I've got a fellow-feeling. I live with my old mum, you know.'

'Well, she's coming along. Still doesn't know me, but talking a bit now. Not always sense, though sentences. She stares right through me. She can recall every word of "Red Sails In The

Sunset", yet not me. It's hurtful. I feel rejected, like the runt of the litter. This is a man going on forty-four. Eerie. You've got something for us, Barry?'

'Your trouble, Manse, you can look on the bright side and cheer people up, none better, but you have to feel loved. Not uncommon. You're the sort who always needs a mother – and a leader.'

'That right? On the dossier about me, is it?'

'It's a problem, old age. I bring some decent news, I think.'

'I do miss her, Barry.'

'Bound to, someone sensitive to people, like you.'

'But, you'll understand, Barry, I couldn't look after her at home. You're right, I think a lot about people and their needs, it's something I'm known for. The thing is, though, I'm single. And my business commitments – never sure when I'm going to be at the house. So, what news, Barry?'

'Of course. Nobody's blaming you, Manse. I've heard a lot of people say there's no blame can be attached to Manse for where his mother's kept. It looks an exceptionally decent place. From outside.'

'It is. Yes, exceptional. I wouldn't settle for anything less for her. Big telly. They keep the pee odour exceptionally subdued. Yes, exceptionally. I'm here every Thursday evening and on a Sunday to do some morale boosting, not just for her but the other fine seniors in there, and I bring biscuits or chewable mints, nothing big and hard that could choke, every flavour you can think of, and we hand them around, naturally. I'm much looked forward to.'

'She's got a son and a half. They obviously thought a hell of a lot of you, picking a special first name. I don't come across too many Mansels. Speaking of the other night, I'm sorry if I was a bit terse.'

'We understood.'

'It was inconvenient.'

'I know, I know. We had a little crisis, that's all. Ron insisted. He can get very urgent.'

'But I heard what you said, Manse. I took note, for action subsequently.'

'Yes, well, we didn't say much, did we? You know what Ron's like about security.'

'He's a laugh, old Ron. In the wrong trade.'

'So, it's wonderful to see you, Barry, but what exactly brings you here? You want me to put you up for membership of the home?'

At a bedroom window above them an old woman stared out and waved and kept waving to nobody in an empty recreation ground. It was hard to feel hopeful about some of the people in there, including his mother, but he did try, and he made sure he always put on a good, noisy show when he was with her. This was welfare, as much as looking after Dean and Tyrone.

Leckwith said: 'I just wanted to let you know I did a little inquiry or two, along the lines you were asking. You wondered whether there was any interception activity under discussion among our people. I don't like to leave you and Planner Preston unadvised, Manse.'

'That's damn British of you.'

'I feel obligated to you, Manse, that's all. And if he's your partner, to him as well. So I made careful inquiries.'

'Thanks – however it turns out.'

'However? What's however? You don't need doubts, Manse. Our people know nothing. That's why I came tonight. I can say it for certain now. No current information. No pots on the boil. Nobody on stand-by – Rob Cotton or Rowles or Synott, none of them. That's what you wanted to know, isn't it?'

Mansel felt embarrassed. 'Thanks again, Barry. I mean it. That's bloody good work, and I know it's tricky. But when I say "however", what I mean is, I have this feeling.'

'Which?'

'A feeling that Ron might decide not to go through with this one. I don't see him for a day or two, but that's what I think he's going to say.'

Not worrying about marking the bush suit, Barry had been leaning against the wall near the plastic bags, very at ease, very pleased with himself, but he straightened up now and, although they had been whispering, his voice suddenly became almost normal strength, and full of edge. Up the lane a dog in one of the back yards started barking, what sounded like a pretty big dog, and then two more followed, or it could be three. 'Not do it? Why?' Barry said.

'Like I said, it's a feeling I have, that's all, but I know Ron.

56

It's a strong feeling. There've been changes. Several – on top of one another. He can't take that. Ron's always looking for omens. You heard how things went bad for him once? It's left its mark. That'll be in the dossiers, too. Christ, listen.' The dogs were still at it, like a husky camp at seal meat time, and in a minute people would start coming out to see why. 'It's great work you've done, Barry – as ever – but this time there might not be anything in it for you, that's what I'm trying to say. We shouldn't have asked you. Mind, I don't want to sound insulting. I'm not suggesting you only help for money. Much more to it than that, I know, but it's bound to be an element, buying a suit like that etcetera. Anyway, I suppose you're all right for funds, really – two jobs.'

'It's crazy, Manse.' He was whispering again, thank God, but a strong whisper, well, a fierce whisper. 'What changes?' Leckwith asked.

'And on top he frets about all sorts – the Collator noting everything that moves and phone taps.'

'The Collator? That's only routine. Every cop's supposed to report everyone he sees who's got a record. It's just so we know where they are, nothing at crisis level. Well, yes, they might be tapping. Illegal, but it's possible. Wouldn't you with someone like Preston on your patch? But they wouldn't get anything, would they? Planner's too cagey to talk on the phone.'

'You know what he'd say to that? He'd tell you police are bound to think he must be up to something because they never hear him on the line. You can't win with him. The other boys think it's his age, but it's not, it's how he's been for as long as I've known him. If I went and complained to him, though, all he would say, nice as pie is, "It works, Manse." It's years since he's been inside, and years since anybody on a job with him has been taken, too. That's a very big argument. So, I trust him, Barry.'

'Which other boys?'

'Other boys?'

'You said "other boys".'

'Did I? Oh, you wouldn't know them. From elsewhere. Good, sincere kids, but that's it, kids. They talk about having a go on our own, without Ron. I don't like the sound of it. Not a bit. I look on the bright side, yes, but Ron's part of the bright side. For me, he *is* the bright side. Like you said, I need a leader.' The dog din had started to fade. All the same, he wanted to be on his way.

'So where was it going to be, this job, Manse? If it's all up in the air, and maybe dead it hardly matters if you say, does it? Never been secrets between you and me before. Oh, I understand when Preston's around you've got to be careful, but not now.'

'What's the point? Why do you want to know?'

'Just that we work together, Manse. There shouldn't be cut-off points, not on either side. Would I do that to you? Is it decent? And Preston's decision – it's so mad. I don't understand what's happened, that's all. What changes, for instance? A smaller take suddenly? Not worth the risk?'

'Bigger.'

'What?'

'That's Ron for you. His thinking. Look, no police dossier is ever going to explain him right. Ron's on his own.'

'But where, Manse? What job? Look at it like this: suppose you did decide to go without him. You say no, but think about it for a minute. You could change your mind. Someone like Planner, he's fine and you're grateful to him, respectful of him, and all that's very understandable and to your credit. But there does come a time, all the same, Manse. And it can come very, very suddenly. One day somebody like Preston is front-line, the next he's a hobbling liability, and he knows it. The point is, I could really check, check double, if I knew what we're talking about. You see what I mean? I could make it two hundred per cent certain you're going to have a free run, and if you're short-handed, that's so vital. So far, I've done a thorough trawl, but it's bound to be a bit hit and miss, yes?' He put his long, bony, copper's face closer, with all that grim skin, and tried to make himself sound like a friend, full of heavy concern. 'We're talking about wages, Manse?'

'I don't want to—'

'Look, it's got to be wages, hasn't it? Is Ron going to do a bank or a jeweller's? Is he, hell.'

Billings felt hemmed in by the sacks and bush shirt and the size of Leckwith and the way he stayed with it, the cop way he stayed with it. How did he get away from Leckwith and go home? 'Listen, Barry, you're a friend, and you're right, there's old times, so, yes, wages. But I don't want to say more. Don't ask me any more, that fair?'

58

'I thought wages. But not too many vans around now, what with cheques and bank payment. Not that are worth the effort.'

'Ron found this one. Oh, he's got his feeble ways, his old-time ways, yes, but he's sharp, too, and sources come to him. That's what I mean about leadership.'

Leckwith looked as if he was thinking. 'I know Harpur's people and the robbery squad take a general interest in wages runs, just in case. The ones I've heard of – Securicor to The Old Foundry? Charles Maitland Ltd? Brand's? Peterson and Crabtree? Leintwardine?'

'What's that mean, for Christ sake, "a general interest"?'

'That's all. They know which firms get a big cash delivery weekly. Well, you'd expect a decent police force to keep tabs, wouldn't you? Otherwise would be neglectful. They don't do a regular watch, nothing like that, but they know. Nothing to worry about, unless they get a tip, and a tip they have not got, I know this, and I'll have another look, for luck.' Just for a moment it seemed as if Leckwith might be going, thank God. He walked a couple of steps towards the end of the lane and then suddenly turned. 'Is it Brand's, Manse? That seemed to get to you, when I said Brand's.'

It was an old police trick that Mansel recognised. They would make out everything was all over and fine, so you relaxed, and then suddenly come up with the question they wanted the answer to all along. Billings picked his way around the sacks and began to walk back towards his car. But, God, he should have ended it sooner. 'I'm not saying, and let's be clear, Barry, I haven't said Brand's, or anywhere else. Okay? It wouldn't be right. You know that. For me, Ron's still the governor, and he wouldn't like it. Simple as that. Can we forget it now? That's all you'll get out of me.' He still had the 'DON'T MOVE' message in his hand and let it flutter away in the small summer breeze. 'Don't come down here again. This is me in my private capacity, and I'm going to keep it like that.'

'I'll be in touch, Manse, when I've done another little survey. I'm taking all your needs and anxieties aboard, so don't fret. I do hope mother continues to pick up,' Leckwith called. That set the dogs off again.

Chapter 8

Iles and Harpur sat at a low table in the ACC's office with Sergeant Robert Cotton's dossier open in front of them, a couple of medical reports included. There was a photograph of him, bringing out the alertness and intelligence of his face. Harpur could have done without it. Iles said: 'Officially, everything is great. The doctors tell us counselling and time have worked and he's altogether fit again. And his shooting on the range is still unbelievable. But people who work with him a good deal say he's—'

'Like you, sir, I understood he'd made a complete recovery and that there was no reason to take away his gun duties.'

'Volatile,' Iles continued. 'People close to him say he's become very volatile since killing Ditto.'

'It might be crucial not to damage his image of himself, at this stage, sir,' Harpur replied at once.

'Image? What kind of fucking quack word is that?'

'Sir, he's working on recovery and—'

'Weren't you telling me recovery is total?'

'Well, yes, sir, but—'

'You've been got at? Is it somehow in your interests, his wife's interests, to keep him happy? I don't see why, but is that it?' His small mouth was screwed up in puzzlement. 'I lose track of the fine points of your love life. Myself, I've other kinds of personal problems. It's a risk, Col.'

'Cotton having a gun ticket?'

'The baby.'

'Oh, I wouldn't worry too much, sir. They take care of any problems very well these days.'

'You're right, Col. If we want it we want it, and we certainly do, especially myself, but Sarah, too.'

60

'I think it's grand,' Harpur said.

'There's nothing that could make a bigger difference at home.' He smiled in a way that came near to happiness, and certainly as near as Harpur had ever seen on his face. Iles took some knowing and not everyone wanted to bother.

'Sarah's keeping well?'

'Absolutely. Of course, I'm a convert,' the Assistant Chief admitted. 'I never wanted children, not at any price.'

'Often the case, sir. People suddenly come round.'

'Well, Sarah spreading herself, bedding herself, the way she was. Your friend, Garland. Then this quasi crook, Ian Aston. That could still be going on, but in decline, I'm sure of that. God knows who else. It meant something, didn't it, Col? Cosmic dissatisfaction. A baby looks the only way to anchor her properly, and I would like her anchored.'

'That will be one benefit. There'll be others.'

Iles, who was wearing one of his tailored shirts and a Force tie, fiddled with the papers on his desk and then said: 'Yes, anchored and steady. But, Cotton: volatile. Do you know what that word means to me, Harpur? It means police gunfire when there's no provable need for it. It means gunfire that might knock over the innocent and ricochets whistling up the jacksy of some old age pensioner, famed for a lifetime raising money for guide dogs. It means, thereafter, endless pious aggro from the Home Office and the dim doves in the Opposition and Lord Gifford and the press and Councillor Tobin and the Court of Sodding Human Rights in Strasbourg. Heard of that at all? It issues proclamations on the side of justice, meaning anti-police.'

'We've gone months without a call for armed officers, sir, and might go for months more. There are no interceptions on the agenda, no scheduled armed raids by gangs that we know about. All the usual feelers are out, but nothing at all. Possibly Cotton won't have to handle a gun on the streets for an age. By then, he could be indisputably all right. Do you have to make your decision now?'

'Or there could be a shout in ten minutes, or tonight, or tomorrow, and he might be one of the only firearms people about each time.'

'They're certainly scarce, sir. And top-class ones are rarer than rubies.'

Iles put the reports on Cotton and the photograph back into the folder. 'Tell me this, Col: do you ever think about yourself?'

'Sir?'

'An outraged husband around, possibly unbalanced by the Ditto killing, trained with firearms, and a supreme shot. Couldn't you quite reasonably feel threatened?'

'Never, sir. I've never for a moment considered things in that way,' Harpur declared at once.

'Oh, I see.' He nodded a couple of times. 'You have, have you? You're very wise, though I don't know what you do about it. You're not going to give up Mrs Cotton, are you, someone warm and so very lovely? But, listen: what the Chief would not want, and what I could do without myself, come to that, is a whizz-kid detective chief super blown away by one of his own disturbed sergeants, in messy revenge for cuckolding. That, also, would not look too great in the *Independent* and might fail to enhance the futures of your seniors. I don't see me working out my career as someone's assistant, and certainly not a someone like Mark Lane.'

'I can't regard Cotton as disturbed. Not in the least. Solid family man, good parent.'

Iles, at his desk, reflected for a while. 'Yes. Sarah's thirty-six. Late for a first child, no getting away from that.'

'It'll be fine, sir.'

'And, of course, I would hate it to be a daughter. How does one know what one's getting with a girl child? Think of Eva Braun, or Eleanor Roosevelt.'

Harpur had heard him on a similar tack several times before. 'Mine are both girls, sir.'

'Of course they are, Col. Forgive me. Thoughtless. But you – you're so solid. You bring a strong, good, shaping influence to bear on your children, even daughters. I don't know if I could manage that. I've always despised stability. It's sour grapes, of course, because I haven't got any. Do I really want it? I mean, the Chief's got stability, hasn't he? Who'd want to be like him, for Christ sake? Oh, look, Harpur, I'm thinking of asking you to be godfather. Or don't you go in for that sort of thing? You've got some religion somewhere, haven't you? I saw it in your papers, alongside the account of that comical education. All right, you're banging someone else's wife, a subordinate's wife, but this doesn't turn you into a heathen, does it? That relationship's long-term, after all, not something merely casual and fleshly. Almost noble. This brings us back to Cotton.'

'He's a very valuable part of our over-the-pavement team, sir. I'd hate to lose him.'

Iles smoothed his face and exercised his mouth and jaw muscles, probably a precaution against age lines. 'All right, as for Cotton, I'll leave things as they are, for the immediate present, Col.'

'It's for the best, sir.'

'But I worry about him. I worry about you. Do I want my unborn son's godfather to be victim of a sleazy killing? Does one wish a baby to start life with that kind of stain? Tell me, have you looked at it like that? How bloody far does your selfishness go, Harpur?'

Chapter 9

'Here's Ron, boys, and he's got some great news,' Mansel said. He had on his biggest and happiest voice, the one Preston used to call 'joy to the world', like an old-time Sunday school preacher announcing the Lord might return tomorrow, and wouldn't it be wonderful when they all were inter-citied to heaven? 'But I won't steal the thunder,' Mansel told them, 'And, oh, this is Hoppy Short. He's going to be with us. I'll tell you more about him in a minute. First, though, the great Ron.'

Mansel made a sound like a trumpet fanfare, then a drum roll. It was humour, but no harm. The other two, Dean and Tyrone, standing near each other in the flat under a snowy forest picture with fancy moonlight, waited like a couple of kids hoping to hear they could go to the fair. They kept the room reasonably clean and tidy, Preston would say that, a bit better than your usual waiting days tip. A lot of these new boys had such nice upbringings.

He tried to look as pleased and excited as Mansel sounded. That was important now. Once you made the decision you had to behave like it was the greatest one ever and was bound to work out handsome. Mansel would call that morale, but it was just to show you believed in yourself. 'The job's on, lads,' he told them. 'No problems. Thursday week we go, go, go. Brian Short here, or Hoppy as he's called, he's coming in to help us, in view of the changes. He knows a thing or two about this sort of outing.'

Dean and Tyrone were beaming. Preston watched both of them, really kept his eye on the buggers, trying to read if he was saying what they knew already, after Grace going out with Tyrone. There was no knowing what a girl would say to a bloke she fancied, even your daughter. The more you told her no, the more she might do it. Thinking of preachers, that was what it meant in the Bible about a child leaving father and mother and going to some smart arse. And if Tyrone knew, Dean would know, and maybe the girl who had been number four in the socialising would know, too – kids with a few drinks in them, all talking big. So, who else knew? Where did this girl, Debbie Something, come from? Had Dean dropped her after that one night and turned her nasty and looking for revenge? So, where was she talking now? That was one reason he had been asking Grace. And then there was the very cheerful thought that someone with a mouth like Wilf Rudd's knew, as well. He came down the house and said a bit and listened a lot, Wilf, that was his special business skill.

But these two, Tyrone and Dean, did look pleased and even breathless when he gave the announcement now, like they had been wondering still if it was go. Of course, they were not dumbos, and especially Tyrone, so they could easily lay on a bit of phoney surprise and delight. Like he had been thinking for a while, *Annie Get Your Gun* might not be the only acting going around here.

Mansel had stopped the fanfare but now started to clap his hands and sing, 'For he's a jolly good fellow'. Tyrone and Dean clapped, too, and joined in the chorus. Hoppy Short grunted a couple of times and stared about in his own style but did not take part. He looked puzzled. This figured, because he did not know about all the argument and doubts that nearly killed this job. One of the things about Hoppy, anyway, he was tops at looking puzzled. His brain did work, but mostly it worked at being puzzled. Hoppy would never be first on Preston's list. Or second, or fifteenth. Just he was the best available in the time. You did what you could. Twice before Hoppy had worked for them and did all right, although he was about three-quarters of the way between too dim, and, Christ, no, much too dim, and you could not rely on him for anything except the heavy stuff. He was like Tyson out of the ring – in need of a shepherd. He did not get scared, and like Mansel said, Hoppy had so much guts a lot of it had to be stored in his head. The words of 'For he's a jolly good fellow', would be tough for him to remember, and some of the words later on like 'and so say all of us' might be too difficult. But, like all of the people Preston had ever worked with, when it was about his cut Hoppy could suddenly think pretty well and count very nicely. There would have to be some tricky negotiations.

The other thing against Hoppy was he had a lot of chicken-shit background, in for little bit burglaries and taking cars and knocking girlfriends about for being brighter, knocking them about with witnesses close, even women witnesses. Not things major enough to interest Harpur or Iles, but things that got in the press and made the dossier bulge and easy to notice on the shelf, all the same.

Although there was all the laughing and clapping now, Preston saw Tyrone did not like the look of Hoppy. He was a bit of a snob, Tyrone, with the yellow frame glasses and no tattoos. He said things like, 'But on the other hand', for Christ sake. Maybe that was the sort Grace liked. Girls could be soft. But Tyrone and all of them would have to make the best of it with Hoppy. Since Wilf Rudd's late news, this had to be a five job now if it was on, three for the driver and guards, one for the lad in the gatehouse and Tyrone driving. If you showed Hoppy just how he had to do it, and told him a few times which were the exact words he had to wait for from Preston or Mansel before he did anything, anything at all, he could still be a sort of plus, as long as everything went just like planned. Preston would handle the thinking himself. That was only the usual.

'We believe there's first-class availability,' he said. 'I had my anxieties, I admit, but that's cleared. Mansel's had some very good information. This is absolutely inside material, and we're dead sure—' He would prefer to keep the word 'dead' out of it. 'What I mean, we're certain, no police will be waiting.'

Dean had on a pair of thick blue braces holding his smart suit trousers up, and he was tugging these, pulling them out and letting them smack back on his body, he was so excited. What you would expect from somebody still a kid, but all right. It was the kind of high spirits that could be necessary.

'So this take, Ron?' he asked. 'This take is what we thought originally, but up three times, at least three times? Are we into decent money at last?'

'There's more money,' Preston admitted.

'Yes, but the information – Mansel's information? Doesn't it—'

'Mansel's information is about other aspects, not size of the take,' Preston replied. 'About priority matters, such as are we going to run into a police gunship with Cotton out in front?'

'What's that mean, cotton out in front?' Dean said.

'Robert Cotton. The Viscount Ambush, himself,' Mansel replied.

'Viscount? I heard of a Cotton, but he's a sergeant in the police,' Hoppy mentioned.

'So we know we're in the clear,' Mansel said.

Preston, still with his eyes on Dean and Tyrone, reckoned they looked not just excited, but frightened with it. Oh, they loved the thought that the job would be on and the money would be fatter, but now the thing was decided they felt scared about it, too. Yes, kids. It did not mean they would turn out useless on the day, only that they talked and dreamed a long way ahead of what they thought. And then, suddenly, the talking and the dreaming had to move over, and the job itself was on the agenda, and in their little boy imaginations they could feel the street under their shoes as they ran at the van, and the metal of it as they pulled themselves aboard among the cash sacks, and could even hear what the shouting and swearing would be like, and maybe an alarm siren and police two-tones. And maybe firing.

Of course, they knew they had to keep up a show now, playing with the braces and yelling and laughing, counting the future wads in their head, but there was something else. The fear grinned through. It might be worse with Dean, but Tyrone had it, as well, Preston could see fear in both. He knew what to look for. He knew from the inside. Now and then he felt it, too, when a job was coming. Well, he had to admit, he felt it about this job. Usually, he escaped all that, now he was not a kid himself. Always, until now, he would have done the thinking before he took the decision, and had made every move, run every step in his mind, heard all the panic din in his mind, too, so he could cope.

This time, it could not be like that. The decision had come out of nowhere. Since Wilf Rudd turned up with the news of two up to three, most of the thinking had told Preston not to do it, and keep clear, go for postponement. And then something else had suddenly grabbed him hard and said. Do it. Well, no mystery about the something else. It was needing to feel young, and trying to bury words like 'past it', and forget such shitty matters as a hair transplant. So, he had wanted to show Grace, and maybe show Carol, the young, pretty one from *Annie Get Your Gun*, too, that he could still make decisions, and still take on tough jobs and do all the thinking and body work that went with them. Of course, the young, pretty one from *Annie* had no idea about any of this, but just by coming into the room and doing the song and taking notice of him she had helped work the trick. That was the thing about women. They didn't know their own strength, women who looked like that.

And then it could be the bloody exact opposite of all this, as well – not about showing he was still young, but about wondering if he had really started fading with age. What if Grace and Dean and Tyrone had it right and he truly was getting old? Well, of course he was getting old, who could dodge that? But what about if they were right and he was getting past it? These were not stupid people. Kids of that age saw a lot and saw it very sharp. So, maybe he better do what he could while there was still time. Perhaps he should be trying to store something hearty for his old age and Doris's old age, and for looking after Devon. That kid down there seemed bright and might have to go to college, like Grace. This would mean funds. When he thought like this, the extra in the van could start to look very interesting, not a turn-off at all, but just what was vital at this time in his life. In other words, he saw he had suddenly dropped up to his armpits in the dream rubbish he always dreaded, the slop that said you should go for the super-take, the 'biggie', because that was the only way you would ever get to put your feet up permanent and live on your fat.

So, if he looked inside, there had been some changes, deep down changes. In his head he still felt something that told him not to try it, but here he was, stuck with a world-class thicko, Hoppy Short, and encouraging the rest of them, like this job was such a piece of cake all you had to do was turn up on the right day and gobble it.

All the same, it made him feel a bit better to see Tyrone and Dean looking nervy. So, who was past it, then? Past it? They hadn't even reached it yet. The other thing he liked was they seemed to be really hearing this decision for the first time, or they would have got used to the idea. If they knew it already, fright would not have hit them so sharp that it got right up into their faces, like measles. Maybe Grace had not opened her mouth, after all, and the other girl knew nothing. Had he been doing Grace wrong? She was a good kid.

Dean sat down with his legs hanging over the arm of the settee to show how relaxed he was and said: 'This is going to take some working out, the shares, Ron. An unknown amount and five now, instead of four. And Hoppy's great, I can tell just by looking and listening, but he's coming into it very late. That's not his fault, no, of course, but I've got a lot of build-up time to be paid for, Ron, and displacement, plus, as you know, the hairy side of the job, the gatehouse. I'm on my own there, cut off. Obviously, there'll have to be a graded system. Well, differentials, really, or what could be called a sliding scale – you and Mansel at the top, Ron, as previously, then myself and Tyrone, then Hoppy. We all want to be fair, don't we? I'm going to admit Tyrone's equal. I want to be reasonable.'

'Ron's brought the armament,' Mansel said.

'You'll see what I mean about expense,' Preston told them.

Mansel had the holdall near his feet and he passed it across now, very delicate, like a bomb or a baby. He could use his brain, Mansel. Mentioning the guns just then and making this big, handle-with-care show was his way of pushing away talk about the shares. That kind of discussion was always trouble. People could not talk about money without going cold in the voice and starting to snarl. It got in the way of thinking like a team.

Preston sat down, with the holdall on his lap and unzipped it. 'There's three,' he said. 'I'll have one. Dean will need another at the gatehouse, we've got to really scare the guy in there. Manse doesn't go much for armament, never has, that's something about Manse, and he's entitled to his own ways, so we'll have to sort out about the third. Tyrone, you're going to be in the car and you'll be busy with that, I expect. Maybe Hoppy?' Jesus. But, yes, maybe.

He brought out the two blue Charter Arms Bulldogs first, one in each hand. 'Pretty? Yes, they look pretty, but a .44 shell, that's quite a size, and it will stop anything less than a tank. Known as a "law enforcement model", as a matter of fact.'

Mansel had one of his best laughs. 'If you can't beat 'em join 'em.'

'Five shot,' Preston said. 'Easy to keep hidden. That's the

beauty. These people, the ones in the van and Mr Gatehouse, they'll all know this Bulldog model, what a nasty little bitch she can be if she gets angry and starts barking, and they won't give provocation. What I don't want, and what I've told you all – except maybe Hoppy, because he's late – what I don't want is blasting off for no reason.'

'They loaded?' Dean said.

'Of course they'll be loaded,' Preston replied.

'What's a gun if it's not loaded?' Mansel said.

'They'll be loaded, but that don't mean I want shooting,' Preston said. 'It don't mean that at all. This is to give those boys in the van and the gatehouse guard something to think about, so they do what they're told and do it brisk. These are handguns, not sawn-offs, because I hate sawn-offs, spewing destruction everywhere. That's chaos. This is controlled.' He gave Dean and Hoppy a gaze. 'What you got to think about is if you're holding a gun you're a target, and more a target if you fire it.'

'Target? Who for? Police are not going to be there, we're told, Ron,' Tyrone said. 'Aren't we?'

'Our information is police won't be there. That's correct. We wouldn't be going if we thought different. But—'

Mansel said: 'Eventualities. You've got to plan for what they call in Sandhurst military academy "the worst scenario". This is basic.'

'All I'm saying, these guns, and my Beretta, here in the bag, are first and foremost for putting the frighteners on. We don't go into this like the battle of Iwo Jima. Of course, if things turn a bit unexpected—'

Mansel said: 'That's what I mean – a gun's not a gun until it's loaded.'

Dean asked: 'If it's police, if this Cotton shows up, we're in a different ball game, yes? This would have to be firing, even if it makes them retaliate? Anyway, what I hear, they don't wait. They're blasting from the start.' His voice was shaky. This babe wanted to sound like no holds barred but he was doing dribbles in his knickers.

'If there's police it's another situation,' Preston agreed. 'I don't pretend anything else. Could be they got to be dealt with, entirely dealt with, so we can reach the car and away.

That's why these are good calibre, the Bulldogs, not some lady's toy.' He placed one of the pistols on the floor and from the bag brought his Beretta Modello 84 Short, a 9 mm, and blue like the Bulldogs. 'This would do the trick too, so I hear. I've never had to try. Considered a man-stopper.' He balanced it in his palm for a few seconds, admiring the lines, though the smooth, cool feel made his stomach turn. 'And I won't have to use it this time, either. Same for the Bulldogs. This raid will go very, very comfortable and there'll be no police until we're miles away, clear in a different vehicle.'

'So why's yours the Beretta?' Dean asked.

'It's what I've had a long time, that's all. The Bulldogs, I told you, new. You ought to be glad. No tracing from the bullets – if you had to fire.'

'Beretta's class,' Dean said.

'They're all class,' Ron told him. 'You can see, they're each lovely.' He replaced the three in the holdall. 'Now, we've got to make another trip,' he said. 'Up to Brand's. This is for Hoppy. He must see the ground and get the feel.'

'What, all of us?' Tyrone asked. 'Again? Look, Ron, this could be noticeable.'

'Hoppy needs to see who does what,' Mansel said. 'We can explain at the spot. It's easier.'

What Mansel meant was Hoppy would not take it in unless they showed him the ground and then also showed him, by pointing and saying it a few times, which of them would do which part of the job, and which part was his, and where exactly they would be when it began, and how to get back to the car. If it had been on, Preston would have liked to do chalk marks on the road for him, like in a stage play. It would not be any good telling him here in the flat that Dean would handle this bit, or Mansel this bit, because he would never remember. If he could look at the street and then see the gatehouse or whatever, it might stay in his head, like in a child's book, teaching things by pictures, 'This dress is red.' Tyrone might be right, it was not good to be going up there again. It was especially not good for Preston, because he had been at Brand's by himself this week already. If you were depending on somebody like Hoppy, though, you had to think about his special needs.

'Then we can give it a rest until the day, except for getting the cars and balaclavas,' Preston said. 'I've got a few things on, anyway – *Annie Get Your Gun* – and Devon.'

'Who's Annie? We using a girl?' Hoppy asked. 'What's she having, a Bulldog or a Beretta?'

'It's just a musical,' Mansel said. 'Ron has to go to it. Life's not all hold-ups.'

'Well, I know it's a musical, don't I?' Hoppy replied. 'Betty Hutton, Howard Keel. "You Can't Get A Man With A Gun." A joke, Manse. What you think, I'm some sort of fucking moron?'

Chapter 10

Mansel Billings, arriving to visit his mother in the eventide home, saw from the entrance of the ward that a man was already with her. He had his back to Billings and was crouched over the bed, patiently feeding her with a spoon from a dinner tray. When Billings went closer he saw it was Barry Leckwith.

Turning, Leckwith nodded to him and, with a very kindly smile, said: 'Here's Mansel, love. We knew he'd come, didn't we? She's eating well, Manse. Semolina pud now.' He gave her another spoonful and wiped her mouth carefully with a paper nakpin.

'What the hell are you doing? I told you not to—'

'Not to see you outside, because of the dogs.'

'I told you, this is my private life.' His mother moved her eyes from Leckwith to him and then back to Leckwith, the same utter blankness applied to each. Billings sat on the side of the bed: 'I'll do that, sod it,' he said, reaching for the spoon.

'Well, of course. I realise I'm just a stop-gap, Manse.' He handed the spoon over. 'Only helping out, wasn't I, my lovely?' he said to her.

Billings began to feed his mother the pudding.

'She likes it better from you, Manse. Anyone can see. Well, of course. You're her boy. I know about that relationship. Same for me at home.' He sat on the other side of the bed, wearing a brown leather jacket that was not bought mail order, and leaned across to speak quietly to Billings. 'I've been doing some digging about Brand's. Looking after you, Manse, as ever.'

'Brand's?'

'Oh, come on now, Manse. I know it's Brand's. And, please, none of that crap about Preston deciding not to do it.' From the tray, he passed a spouted cup with milky tea in it for Billings to put to his mother's mouth. 'Food looks grand here. You've sorted out a first-class place for her. Just what I'd expect from someone so caring.'

'Why don't you just fuck off?'

Leckwith frowned. 'A charmer, when he wants to be, isn't he, Mrs Billings? You never taught your son such language, I know. But there's no real harm in him. Manse, you'll have heard the van's calls have been upped to three. Well, of course you have. Planner Preston's done a very classy bit of research there. But have you heard the amount? I don't think so. You couldn't. This took me a lot of getting – locating an old contact, and winning his confidence again, really winning it.' He leaned further over the bed, so he could whisper close to Billings's ear. 'Oh, sorry, sweety,' he said, because he had been bearing down on her legs. Leckwith carefully repositioned himself. 'Three hundred and twenty thousand pounds, Manse.' He sat back, nodding. 'This is Planner moving up a couple of gears. Good luck to him. Obviously, to take the lot you've got to hit it at Brand's, before any unloading. And I don't see why not. Nothing I've found says there'll be a problem.'

'I don't know anything about Brand's. I've told you.'

'Not so loud, Manse. Some patients here have still got their wits. And there are visitors.'

Billings gave her some of the tea, and Leckwith waited.

'Manse, I had to see you to say that in justice there's got to be a due percentage for Barry in this outing. Bound to be. This is a lot of money, good shares all round. I've really put some work into it for you, knowing you were worried about your mother, and the bills for this place. I realised exactly how important it was to be sure there's a clear run, no opposition waiting – Harpur and his specialists. You don't worry as much as Planner, but you do worry, despite that jolly exterior, and I felt I'd better get to you as soon as I could, now I know the target, to confirm that you're absolutely in the clear and due for a beautiful pay-off. All right, I could have phoned. But I can't be super-sure they're not listening to you, too, so another meeting seemed in order, especially as I could combine it with good deeds.'

'No, it's not right. You shouldn't come here. You know it. This place – well, it isn't to do with any of that.'

His mother heard a man visiting another bed say something

74

about 'the amenities' where he lived, and Mrs Billings began to repeat, 'Yes, amenities, amenities, amenities.'

'Good, Mrs Billings,' Leckwith exclaimed. 'What's her first name, Manse?' When Billings did not reply, Leckwith looked up at the name label over the bed. 'Yes, good, Ida. Nothing wrong with your articulation now. So, Manse, what I want is an undertaking on this cut we were getting near to discussing. I would say ten per cent is pretty right. You boys will do the work, no disputing that, and you rightly earn the bulk. But—'

'Bulk,' Ida Billings said. 'The bulk, bulk.'

'Right, love,' Leckwith went on. 'Manse and his friends are certainly entitled to a share of that. Me, I'm talking about thirty grand, that's all. In fact, a fraction under ten per cent. We'll let that go, though.'

A woman took the dishes and tray and put them on a trolley.

'If you like, I mean, if you haven't got say-so, I'll talk direct to Planner, Manse.'

'Talk to Ron? About what? Christ, no.' Again his voice had gone up.

'Panic not. Ron doesn't know we've been having private confabs? Fair enough. I had considered that. All right, a promise from you, now, will be enough for Barry,' Leckwith said. 'We've worked together before, and you do things right, I know. Manse, look, thirty grand might sound like nothing to your crew, but it could make a hell of a difference to me. Maybe a third of the way to a small but decent restaurant for myself. Not like that clip-joint, Wankers. I mean a real restaurant. A year or two from now, Manse, I could be employing a chef, not doing moonlight cooking myself.'

'How can I promise, for God's sake. How? How?' Billings replied.

'How? How? How?' Mrs Billings said.

'I can't say to Ron you've got to have thirty grand, can I, Barry? It would be off again if he knew you knew.'

'Knew you knew you knew you knew,' Mrs Billings added.

'So it *is* on then, Manse?'

'It could be. You bastard, you know that.'

'Of course it could be. Yes, I did know. Well, I assumed. Who's going to sniff at this much loot?'

'That's not why. I don't know why. It came from nowhere.'

'You say.'

'It's true. You know what Ron's like.'

Leckwith leaned across Mrs Billings again. 'Manse, I don't give a shit why it's on, as long as it *is* on, and I couldn't care less about fascinating aspects of Planner Preston's personality. I've got to have thirty grand, and you'd better say, now, that I'm going to get it.'

'How can I promise without talking to Ron? And if I talk to Ron—'

'He'll cancel?'

'Of course. And God knows what would happen to me. I'm talking to police, that's how some of the others would regard it. You – you're police. They wouldn't see there were special reasons, wouldn't want to. There are some unpredictable people involved in this, not just Planner. Youngsters from out of the area, smooth and hard. No, Barry, I can't. And as for Ron, all he would see is that a cop knows about it. I could tell and tell him you're all right and completely straight, but he doesn't really know you, and to him it would be only a cop knowing, and if one knows they all could know.'

Leckwith stood and came around the bed to sit alongside Billings on the other side. 'I understand all that, Manse. Of course I do. But what I'm saying is that after it's over, at share-out time, you tell Ron the situation, and what I've done for you. Explain why I'm due. He'll see the force of that. He's a thinker. Famous for it. And he takes notice of you, you're old confeds. Part of the situation then will be that I'll know who did the job on the van, won't I? Manse, I'm a friend of yours, and as you so decently say, I play very wholesome, but I do also have certain obligations to colleagues – Harpur, Cotton, Iles. If I'm stuck in the police for the rest of my life, I'd better think about impressing the brass, hadn't I, and this sort of information could bring me credit. You don't want people like Harpur and Iles around your place immediately afterwards looking for cash and dungarees and balaclavas, do you? Those two, they tend to find what they're searching for, somehow or another. That's why they're where they are, and not getting thumped by football hooligans. You'd all go away for ever. Consider, there could be shooting, maybe even a death or two. Iles, Harpur, they don't give up. And then Cotton, apparently recovered now after trigger

76

trauma, but who knows, really knows? Any party visiting your house would be armed and edgy, because they wouldn't know what to expect. You see how things are? I'm being reasonable, Manse, not greedy. After all, this is a case where there's very good availability, exceptional availability.'

'Availability, availability,' Ida Billings said, coming round from a little doze.

Chapter 11

Iles said he thought it would be what he called 'a telling gesture' if he and Harpur went down to the range and watched
Robert Cotton shoot, now the Sergeant had been informed he
could remain on the gun register. 'Col, as you know, I'm deep
into *noblesse oblige*. People do appreciate having a close interest
taken in them, especially a star, like Cotton. It won't disturb you,
all that fierce flying lead?'

They sat in the glass-fronted gallery while Cotton worked with
a Grande Puissance Browning, standing, lying and kneeling. He
wore ear pads against the din, and from above Harpur saw how
Cotton's fair hair stuck out thick and healthy from under the
harness. Lately, Harpur had come to fear that his own mop was
beginning to thin. Only this morning his younger daughter, Jill,
said she thought he was 'showing an obscene amount of forehead'.
Kids would always rush to pay off old scores, and they knew how
to hurt.

Cotton was shooting with a couple of other top people, Sid
Synott and Ambrose – Laissez Faire – Rowles, and their tallies
went up on an illuminated board at the end of each volley, like
hymn numbers in a trendy church. Cotton just about kept ahead,
though he must be short of practice after the lay-off.

The gallery was sound-proofed and Iles and Harpur could
talk. 'On second thoughts, I do take your point about Cotton
and "image",' the Assistant Chief said in the sweet-reason tone
he could occasionally fall victim to. 'One can see why guns would
be crucial to his self-esteem. It's obviously his way of imposing
his will on the world.'

'Oh, I wouldn't say that, sir.'

'No?'

'Hardly. I meant his image in the sense that this skill is part of his trade, and important for that reason. But gunplay can't be a personal thing with Cotton, or with any police marksman, can it?'

'No?'

'He, and all of them, shoot only within a very disciplined and very clear set of conditions.'

'Yes? I'm glad to hear you can think so,' Iles replied.

The tally board twinkled and Cotton's score moved ahead.

'The personal, the professional, they're not always easy to separate, Col.'

'How's Sarah, sir?' Harpur asked.

To his surprise, Iles sounded less serene about her today. 'She'll be all right, in due course. She'll settle down, I know it. This is not something that will happen overnight, and I might have been foolish to assume it could. She has formally to sever connections with that other, unfortunate part of her life. I do understand: motherhood, once it comes, tends to take over so comprehensively. It has to be a boy. As to names, I think you know I always regretted my parents failed to call me Beauregard, and I still have a hankering, though I can't see Sarah allowing that for ours. By the way, the babe is mine. No question. Sarah and I have been over dates together, quite carefully. And Mrs Cotton?'

'There's a lot to be said for not having children too early, sir. I've always maintained that.'

'Have you? Have you?' Iles nodded thoughtfully. 'These family chats, I love them, don't you, Harpur? What life is really all about.' He watched Cotton for a while. 'I'm fond of the Grande Puissance pistol. Never lets you down. The only handgun manufactured and used by both sides in World War Two, you know. Oh, Sarah's probably still seeing Aston, off and on. These things don't finish just like that. Well, do I need to tell you of all people, Harpur? But she wants the child, definitely wants our child, and I see that as resoundingly meaningful.'

'I agree, sir.'

'Adultery: so often it burns itself out, Col. Please, I'm not getting at you. I've no wish to do a Mark Lane papal sermon. One has experienced these sexual things from both sides. But the institution of marriage means a great deal – I mean literally, the institution. I don't put this forward as a new thought, but as a thought.'

'They all count, sir.'

Iles somehow made his lean, domineering face become mild, even pitiable. 'Now and then, when she's out late, Col, I'll go up and sit in the car outside Aston's flat just to see if she's around. Or that club, the Monty, run by Panicking Ralph, where Aston's a member. I've never spotted her at either place and I wouldn't do anything – I'm sure of this, absolutely sure, oh, yes – even if I did see her.' Suddenly, he was shouting. Once before Harpur had heard the ACC's voice take on this pain-filled, metallic, murderous edge when talking about his wife and Aston. 'I'm not proud of these expeditions, Col, but I quote it to prove my point, about the power of a marriage.'

'This is impressive devotion, sir.'

The shooting finished. Cotton glanced up to the gallery window, the pistol at his side, and gave a small nod to Iles, perhaps gratitude, perhaps an assertion of pride in his performance. He did not look at Harpur. That was usual, even welcome. To Harpur, Cotton appeared calm and balanced, wholly in control of himself, and that was a relief.

'I should go down and talk to him,' Iles said. 'These things do make a difference. It might be better if you didn't come, Col. This meeting's for cuckolds only. Men like Cotton and I have instant rapport.'

'I'll wait here.'

When Iles returned he said: 'I gave him the full history of the Grande Puissance. He was riveted. And I stressed your part in persuading me he should stay on firearms.'

'Why did you do that, sir?'

'I don't want anyone thinking you're a total shit, Harpur. Saving graces.'

'Thank you, sir.'

The range inspector came in. 'That was much appreciated, sir – the few personal words,' he told Iles.

'These are simple but worthwhile duties,' the ACC replied.

'Extremely worthwhile, if I may say, sir. Cotton's had a rough time since Ditto. Fools tormenting him, asking when he'd be doing another over-the-pavement job. You know the sort of crude stuff, sir. Makes you despair of police, almost. And always from people who've never held a gun, let alone pointed one in anger. That's the real pain. People like Barry Leckwith, in some desk job. This sort of thing did get to Rob Cotton. But I know he's all right now, and your presence here today, I mean both of you, that really clinched it.'

'Harpur's first class on this sort of team spirit thing. It was his idea to come. I learn so much from him about man management.'

In the car on the way back to the station, Iles said: 'What's Leckwith doing, asking Cotton if he had a gun job coming up?'

'As I understood it, this was just a tease. Taking the mick because Cotton was off colour after Ditto. Not quizzing him, sir.'

'Maybe. Why tease? He wouldn't know Cotton was in danger of losing his ticket, would he?' Iles drove on silently for a while. 'Tell me about Leckwith, Col.'

'Clerking in Personnel – a flower-arranging job. Moonlights as a chef at The Calaboose.'

'He bloody what? Is that known?'

'Known to me. It didn't seem worth making official trouble for him about it.'

'No? Oh, I see. The old game. One for your collection: someone else you could silence if he ever stumbled on unhelpful stuff about you. What's called career strategy, I believe.'

'Cookery's harmless, sir.'

'So, double wages. We pay Leckwith too little for his lifestyle?'

'Apparently. Nice dresser. But he's not unique, is he, sir? There are police plumbers, and police electricians, police chippies, police coach drivers.'

Iles parked in the yard, then sat still for a moment. 'So, if he needs money, might he be into something else – something that could pay a bit more than cookery?'

'What else, sir?'

'Why quiz Cotton about possible interceptions?'

'Just fun, sir. Kicking him while he's down: normal breezy, comradely police humour.'

'It could be made to sound like that, couldn't it?'

'Leckwith as a tipster to someone outside?'

'Have a look at him, Col. See if he's talking to anyone, would you? Who might be interested in where Cotton's working next?'

Chapter 12

'There'd be something very commensurate in this for you, Ian,' Preston said. 'I'd be ready to go to five per cent.'

'This sort of information, it's difficult,' Aston replied.

Preston had never liked the look of Ian Aston – another one too boyish, too bright, too bloody self-satisfied, but you had to use what there was. These days, did he like the look of any man who seemed young? 'Difficult? Don't I know! Why I'm here, Ian,' he said. 'Look, I'll level. Mansel was supposed to have someone inside the police, I mean, really inside, and able to keep us right in the picture. All I'll say, Ian, I met this source, this so-called source, once, and it was total dead loss. This guy, this moonlighting cop, did not want to know. I said to myself then, "Right, fuck you, my lad. I'll look elsewhere if I want to find out anything," which is why I had the idea this morning to come out to here and see if Ian Aston was still a regular at the Monty club and maybe put a proposition to him. What I mean, I need somebody professional, Ian, somebody who knows what's expected. It's manners, really, simple as that.'

'Look, it's great of you to think of me, Planner, but—'

'Well, let me get some drinks, first. Brandy as usual?' Preston went to the bar.

'An honour to see you back in my little place, Ron,' Panicking Ralph Ember said, pouring the two big Kressmann Armagnacs, no fussing with optics. 'We miss you. I like to see people of calibre here. Good for the Monty's image. I mean, where would White's be without the whites?'

'You're looking great, as ever, Ralph,' Preston replied. And it was true. The old knife scar along Ralph's jaw had worn down so it was paler, and you almost did not notice it in this light. People said Ralph looked like Charlton Heston without the money. Preston was fond of the Monty. It did have something. What it had was not class, naturally, but for a shit-heap the panelling and real brass fittings around the bar were extremely passable. And in the old days, anyway, Ralph managed to keep fair order here, despite the kind of people he had in night after night. Once in a while something terminal could happen, and there would be a cloud for a month or two. Ralph always seemed to weather it all, though.

Preston went back to Aston. 'What it is, Ian, I've said I'll do a certain job, said it as a fact. I won't bore you with the details, and I know you wouldn't want to hear, anyway, you object to getting involved. That's very important to your style, and I fully respect it. I had big doubts about this job, but I don't go back on something like that, once I've said it.'

'You're known for sticking to your word, Ron.'

'Well, I hope so. That's what leadership is all about, among other things. So I need a top-quality scan, to know for sure we're not going to meet opposition. This was supposed to come from Mansel's friend, who would be very well placed, but no joy, and I wouldn't trust it if it did come, now. You, Ian, you keep clean, very clean, and, as I say, I respect you for it. You stay out on the edges, but you do hear what's on the cards sometimes. Well, that's your special business, yes? Which is why I say a fee as high as five per cent, no messing. And, pardon me for coming out with this, but this thing you've got with Mrs Iles, naturally I've caught glimpses. A serious, worthwhile relationship of duration, no fly-by-night sex and farewell matter. This is unique, and is bound to bring certain information now and then, surely. Or do I speak out of turn, mentioning the lady?'

'You mean anything about possible police street operations?'

'Exactly. I knew you were the boy to visit, Ian. You've got grasp. Is she coming tonight? I mean, if so, I'll get out of the way. You wouldn't want to be seen with someone like me.'

'What's it five per cent of, Planner?' Aston replied.

'I got quite a team to accommodate, Ian, and commitments.'

'My trouble— Look, Sarah Iles would never speak about anything like that. She wouldn't even know, Ron. No, I don't mind you referring, but she and Iles, they don't talk a lot, and even less about his work. They discuss *The Times* crossword clues.'

'But if you were to—'

'And all that with Sarah might be closing down slowly, anyway. As you say, this has been going quite a time. It's a grief, but that's how it looks. She's pregnant. Insists on having it. Don't ask me whose, but obviously the husband takes first claim. That's only decent. No, she won't be here tonight. Given the circumstances, she's drifting back towards being full-time Mrs Assistant Chief Constable and one of the pillars of Rougement Place. There are all sorts of reasons I don't want to talk about it. Some sensitive areas, as you can imagine.'

'I'm sorry, Ian. That's real tragic. You sure?'

'Probably, it was always bound to happen. Christ, what am I, after all? A sort of nobody go-between. You say nice things, but that's what it amounts to, really. Anyway, I'm not Rougement Place quality, whatever else.'

'Don't say that. I think of you as—'

'So let's leave Sarah out of it, shall we? Look, I've got other sources. I do hear bits and pieces on my travels, even police bits and pieces. If you like, I'll listen and do some follow-up if I scent anything. It's risky, Ron. It's the kind of work where you can easily put a foot wrong and people see what you're up to. Eternal grudges are borne. That's what I mean about five per cent of what.'

'Can you take my word it will be very commensurate? There's really excellent availability.' Disclose the money details and, often, they could work out the job.

Aston stood. 'I don't hang about here too much now. There've been one or two unpleasant episodes late on. All sorts of rubbish has joined. Out and outers. The Armagnac's still beautiful, but the Monty's going down.'

Ralph waved as they left together and mouthed, 'Take care.'

In the street, Aston said: 'Yes, I'll look at it for you, Ron. It's a pig in a poke, but work's short. Make contact through Ralphy's? You're still worried about phones?'

Chapter 13

'Manse, you've got to make Dad call it off.' Grace had her head lowered and was speaking down at the little, formica-topped kitchen table, her voice hopeless and dead. It was the way people talked when they were too worked up to meet your eyes.

'Me? I'm the boy who jollies people along, aren't I, Grace?'

'For Christ's sake stop fooling and dodging things, will you? People are going to get killed. You know I'm seeing Tyrone?'

'This is crazy.' He found a laugh from somewhere. Jolly Manse. 'Do you really believe your dad would go into a job if he thought people would be killed – any people, not just ours? Or I would? Your dad and I, we've worked a lot together, and we cut the risks right down.'

They were alone in the kitchen of the hide-away flat used by Tyrone and Dean. Arriving here to give the lads another of his welfare visits and pass on the bright news from Leckwith, Mansel had been appalled to find Grace present. Now, he heard she had something on with Tyrone. And not only Grace, there was another girl around as well. God, what had happened to security?

Grace went on talking down at the table, her voice almost gone, like she was afraid to speak her thoughts: 'Stalked by that Harpur, and his gun team.'

'They know nothing. Couldn't. This is a totally secret operation.' Except he was having to talk to her about it.

'Manse, I think my dad only decided for this job because of mad things I said about him getting old and past it.' She started crying, but made no sound.

He laughed again. 'That's what's bothering you? Well, it needn't. That's not how Ron operates. He works everything out before he settles yea or nay. There were good points, there were

85

bad. He had to weigh up the two sides, that's all. And when he weighed them, the balance showed we could do it. I don't know what you said to him, love – about what, his age? Forget it. That wouldn't bother Ron.'

She could have this right, and although he was no worrier, it scared him. The way Ron came round so sudden to the job, even when the information was problematical, had to be a right mystery. Maybe Grace had the answer. But he told her: 'You say your dad's getting old, and he is a bit, of course, we all are, but getting old means getting wiser, too. It means coming out of something like this without any bother or blood.'

She put some tea in the pot, tears still running down her face, and her body all tensed up and shaking now and then, like someone sick. 'Do you understand, Manse?'

'Understand what, love?'

She spoke slowly, like a kid reciting a lesson, and yet he had never seen her less like a kid. Since he saw her last she seemed to have started being a woman and full of cares. 'Is it too late? I don't think Dad would have done it, and then because of what I say, he does. You'll tell me different, but I won't believe you. I saw it happen, the change-over.'

Then she did start to make a noise as she cried and sobbed. He hated it when women wept, never knew what to do, so he stood still on the other side of the kitchen and waited. After a couple of minutes, she quietened down and then pulled a big sheet of paper off a roll fixed to the wall and wiped her face. She sat down at the table and waved a hand to show he should take the place at her side. That wasn't like a kid, either.

'Why don't you want it to happen, Grace?'

She did not answer at once. Then, with the piece of kitchen roll still up at her face, like someone dabbing a wound with a pad, she said: 'Something could go wrong, couldn't it? Dad thought something might go wrong, and he wouldn't give the okay. Then I say my stupid piece, and he turns himself inside out, because he thinks he'll look like a carefree, hard youngster that way. You ask me, he fancies one of the girls in *Annie Get Your Gun* and needed to tell himself he wasn't over the hill.'

'Grace, it's only natural you worry about your dad, sweet-heart.'

She lifted her head slowly and took the kitchen paper away

from her face. For a couple of seconds she gazed at him, her eyes swimming and full of grief.

Mansel read it all and suddenly realised what she meant: 'Oh, I see. Of course. Not Ron. You're scared for Tyrone.'

'Manse, I'm afraid for all of you, honestly.'

'But mostly Tyrone.'

'But mostly Tyrone.'

It reminded him of the way his mother in the residential home would echo everything.

'Always it's someone not too important who gets hit, yes, Manse? There was that Ditto – I mean, a complete dogsbody and dim as dusk with it, but he's the one who picks up bullets from Sergeant Cotton.'

'What are you saying, Grace? Tyrone's a dogsbody and dim? Does he talk like that? Is that the sort of bloke you go for?'

'No, all right. But he's an assistant, isn't he? Not management. He's the driver, yes? Tyrone sits in the car waiting while you others do the collecting. He's not moving, Manse. He's just a lovely head and shoulders target through the car window. This Cotton, he knocks a couple of holes in someone like Ditto Repeato when Ditto's running. What's he going to do to Tyrone who'll be sitting still, like a dossier picture? And if they want to make sure the money doesn't disappear, what's the easiest way? Stop the vehicle before it starts. How? Spatter the driver's head.'

As analyses went he had heard worse. 'But Cotton's not going to be there,' he crowed. 'Nor any of them. We've got a handful of amateurs to cope with, that's all, one of them ancient – fat and seedy. Anyway, what does Tyrone say?'

'I haven't told him one bit of this. I couldn't, could I? Can I let him know he's on a job that's just a face-lift for my dad?'

'No, it's nothing like that, Grace. Would I . . . ?'

She stood up and went to the stove to make the tea. 'I could say all this to Dad or to Tyrone himself,' she told him. 'I haven't yet because I don't think Dad could back down now. It would be like admitting what I said was true, if he cancelled. And if I talk to Tyrone, he's going to think my dad's a fool and rubbish, and I won't have that. I won't. Listen, Mansel, here's the situation as I see it – I meet a bloke I go for, and I send him to his death.' Her voice went to a whisper now.

'That's nonsense, Grace. This is a job of work, nothing more.'

'Business. I know. But a business that people don't always come home from. Manse, you could stop it. Dad listens to you. Tell him you think it's been blown – that you've heard whispers Cotton and the rest will be waiting.'

'Grace, that's just not on. I can't go to—'

'Please, Manse, oh, please.' She stood there, the kettle in her hand, ready to pour into the pot, and starting to weep again. It was a mixture, almost comical, the ordinariness of making tea and the grief and despair. He did not laugh. This needed handling. If the despair really took over she might turn crazy and speak her piece to Ron or Tyrone, regardless. That could kill the whole outing. She said Ron would not be able to turn again, but Mansel was not so sure. Ron could be so bloody reasonable, he might see the point she was making.

And then there was another way she could destroy everything, maybe not a way you would want to associate with a daughter of Planner Preston, but girls in love, as they called it, could do all sorts. An anonymous tip here and there that Ron was about due to go active again, and the rumour and guessing would soon build up. In no time, the feedback would reach Ron, and he would put the stopper on again, this time for keeps. If Grace did that, nobody would be betrayed or hurt but it would see to what she wanted.

She handed over the cup of tea in a special, close way, putting her hand on his for a minute, trying to say they were friends from her childhood, and that she knew he would do all he could for her. Yes, she had brains. She knew how to be crafty. God, he almost wished he had not come here today. There had been no real need. All he had thought was he should make another cheer-up visit to Dean and Tyrone. Now they knew for sure the job was on, tension would screw them harder every day and it might help their baby souls if he took Leckwith's confirmation of no police. Someone had to think of these things, and he was the someone. When the time came, the kids must be in good shape, not wrecks through fear.

Another thing – he had wanted to give Ron a special build-up with them. That day when he said yes, Planner had seemed bloody old and shaky. His voice was weak, not a winner's voice, even though he tried so hard. Oh, sure, he had smiled a lot to show brilliant enthusiasm, but you could see the jibber in his jaw and his hands and his eyes, and feel doubt sweating out of every inch of him. Dean and Tyrone had whooped and yelled and given him meaty applause, and yet they would spot those signs of break-up. It was what they would expect, this couple of smart, cruel youngsters, and it could be bothering them now, even more than when the job was still only a maybe. So, Mansel had reckoned he must make sure they realised what a great street-scene operator Ron had always been and still would be for sure once the action started. They could bank on Planner.

Then, when he had reached the flat he was astonished to find Grace there. This was supposed to be a really confidential waiting station. She had been crying, that was obvious, though she tried to hide it. He must have looked shocked because Tyrone said: 'It's all right, Manse. Her dad knows she comes here.'

'None of my business,' Mansel said. Grace was pretty and full of fun, but Ron always liked to keep her very separate from all this. Or until now, he did.

'If Planner Preston's daughter doesn't know how to keep quiet I don't know who does,' Tyrone went on.

'Right,' Mansel said, but he was dazed.

A lavatory cistern had begun to fill somewhere in the flat. 'There's another girl, Dean's girl,' Tyrone said hurriedly, 'but she doesn't know a thing, Manse. Not one little thing. She's great, but an outsider.'

'Just a friend, Manse,' Dean had said.

So it meant that if this other one was Dean's, Grace was Tyrone's. Mansel did not like it.

In a moment, the second girl had come into the room, a tough-looking kid about nineteen, very good body, of course, and wearing a red leather skirt and white T-shirt, no shoes. 'Who's this?' she asked.

'This is Manse,' Tyrone said. 'Manse is a good friend, who cossets us.'

'Manse?'

'Mansel,' Tyrone had explained.

'Hello, Mansel. I'm Debbie.'

A treat to have your name familiar to some bird from who knew where, especially a very traceable name like Mansel. Jesus, though.

'Manse brings us news. That's one of the great things about him,' Dean said. 'We'd be lost without Manse.'

This was a patronising little shit, but let it go for now.

'What news?' Debbie asked.

'Good news,' Dean said. 'It's good news, isn't it, Manse?'

'Yes, good.'

'We can rely on Manse to bring us joy,' Dean said.

'Manse is upset, finding girls here, that's a fact,' Tyrone told them.

'Why? Don't you like girls, Manse?' Debbie asked.

She had said it straight, like asking someone if they took sugar.

'It's a matter of timing, that's all,' Tyrone said.

'No harm,' Mansel replied. 'I'm sure no harm.'

'Doesn't sound as if you're sure, Manse,' Debbie had said. 'Are you the landlord? No girls on the premises, that sort of thing?'

'Of course he's not,' Dean told her. 'He's a business partner.'

'Who's afraid of girls,' Debbie said.

'Just timing,' Tyrone replied.

Grace had said suddenly: 'Anyway, I want to talk to him, on his own.'

He could tell her voice was still full of tears, and near to cracking.

'Alone. Wow,' Debbie had muttered, working for some gaiety.

'What's up, Grace?' Mansel asked.

'We've been having great times,' Dean said. 'Not too much booze. Well, do we sound like too much booze? Me, I feel sharp as a bacon slicer.'

There were a couple of cans about this time and a bottle of sweet vermouth half empty on the table, but nothing too bad. He had seen much worse waiting camps.

'Improving ourselves with a learning game called Trivial Pursuit, as a matter of fact,' Dean went on, pointing to a box. 'Debbie brought that.'

'Well, my friend Helen and I play that with my mum and dad sometimes,' Debbie said. 'It's a laugh.'

Dean said: 'There you are, Manse, nothing to worry about – Debbie's parents live not too far away. She sees a lot of them. She's a good girl. Debbie knows history and a lot more, don't you, Debs? Everything very well regulated and healthy, Manse.'

And, he had to admit it, all of them, except Grace, did sound in good form, better than he expected. Dean was the one who used to sound nervy and worried but today he seemed fine, not high, just on top of it all. Maybe this Debbie really had something good, something for a man's spirit, as well as all the obvious. She was bright and noticed everything. Although Debbie could look tough, Mansel thought there might be some warmth and feeling there, too.

Grace had suddenly started to weep openly again. Tyrone moved across and put his arm around her shoulders. 'It will be all right,' he said.

'We can't sort out what's wrong with her, Manse,' Debbie said. 'Well, I can't. My friend, Helen, she's great at that, seeing what's wrong with people, but me, I haven't got a clue with Grace. Mind you, now and then I get the idea I don't know what's going on here at all, like I'm number four in a family of three. You know what I mean? What is it, Grace, love?' Debbie sounded really worried and she went to Grace, too, and bent over her where she was sitting hunched up in an armchair. Debbie did not touch her, though.

'I want to talk to Manse. On his own,' Grace repeated.

Tyrone said: 'Well, I'm not sure that's—'

She had put her face up and glared at Tyrone. 'Now. On his own,' she shouted.

'It'll be all right, Tyrone,' Mansel said. 'I don't mind. I can give you the news in a minute.'

'Great,' Dean said.

'What news?' Debbie asked. 'The students in China?'

'See what I mean – history, politics, Debbie Simms knows about it. No, it's re the business, I expect,' Dean replied.

'Yes, the business,' Mansel had said.

'You'd be bored, Debs,' Dean told her.

'Would I? Try me. Some business,' Debbie said. 'You're in here hanging about all the time.'

She could have let it drop now.

'Shut up for thirty seconds, will you, Debs,' Dean told her, his voice very flat.

'Oh, nice,' she said. 'Grace is not the only one worked up about something, you ask me.'

Dean turned and stared at her. 'For Christ's sake, Debbie, will you—?'

Tyrone held up a hand and smiled at Debbie: 'Honestly, love, it would be so tedious explaining it all. There's a bit of stress, that's obvious. This business we talk about, it *is* a business, but the main part comes later. Why we're waiting here. That's all. We have to be ready to pull off quite a tricky deal, so there's some anxiety.'

'Why do you have to be sticking your fucking nose in all the time, Debbie?' Dean asked. 'It's not clever.'

Debbie took no notice. 'Grace has to help pull off a deal?'

'Grace knows what's involved, that's all,' Tyrone explained. 'Some of what's involved. These deals, they're full of technicalities, so even Grace doesn't understand it all. I'm not sure I do myself. But Manse, he understands. That's why he so graciously comes to visit, to explain things to us.' He laughed. 'There you are, now you know nearly as much as Dean and me.'

'I do?' Debbie asked.

This boy Tyrone, he had the gift, no question. It made you wonder when you heard him talk why he was into this work, rough work and hairy sometimes, when he should be able to chat and charm his way to a fortune. That was great the way he seemed able to take the roughness out of the moment with Dean. Yes, he was a kid who did some thinking. Mansel could see why Grace might go for him.

'Come on then, Grace,' Mansel had said. 'We'll do the washing-up.'

He had taken her hand and they went to the kitchen. Everything in there was super-tidy, like the mother-in-law was visiting. No need for dish-washing. These were very unusual lads. Grace shut the door and had started right away with her worries.

They were dangerous, no question of that, and could lead to difficulties. To calm her, Mansel said now: 'Grace, suppose I could prove it to you, really prove it, that there isn't going to be the slightest trouble on this job and that Tyrone will come out of it fine, and a lot richer?'

She looked disappointed, as if he was trying to soft-soap her. 'Prove it? How can you?'

'Look, I shouldn't tell you this, but you're Grace Preston, not some nobody, and you're suffering, I know, and Tyrone's a lad I've got a lot of time for. I don't want you fretting when it's not necessary. I'm prepared to stretch a point. What I've got, Grace, is a brilliant contact in the police.'

She spoke wearily: 'Oh, Manse, I've heard this sort of—'

'Believe me, this boy knows what's what. I've never proved him wrong yet. He knows what's on the operations board for the police, I mean, even the most hush-hush stuff.'

'And he says there's nothing?' She paused, and when he nodded said, 'Manse, you pay this guy, do you?'

'He gets his take, naturally.'

'So, of course he's going to say the job will work, yes? If you don't do it, he's without.'

'God,' he said, 'you're not Ron's daughter for nothing. You don't trust anyone. You've got the X-ray eyes, just like him. Fair enough. But this officer has to think long-term, Grace. He's clever, and he's got ambitions. He wants to set up a business, buy a restaurant one day. It wouldn't do him any good to land us in a trap, now would it? He'd get nothing out of that job and nothing ever again. On top, any of us who survived a mess-up like that would be looking for him afterwards to let him know with underlining we didn't like his information.'

'Manse, I don't trust anyone. I don't even trust you. Sorry. All of you want this job, don't you? Really mad about it. What I gather, and, look, this is only me guessing, there's no gossip from Tyrone – what I gather is there's a lot of extra money this time. You're looking for a long lay-off, are you, Manse? You want it so badly you'd tell me any old lies to shut me up, wouldn't you? Oh, I should have known. This never-failing police tipster who loves you like a brother – that could be half bullshit, or even all bullshit. Manse, I can't believe it. I'd like to, but I can't. There's someone's life involved. I won't let this job happen, Manse. If you won't stop it—'

'None of the bleak stuff is going to happen, not to any of us.' But he saw he would have to go the whole way, though Christ knew what Leckwith would make of this. 'What I was going to tell you, Grace, and you've got to realise I'd never say this to anyone I didn't know as well as you, what I say is, I can take you down to meet this officer one night. You can't believe me, so hear it direct from the source. Ask him what researches he's done. You'll see the thoroughness. Hear him and you'll know you can rely on his words.'

She drank a little tea and he could see he had made a small advance. 'Meet him?' she said. 'Is that safe? Secure? At his house, you mean?'

'We can bump into him where he does some moonlighting. Nobody's around at night. You can take your time quizzing him there.'

Chapter 14

It might turn out mad, but Preston took Hoppy Short for some gun practice in the hills just beyond Georgeboon. They went to an abandoned quarry, enclosed, safe and remote, which now and then Preston himself used as a range when he felt rusty. Although he loathed the countryside, and especially these stony hills with their fucking ridiculous green ferns, he regarded the trips as necessary once in a while. He loathed shooting, too, but nobody could do without the basic skills. If things went wrong, you could be up against beautifully trained people smart at killing, so get some training yourself. That was as simple as life and death.

As always, he drove to the quarry cursing in his head the scrounging lambs and the trees and wet hedges, and vowing that once he had enough to give up the business and gun practice he would never look at nature or wellington boots again. What the hell had nature ever done for him? Alongside him in the car, Hoppy seemed quite interested in all the sights, but Hoppy was a dumbo, though he did not look a dumbo, or even ugly. Preston had seen royalty on TV much worse. Hoppy was young and had a lot of black hair, which he spent plenty on. And he shaved very close, always a help. You might have thought he was in a good office job, such as financial services, something like Dean. Preston believed in letting people find their own way, no pampering and fussing like Mansel, but when it came to guns you had to give help.

Preston had argued with himself a long while before bringing Hoppy out here, and even now he wondered if it was wise. Two big questions. First, did Hoppy get weaponry on the day at all? Second, suppose he did, would it be better or worse if he could use it right? The first was more or less settled. Hoppy lacked a hell of a lot of polish and areas of grey matter, but he had to be armed. After all, he would be front-line, and the more guns they could wave the quicker that wages team might cave in. Ever since Wilf Rudd came down to say three not two in the van it was obvious they had to be frightened fast.

Then, there were the two Bulldog revolvers to go around, and Preston saw no way out of allocating as he first planned – Dean and Hoppy. Tyrone was Wheels and it would be a waste to give him one. Mansel did not touch firearms, the way priests did not touch girls' tits, and then more. But, what you had to ask yourself was, if Hoppy thought he could use the pistol fine after a learning session here, did it mean he would start banging away regardless as soon as he smelled van cash? Could someone as addled as Hoppy see that if you took trouble to teach him how to use a pistol this was not the same as telling him to use it? Looking at it from the other direction, though, if he was clueless about guns but still had a Bulldog in his fist, might he bang away just the same, being that sort of rather outgoing person, and maybe hit anyone near, friends or enemies or the zebra-crossing lady?

In the car, Hoppy said: 'This Tyrone.'

'Oh, he can sound poncy, but underneath he's all right.'

'*Is* he all right?'

'What? Reliable?'

'All right. You looked into him? You asked enough questions about where he comes from? So, where does he come from?'

'What? What you saying, Hoppy? Of course I've done antecedents.'

'Them glasses, for instance. They real? Yellow frames? They got real glasses glass in them or just glass? I've seen all sorts do that, put on glasses with not glasses glass but just glass in them, so the glassess will do something to a face. Glasses, they can help people seem harmless, like a student or from working in a shop, somebody human. Or like Tyrone.'

'Tyrone? That's bloody daft.'

'Could I ask you respectful, Ron, you had a look through them glasses to see if it's glasses glass or just glass? I'm only asking. I can tell you a tale. I had a friend who was into very decent cocaine trading. He's working with a team and especially one mate. This was very close. Then, suddenly, he finds this mate's not a mate at all. He was put in there from another team altogether, and when it came to the big collection, this lad disappears with all the gains

– just the lot. This lad had glasses which was not glasses glass at all, only glass. They found out after, because when he went with all the earnings he left them glasses behind. That was all he did leave. Glasses can give a new tone to a face, that's the problem.'

'I asked questions about him, for Christ sake,' Preston replied. 'How long do you think I've been in this business? Of course I know where he comes from, what work he's done. First thing I ask myself about someone new is, Can he be trusted? Tyrone's a gem, I tell you.'

'Look at that,' Hoppy said. 'That's lovely.'

Preston glanced from the car window and saw a couple of greasy swans making a long skid as they came down on a pool of black, still water. 'Sodding animals,' he replied. 'Animals are everywhere up here.'

'Well, if you asked and you know about him, that's all right,' Hoppy said. 'It could be real about his eyes and the glass could be glasses glass. Sorry I spoke, but I've got ambitions you know, Ron.'

'Tyrone a plant from some other outfit? Which outfit? Jesus, Grace, my daughter's fixed up with him. Do you think she'd make a mistake like that? Do you think she wouldn't spot there was something wrong?'

'Never. It's got to be all right, then.'

This stuff about Tyrone would be Hoppy thinking he must make himself sound smart and careful because he knew people had him down as brain-damaged. Just grab any idea. It was forgivable, poor sod. Preston said: 'I know the people in every outfit around here. I'd spot anything like that, glasses or not. That's part of routine admin and planning. What you talking about, ambitions?'

'This one I'm telling you about, who did for my friend, he came from miles away. That's what I mean. The glasses wasn't to give him a disguise, not hide who he was, glasses can't do that. They didn't know him, anyway. But the glasses was to make him look like he was a bit soft, not a pirate.'

'But that's drugs, you said. That sort are always fighting each other, conning each other. It's not going to happen here.'

'I'm only mentioning it, Ron. I feel a bit wide open after that tale. I see glasses and I turn anxious. I got these ambitions, and I don't want anything to foul up. People with glasses, I try to come round behind them and get a look through past their ears and see if it's glasses glass or just glass. You can tell because glasses glass makes things bigger, because of weak eyes, but glass is just like looking through a window, not bigger at all. I didn't get a chance with Tyrone because he wasn't doing no reading at the time.'

'Well, don't let him hear you've been talking like that. He can turn nasty.'

'Now I'm really shaking. I never had confrontation from anyone called Tyrone with yellow glasses. Ambitions? Oh, travel. There's towns I hear the names of that I want to see. Jima. Tierra del Fuego. These are places that need money to get to, and the special hot weather clothes in nice luggage.'

Before they climbed down into the quarry Preston explained to him about the .44 Bulldog. He would have five bullets in the gun and another ten in his pocket, and Preston went over with him how to swing out the cylinder and reload, in case it came to that.

'We'll do it when you've had five shots at targets down below, Hoppy. Empty it, then push out the cylinder and put the new rounds in fast. That could be important.' Which brought him right up against the problem. 'But listen, I say again, I don't want shooting on the day. I'm showing you the Bulldog and how to reload, but I'm not telling you to fire. These guns, mine just like yours and Dean's, they're lovely things and they're frighteners, that's all. Tactics. Those boys in the van got to be able to tell their chiefs and insurance they had no option owing to being unarmed. As soon as they see weapons they can give up and hand over.'

Hoppy took one of the Bulldogs. 'Neat.'

'For a handbag or a pocket. In the States they can't even go to the toilet without carrying one in case of intruders after cash for a fix.'

'Another place I want to see, Ron – São Paulo. That's a name with a kick to it. I've been in gun work before. But a big, heavy thing. Don't ask me what.'

'You've used a pistol?'

'Carried. I never had to fire. But I had some practice.'

'When was that?'

'Oh, a couple of years. Not here. We took a few grand. It was a fair job.'

Preston very badly wanted to believe him, especially about not opening fire in the raid. 'That's exactly it, Hoppy. We'll do a fair job, too, and no shooting. Great. Show the weaponry and this does the trick.'

'Ten spare shells.'

'Just a precaution.'

'Fifteen shots altogether.'

'It's like Mansel says, a gun's not a gun without ammo.'

'Even a gun you're not going to fire?'

You had to wonder now and then was Hoppy as far-back retarded as people said.

'Mansel – he talks about guns but won't use one,' Hoppy went on.

'Mansel can do tactics and morale. Guns, no. It's something to be respected. Principles, and he's got an old mother he thinks a lot of.'

'How's he going to look after my back?'

'There won't be trouble, Hoppy.'

'If I'm reloading this bloody five-shot Bulldog and we've got trouble – you'll tell me no trouble, but say there's something that looks a little bit like trouble, such as police blasting away at us from an ambush. Who's giving me cover if Dean's in the gatehouse and you with the grand, twelve-round Beretta are too busy looking after yourself at some other spot where there's no trouble, either, only Cotton and Synott or whoever trying to pick holes in your boiler suit and get more scalps on their belt?'

'Why I'm getting a double double check those boys won't be around on the day. Information from two sources.'

They began to climb down. Preston went first. He had to look nimble when someone like Hoppy was watching.

'Jima or São Paulo, I'll be taking a girl,' he said. 'She thinks the world of me, says I'm laid back. That's like in fashion, to be laid back. I promised her big travel, Ron. I can't stand being by myself abroad – see them dipping lumps of bread in coffee at breakfast. Christ.'

'There'll be plenty for you, enough for two, don't worry.'

'Worry? Ron, not me. I know you'll see me all right. One thing everybody says about you. I'm lucky to come into your outfit. You all right?'

Preston had slid a few yards because of the bloody rubber

boots, no grip, and he was awkward through carrying a bag with ammunition in and empty beer cans for targets. Hoppy hurried down and helped him get steady again.

'It's the bloody boots, Ron, that's all. And that bag.'

'Well, of course it is. I was just going to say that.' His breath had gone for a moment.

'Of course it was.'

'Bloody mud, red mud. Like a mass grave.'

'Travel's interesting, Ron. You've got something to talk about later. When I'm eighty, do I want to be stuck in front of the telly wondering what it's like in Jima? I'll know. I'm the one to ask. If this girl, Sandra's, still around she can say I'm not shooting the shit, I've been there. When I'm eighty she'll be seventy-eight.'

'That's total rubbish, what you said about Tyrone. Sick. A fantasy.'

'I expect so, Ron.'

'You've got a thing about glasses. I don't like them, but you, you're a bit poisoned.'

'Could be. Off balance about glasses, maybe.'

'Tyrone won't even have a gun.'

'Well, not from you.'

'What? What you saying now?'

'Nothing, Ron. You got to be right. I'll buy it. Haven't I said already?'

Preston set up the cans on a ledge and they went back twenty-five yards. He had a full twelve in the Beretta but fired only four from a two-hand stance. He knocked over three cans and chipped the ledge close to another. That would do for now. They were not here to show off his gunplay but get Hoppy into shape. Preston went forward and arranged five cans on the ledge.

Hoppy fired one-handed, his arm stiff out in front. Two of the cans fell. The other three rounds went to São Paulo.

'Reload,' Preston called.

It took him too long – slob fingers such a distance from the slob brain, like two deafies having a conversation across Niagara Falls, but eventually he was ready again and fired five more. This time he had only one hit.

'Reload,' Preston shouted.

Hoppy moved quicker now, did not fluster even if he was so

sodding awkward, and took the remaining two cans with three shots. He brought the Bulldog down to his side.

'Not bad,' Preston said. And he meant it. Especially he felt good that Hoppy ceased fire when he had done what there was to be done, and did not just blaze off like the SAS. That might mean he could prevent himself starting, too. Preston set the cans up again. Hoppy knocked two over with his remaining shots. 'Great,' Preston said. He raised the Beretta and smashed the remaining three. Then he gave Hoppy another twenty rounds and set up some new cans.

They spent a couple of hours there and at the end neither was missing much and Hoppy had brought the reload time down to a few seconds.

'That Beretta. Lovely,' he said. 'If anyone's looking after my back, Ron, I hope it's you.'

'None of it will be needed.' He was gathering up the wrecks of the cans and as many of the spent shells as he could find. The fewer the traces the sweeter he would sleep.

'But just if,' Hoppy said.

'If there's trouble I look after my people, all my people,' Preston replied. 'Count on it.'

'That's all I want to hear, Ron.'

They began to make their way towards the top again. Preston felt easier. Yes, it was the best he had been since the day Wilf Rudd arrived at the house to talk about the changes. This boy Hoppy could shoot a bit, and he could stop shooting.

'My turn to take the bag,' Hoppy said.

'Nothing to it now most of the ammo's gone.' But he let him carry it, all the same, for the climb up.

Chapter 15

When he had considered for a while, Mansel Billings decided it might be best to ring Leckwith and warn him he would be turning up that night in the lane behind Wankers with Grace Preston. If they arrived out of nowhere there could be stupid aggro again, like when he went with Ron. And this would not bring Grace the sort of calm and confidence to keep her quiet, which was the whole intention.

One of the basic rules from far back was he never rang Leckwith or vice versa. Too bad. Billings believed in taking care of his contacts, just as he believed in looking after everyone close to him, but things had to be settled fast now. Even so, he could not risk the police switchboard, so he called Wankers early in the evening and after a while they brought Barry to the phone. Far in the background, somebody talked non-stop, a sing-song voice, like a magician's patter, so maybe they were making caviar from lumpfish roe.

'It's Mansel. This is vital, or I wouldn't have.'

'You flipped, for God's sake?'

'All right, I've apologised. You put strains on things, too. Feeding my mother.'

Leckwith turned from the receiver and shouted something about spring cabbage.

'Barry, I'm bringing a girl down there, Preston's daughter, and you've got to tell her it's all going to be bloodless. Well, not that word. Don't even raise the idea of injury. Just say "troublefree". Keep on saying it. I've got her believing in you, but it's touch and go.'

He answered at once: 'No, not here. It's too risky.' For the final word, he lowered his voice, so that Mansel hardly heard it above the other jabber.

'We must, Barry, or it's not on.'

'Not on? Again? What the fuck? How can his daughter stop it? Why? How the hell did I ever get mixed up with you people, anyway?'

'Oh, money, I think, Barry. Look, just say to her what's true – you've had a look around and it's clear and harmless. She knows she's not to tell Preston she's seen you.'

'How does a girl come into it? A girl? How old? And she's running the bloody show? I can't believe this.'

'A couple of minutes and you can say it all. We won't hang about.'

'Listen, have you thought they could be watching me? I've been asking a lot of questions on your behalf, you realise that? I'm asking people who know what's what – like Cotton. People whose nerves are raw because of all sorts and who notice things. I'm careful, but even so. I'm very exposed. And then, you ringing here. Jesus.'

'Noticed? You've spotted someone watching?'

'No. Well, probably not. I'm tensed up, so I could be imagining. Don't do your nut. There's enough problems. But it's possible. I keep looking. Maybe they know I chef here off and on. These are clever people. They might shut their eyes to the moonlighting. Everyone's at it. But not something bigger.'

'Barry, you recognise all of them. You're a pro. Someone behind you, you'd pick it up right away.'

'Maybe. I told you, they're clever. I know. I worked with these sort of boys a long time ago. They don't miss a trick.'

'In a few days we're going to take care of you extremely nicely, Barry. Yes, I know the full ins and outs of what you've done for us, and I'll see to that. But I can only see to it if the job goes ahead. Why you're vital.'

'Nicely means what? Are there figures yet? Real figures, no percentages?'

Other voices behind seemed to have joined in the chanting, like reaching a crisis. It must be near opening time.

'Figures? I can't now, Barry. I could say a figure, but you know I've got to consult, so it wouldn't mean anything. A guess. I wouldn't insult you. What I'm saying is, this sort of special service on your part, I'm going to be mentioning that in due course as demanding reward.'

'And mentioning to Preston that we worked on his daughter?'

'When it's all over and we're laughing, he'll see the point, Barry, won't he? Success smooths out all these things. I'll count on you. All right? You'll comfort the girl? In your gear you look so wholesome and reliable.'

Leckwith did not speak for a while. Then he said: 'No, not in my gear. I'll do it, sod you, but not here. It's too dicey. If they're observing, it would be at the back. They'd know my routine by now – a couple of breathers at set times out there every night, late. I don't want you and yours around again. They'd probably get a window-spot somewhere opposite in one of the warehouses. Couldn't be easier for them. So send a taxi to the front of the restaurant now, right away. It's just seven o'clock. I can disappear from the kitchen for half an hour before the rush. There'll be ructions, but that's my problem. You hear? Can you get hold of the girl now?'

'Well, I'll have to try. Hope she answers the phone, not Planner.'

'Careful what you say on that line.'

'I know, I know. I hear it all the time from Ron.'

'Half an hour only. I've got to be back here before eight o'clock. Before eight o'clock, you hear? This has to be very big pay, Manse. This is messing about with two jobs. Meet around your mother.'

Mansel was able to reach Grace and arrange to pick her up in the street and the two of them were already at Mrs Billings's bed when Leckwith arrived carrying a huge bunch of carnations. He had on his brown leather jacket that looked like a month's pay for a geriatrics consultant. This boy was a liability, blaring his need for cash.

'And how is she now, Manse?' he asked, his voice extremely caring.

'She's sleeping.'

'Well, we won't disturb her. Doesn't she look serene? I'm sure she's coming along.' He skilfully arranged the flowers in a jar and then stood back gazing fondly at Mrs Billings.

'You knew her – I mean, know her?' Grace asked.

'From way back,' Leckwith replied. 'Dear lady.'

'This is what I mean, Grace,' Mansel said. 'This man I've known since I can't recall when, and my mother. She thinks the world of him. He's here so often. No need, but he won't stay away. It's what I've been telling you about reliability.'

'I'd do anything for either of them, love,' Leckwith said.

They sat down on the bed, Leckwith one side, Mansel and Grace opposite. Mrs Billings snored quietly between.

'And you're police, really police?' Grace asked.

'Afraid so.'

'Have you got a warrant card?'

Mansel laughed. 'This is Planner Preston's daughter, as you can see, Barry. Things have to be done properly.'

'Very wise,' Leckwith replied. Shielding the card in his palm, he showed it to her across the bed.

'Okay,' Grace said. 'But you really know what's going on? You're just a constable and you know what's going on? Pardon me, but—'

'Perfectly understandable, love. How does a nobody get inside information, right? In Personnel. We know everything, Grace. And I make it my business.'

Mrs Billings opened an eye.

'Ah,' Leckwith said. 'Here's a treat, she's waking up.'

'Here's Barry, Mother.'

'Barry,' she muttered.

'That's it,' Mansel said. 'You see what I mean, Grace?'

Mrs Billings slipped back into sleep. Beyond her, through the window, Mansel could see all sorts passing on their way to the home, and glancing in. He felt unpleasantly exposed. Stress must be getting to him. That was not usual: more like Ron.

'So tell me,' Grace said to Leckwith. 'Speak to me from inside.'

'Glad to, quick as poss. The taxi's waiting. I've got to be back in ten minutes. So, then, this is it: no leaks, no hints, no over-the-pavement operations scheduled. This is checked three ways, through contacts and on the spot. Particularly on the spot. Not a sign of anything. Total blank. Don't worry, I know what's involved.'

'I haven't mentioned your personal concern,' Mansel told her, 'but Barry's very aware there mustn't be any mistakes. Troublefree.'

'Troublefree, yes. Well, I can see you'd be worried about your dad, naturally.'

'That's it, worried about her dad,' Mansel said, smiling at Grace.

'And I am, of course I am.'

'There's something else? Somebody else?' Leckwith asked, preparing to leave.

'Let's just say it's important nothing goes wrong,' Grace replied.

'I told you – Planner's daughter,' Mansel said. 'She plays it all close to the chest.'

'Very nice chest,' Leckwith replied.

'You can cut that out, copper,' Grace said. But Mansel could see she had been reassured by him and had lost that look of helpless panic.

Chapter 16

Harpur was listening to a talk on 'The Novel That Knows It's A Novel!' at one of his wife's literary discussion groups when there was a telephone call from Iles. The intrusion irritated Harpur. He felt he often learned something worthwhile at Megan's monthly meetings, and for this evening had taken the trouble to read some pages of the book in question, a two-hundred-and-fifty-year-old work called *Tristram Shandy*, where the writer kept arguing with the reader about the best way to tell the tale. Harpur genuinely wanted to know how the hell it had survived so long, even if only for discussion groups.

Harpur's older daughter, Hazel, knocked heavily then put her head around the door of the lounge. She did a big mime job with an imaginary receiver to call him to the telephone, mouthing the words, 'The feral loony', her term for the ACC. Harpur waited a moment while the speaker finished his gleeful point about the unflaggingly exuberant, self-aware humour, and then made his way with apologies through the little gathering. Megan sometimes accused him of deliberately arranging for telephone interruptions, so all could see what a martyr he was to the real world, while they gaily intellectualised. True, he was occasionally happy to escape, but not this evening.

'Col, sorry,' the Assistant Chief said. 'Your daughter told me you were "egg-heading".'

'Literature.'

'I can take it or leave it alone. I like to find you safe at home, though, Col – not out risking revenge from trigger-happy husbands. Harpur, the Barry Leckwith matter.'

'Yes, sir?'

'In my dilettante way, I've done a few inquiries.'

'Yes, sir?'

'Don't audibly wilt, okay? Yes, I hear he's had some feelers out with a possible view to buying his own restaurant. It's a long-term ambition, and you probably know about it, but apparently the pace has considerably quickened recently. So, where's the money coming from? I grow more and more interested in him. My information is estate agents' gossip – in the Lodge. Might be something or nothing. Are we watching him?'

'Oh, yes, sir. As you suggested.'

'I wondered.'

'Sir?'

'I had the sudden urge to check, and so the home call. I got the idea you thought my worries about him were balls.'

'Not at all, sir.'

'Good. Anything showing?'

'Nothing, sir.'

'As you expected.'

'It's a tricky job.'

'Yes, I know it's a tricky job. You're there to handle tricky jobs.'

'For the officers tailing him. He knows all our best people, of course. Used to work with some of them, when he was in plain clothes. And if he really is into anything, we don't want to alert him and those he's working for. Whoever.'

'I *have* thought of that.'

'And I can't bring new faces in from outlying areas to watch, because they wouldn't recognise any town villains who contact him.'

'I've thought of that, too. You're giving me what Mr Kinnock might call a "bloody Workers' Education Association lecture", Harpur. You'll keep me posted?'

Harpur was not drawn irresistibly back to the book that knew it was a book, and which found this so unflaggingly funny. Instead, he drove down to the lane near Wankers restaurant where tonight Erogynous Jones should be keeping observation from a lavatory window in the rear of the crumbling warehouse opposite. Iles was right: Harpur had not thought much of the case for putting tabs on Leckwith, but, if the ACC's new material rated, things might be moving.

In the adjoining street, he hammered on the front doors of the warehouse and eventually Erogynous let him in. They went up a couple of floors to the lavatory together. There was no seat and Harpur stood on the porcelain rim for a while and observed the back of Wankers.

'He comes out two or three times late in an evening, sir,' Erogynous told him. 'A smoke and taking the air. He appears first around about nine forty-five, after the first restaurant sitting. Nobody's contacted him in the two days he's been under observation.'

'This is not ideal,' Harpur said, over his shoulder. There was a small frosted glass window, open a couple of inches at the bottom.

'We can't get closer, sir. He'd recognise me, and any of the other people.'

'The front of the restaurant?'

'We don't think he ever uses it to come and go.'

'Unless he began to think we were out here and wanted to lose us. He could be in and out of there every night, and we wouldn't have a clue.'

'Right, I'm afraid, sir. It's a chance we must take, or you'll have to allocate two people.'

'This looks like him now,' Harpur said.

'Yes, about his time. Nine forty-eight.'

Harpur shifted his feet to one side and Erogynous climbed up alongside him on the lavatory pedestal. Leckwith stood against the wall in his chef's outfit and smoked a cigar, looking very relaxed. He certainly did not seem aware he was being watched, or that he might be, but who could tell? He was a cop. You couldn't trust them. He might be giving a performance.

'Routine.' After a few minutes, Erogynous stepped down and went to make some tea on a small canister gas stove near the lavatory door.

Nobody approached Leckwith and just after ten o'clock he threw away the cigar and went back into the kitchen. Harpur came down and he and Erogynous sat on each side of the lavatory basin, as they had previously stood, and took turns to drink tea from the one mug available. What sounded like rats cavorted above them in the roof.

'This would be what's known as one of the unglamorous aspects of police work,' Erogynous said.

'The ACC's very keen on this surveillance.'

'I hear he's quite often right, sir. Who are we expecting to approach Leckwith?'

'We don't know.'

'But some idea, sir? I mean, if I'm spending my career in a wc I wouldn't mind knowing why.'

'No, no idea at all.'

Outside it was almost dark and they could use no lights in the warehouse without giving themselves away, but Harpur made out well enough the look of disbelief on Erogynous's face. 'So, what's the basis, sir? Why am I snooping on another cop?'

'The ACC's perturbed by some parts of his behaviour.'

'The flash clothes? Five hundred quid leather jacket? Leckwith's always been like that. He's single. Nothing else to spend on.'

'Not just the clothes.'

Erogynous climbed back on to the pedestal and gazed down into the lane. 'I don't like it, sir, and, in any case, it feels to me like a dead loss.'

'Yes, it does, doesn't it? Like to tell Mr Iles, though?'

When Harpur left him he drove up past Ruth Cotton's house in Canberra Avenue, but her husband's car was in the drive. Had Cotton been working Harpur might have rung Ruth from a box to ask if she could slip out for a while. It seemed a long time since they had seen each other. As it was, he continued on his way home. The literary discussion and post-meeting drinks were over and people just leaving.

The speaker said: 'Pity you had to go, Harpur. We've had a mild success here, I think. I do believe we could start a *Tristram Shandy* fan club.'

'I'll stick with Elvis.'

Chapter 17

Suddenly the doubts came back to Preston about this job and hit him like an illness, though he knew he could not abandon it now. For a true and worthwhile leader, that was impossible once the final decision had been given. There were responsibilities. But dread dragged him down, and he felt weak and doomed. To find some comfort, he would have liked to talk about it to Doris, but she had become edgy as *Annie Get Your Gun* drew nearer, and it would be wrong to bother her. Doris had her own life to look after and for the moment this show was every bloody thing. God, the fuss about her pony-tail. And he was sick of 'My Defences Are Down', too, but did not want to upset her by groaning. Well, it might still be possible to get to Devon for a couple of days' break before the raid, and in the meantime he must take another trip to Panicking Ralph's club in case Aston had found something decent and soothing to help him out of this palsy.

Once or twice in the past he had woken himself up in the night before a tough project yelling with terror, sweat coating his body. This was part of leadership too, and he had accepted it. Lord Kitchener used to be like that, he had read somewhere. Now, though, these sweats had started coming in daylight, abruptly arriving from nowhere and taking over when he was doing ordinary, absolutely no-stress things, like making a pot of tea, or reading the racing. He knew he was out of control at these times. Jesus, what would happen if he broke up like that on the day? Driving Doris to the *Annie* dress rehearsal, he told her over and over she was worrying too much and it would come great on the night. This kind of cheer-up Preston might have appreciated himself, but his rôle now was to give comfort, not get it. You had to humour the *artistes*.

Afterwards, he made for Ralph's place. Where had it come

111

from, this new rush of crippling anxiety? As he drove, he tried to run his mind back and soon began to fear it was Hoppy Short's suspicions of Tyrone that had brought the poison. Crazy. If the words of a moron like Hoppy could shake him so much he must really be getting old and feeble. Hoppy sees a pair of glasses and goes bananas, so at once Tyrone's made into an intruder and a spy. Hoppy had no facts, for God's sake. Who'd give anything confidential to Hoppy? He said the first thing that came into his head, and there was bags of space for it there. Forget him. Forget his sick dreams and hates.

The doubts stuck, though, and he could still think only of the shadows that began closing around this job from the day Wilf Rudd mentioned the extra man. Other dark factors had piled up since, and maybe Hoppy's notion was the ultimate. Preston urgently questioned himself again, but now from the other end. How the hell had he agreed to do the raid? Had it really been on account of a few playful words from the girl in *Annie*? Was he putting God knew how many people's skin on the line, his own included, because some kindly young bird for half of half a second looked interested and crooned him a corny song? Probably she was very sweetly shacked up with someone her own age, or even married. A good-looking girl like that? Legs. Of course. He would probably never get any nearer to her than a few flirty words and a bit of a tune for a has-been. 'There's a place for us!' How soft could you bloody get?

The Monty had a fair crowd in and he glimpsed Aston drinking alone in a far corner, but did not go to him at once. That might look prearranged. Ralph, on his own behind the bar, gave Preston a rich smile of welcome. Ralph came bloody close to being human, and seemed to be improving all the time. Although he was not quite all heart, he would probably never do bad damage to anyone he had known for a while, unless it became truly unavoidable. He and his wife were bringing up a good family, with daughters travelling right across the city to a fine private school. Another thing was, now and then you could feel he really regarded some of the regulars in the Monty as friends, not just customers. Ralph had a definite warm side to him, and a lot of decency. One rule he always stuck to, everyone said, was he would never shag another woman in his flat above the club, and, in fact, not on Monty premises at all, even when his family were all away. These were the old kind of values, and you had to respect him. Preston called for white wine and bought Ralph vodka.

'This is the best time in the club, I always think,' Ralph said. 'Companionable but not crowded. A man can hear his taste buds sing. Up here to see someone, Ron?'

'No, just drifted in. I was around these parts. I never miss a chance of visiting you, Ralph.'

'Too kind. Ian Aston's here.'

'Yes? Aston? Is he the one . . . Is he still doing something with the police wife?'

'What does he say, Ron?'

'Never discussed it.'

'This is a sensitive area.'

'Yes?'

'Oh, yes, delicate. A bit off and on. She's a headstrong lady.'

'Yes?'

'And there's the matter of a babe.'

'I heard.'

'Very delicate. This is a VIP officer, not some ranker. It could turn into a highly controversial situation. I'm fond of all three of them, though I have to say Iles can be a trifle ungovernable.'

Preston moved across the room to Aston and sat next to him. 'Ron,' Aston said at once, 'I bear great news.'

'I could do with it.'

'This is from the horse's mouth.'

'Which?'

'The horse's mouth.'

'This is Iles, through his missus?'

'The horse's mouth, Ron. Can we leave it at that? This is a—'

'Sensitive area?'

'Well, yes, it is. Sources always are, yes?'

'But you're sure this is real inside stuff? What I mean, you did say Iles would never talk to her about something like this. So, this is really inside?'

'It's as inside as inside can be, Ron.' Aston looked really excited and pleased. He had a face like a kid's, smooth and fresh and not a mark on it, even though he did this sort of unprotected, one-man work. Maybe Mrs Iles went for youth. 'Here we are, then,' Aston continued. 'You're all right. That's the message. They've got no pointers to jobs coming up. Definitely not. This took some getting. Not something you pick up the phone and find out from recorded information like the cricket score.'

'I know it's difficult. I'll be keeping your work in mind, don't worry. This is good research, Ian. So you're still seeing her?' He wanted to know for sure where this stuff came from. Bastards like Aston were not BBC news. They could cook it all up if that suited them.

Aston laughed and it made him look even more like a happy teenager who had won the Bible class prize. 'You don't give up. I'm telling you it's a first-class source. That's all. I wouldn't say so if it wasn't true and proved, you know that.' He stood. These days, he always seemed to be on his way somewhere when Preston wanted to dig into a topic with him. 'I was just going, Ron. I don't hang about here any more, as I said. Get out before the dregs arrive.' They left together again.

'I'll be in touch,' Preston said.

'When you're ready and no complications to follow, Ron. I can wait. Five per cent we agreed?'

On the way home, Preston felt only slightly less troubled. So, was this really from the kosher top? Going over things in his head, he thought he heard echoes. Rumours floated around and could be picked up by anyone and handed out as if they were new and the truth. Yes, that boy could babble what he liked and never come unstuck. In his sort of line there was no responsibility. He could run things just as he wanted. Then, if the job went nicely he could say he had promised it would, and collect. If it didn't, he would miss a collection, but there would be nobody much left to give him heavy reproach, either, and what had he lost but an hour or two?

Then, as Preston pulled up at his house, one of those sweats suddenly started and his scalp felt as if it was on fire. His breathing became tight and noisy. All at once, as he went over the words, it had struck him that Aston might use exactly the same source as Mansel – Leckwith, the cookery cop, even though Preston had said he was a failure. Jesus. That could happen now and then in this game. For certain sorts of information, there would be just one talker and everyone would go to him, regardless. You might want to confirm something so you'd send out on a repeat research, but what you were really getting was the same sodding story from the same sodding tipster. Then, if it was wrong, you had it super-wrong. Wrong twice.

He sat in the car for ten minutes until the panic sank a little. Wilf Rudd's car was outside the house and when Preston eventually went in he found him talking with Grace in the kitchen. Preston felt disappointed. He had been hoping to find his daughter on her own one of these days and lead her into a little chat about Tyrone, just in case there was something in what that dim bugger Hoppy had said. Somehow, he might have got hold of a fragment of a hint, and somehow understood it right and remembered it. Preston reckoned he would sense it at once if Grace had come to suspect Tyrone was phoney. But he could not talk to her about all that with someone else around, especially a mouth like Wilf.

'I just looked in to see everything was okay for the *Annie Get Your Gun*, Ron,' he said. Wilf had on a jacket which was sort of cleaner than the usual, his sort of cleaner.

'Yes, tomorrow, Wilf, as starters. Possibly a second visit, too, to keep the numbers up? We'll all go tomorrow. I'll be with Grace. Maybe it would be better if you sat somewhere else in the hall. The tickets aren't numbered. Harpur could be there, because of his kids in the show. *Annie*'s on four nights, but he might choose tomorrow, too.'

'Why I came to ask. Christ, though, I don't like the idea, being in the same room as that one.'

'We're entitled, Wilf. This is a public place. It's great of you to make up the numbers. Doris says you're really grand. Sitting separate's just a precaution. I mean, at this time, in the circumstances.'

'Of course. So it *is* on, Ron? The job, I mean, not *Annie*.'

'Both.'

'Great.'

That's what Wilf would really be here for. Another one checking on his cut. Hired hands behaved like that. It was understandable. There weren't any signed, sealed and witnessed contracts in their game. 'You shouldn't drive here, Wilf. You know that. I don't want your car outside. It's a link.'

'Well, I usually walk, around the back. But I thought, as it's only about *Annie*.'

'It's still not good, Wilf. Things are very near now. How do they know it's supposed to be about *Annie*?'

The bugger looked scared and sorry. 'Shall I go the lane way when I leave, Ron, on foot?'

'The damage is done. And I don't want your vehicle there for the rest of the night, do I, you thick prick?'

Chapter 18

From a taxi Mansel Billings watched Preston's house on the Ernest Bevin council estate. He saw Wilf Rudd call and Grace open the door and let him in. She still looked reasonably happy, thank God. The meeting with Barry Leckwith seemed to have done the trick. Not long afterwards Preston arrived and sat for a while in his car outside, crouched forward a little over the wheel, as if ill. What the hell was wrong? In about ten minutes he seemed to pull himself together and then went into the house. Later, Wilf Rudd came out and left in his car. Mansel stayed for another hour but saw nothing else. He told the taxi driver to take him home.

It had been a bloody expensive outing, and worth it. Despite anxieties about that mysterious, helpless spell in the car that Ron seemed to have suffered, Mansel felt happier now, almost back to his usual, bubbling self. He had been through a bad time. The run-up to this bloody job was knocking some of the usual high spirits out of him. Although Leckwith had soothed Grace so well the other evening, the policeman's fears that he might be under surveillance had deeply troubled Mansel. There were some very rough possibilities in that. If police really were observing Leckwith, how long had it been going on? They might be logging his contacts and keeping them under watch, too. That could include Mansel himself, and Preston. Both had visited Leckwith at the back of Wankers.

So, for a complete twenty-four hours, Mansel had carried out a very careful check and satisfied himself he was not being tailed. He felt certain he would spot anyone behind him. Then, today, he went up to Ron's and did his stint there for a couple of hours, with the meter ticking away. It would not have done to use his own car, and to hire would be dearer still. He took a long look at everything parked in the street and at everyone who walked past the house. Eventually, when he left, he felt confident there was no police presence there, either. They might suspect something was wrong about Leckwith, but they did not seem aware he dealt with Planner Preston and himself. Mansel had needed to discover this personally. Had he told Preston about his worries they could have been turned into another reason for cancelling. In any case, Ron did not know Mansel was still talking to Leckwith. Preston might panic if he discovered how much that sod Barry had guessed about the job. That could be yet another argument for backing out.

At home Mansel picked up his car and drove down to the home to see his mother. She was in good form this evening and they did three songs at the top of their voices to exercise her memory: 'You Always Hurt The One You Love', 'Where The Bee Sucks', and 'The Rose of Tralee'. A few of the other old dears joined in, too. One of the nurses conducted with big waves of her arms. To Mansel it was another tonic, showing how you could squeeze a bit of happiness out of even the saddest places, and he really enjoyed himself. He felt useful here.

But near the car park, Barry Leckwith was waiting again. 'There've been developments, Manse. I didn't come in. You know, old son, I get the feeling sometimes that you resent my presence at the bed with you. That's perfectly all right. Don't blame yourself. The relationship between a lad and his mother is unique, and very private. Aren't I familiar with that notion from my own experience? But I did take the liberty of glancing in through the window. A sing-along? Music's a therapy. Well, I don't have to tell you. I think it's sweet the way you devote yourself to her needs. That's really a lovely home. I've inquired about the costs and, my God, no wonder you want this job to go ahead, Manse. I intend to do everything I can to assist.'

'What developments? You have assisted.'

'Oh, I've done a few things. Grace Preston? All I did was tell her the truth. I claim no credit.'

'We'll see you right. You don't have to keep rushing here.' Billings looked about the car park, recalling that feeling from the other night with Leckwith and Grace, when he had feared for a second that they were being watched. He did not feel that now though and, in any case, spotted nobody.

'No rush this evening, Manse. My night off from Wankers. I

came from home. In the clear. Yes, a development. But perhaps you know.'

'What is it, for chrissake?' Mansel's good spirits had begun to evaporate again as soon as he saw Leckwith. Now they disappeared altogether. He gazed into the policeman's long, crafty face and saw nothing but threat. And yet, at the house they shared, Leckwith's mother must look at him and find loving concern in those features.

'Someone else came to see me, Manse. I'm the centre of attraction, suddenly. No money to date, but lots of visitors. This was a lad called Aston. Ian Aston. Messenger boy and dogsbody for all sorts of villains and fellow-travellers. Doing a bit they reckon with the ACC's wife, but that could be gossip. You know him, Manse?'

'Aston?'

'You didn't send him? Are you sure?'

'What did he want?'

'Absolutely the same as you: clean bill of health for some imminent caper. Did I know of any ambushes in preparation? No details about the job again, naturally. Nothing about what it was or who he's acting for. That's why I thought it might be you.'

'Me? Why would I? I can talk to you direct.'

'So you can, Manse, so you can. But don't sound so fucking miserable about it. I didn't mean you'd asked him to come to me. I wondered if you were running a double check and told him to find what he could. So, he thinks of Barry Leckwith, not knowing you've already done that. It's a small world.'

'No, I didn't ask him. No point. As far as I'm concerned, everything's fine. I don't need a double check.'

'That's like you, Manse,' Leckwith cried, his voice full of friendship. 'Admirably like you. A real impulse for looking on the positive side. So, might it be Preston? They don't call him Planner for nothing. Mr Careful in person.'

'Ron? No. He's satisfied. The job's going ahead.'

'Planner's never satisfied. You know that.' Leckwith shook his head a few times, because of the puzzle. 'Anyway, I gave Aston just what I'd told you and Grace. What else? It's as things are. But I thought you'd like to know, Manse. You and I – we always level with each other, in full. It's one of the grandest aspects of our relationship, I always think.'

'Oh, yes. Yes, thanks, Barry. Good of you.'

'It's got to be Planner, hasn't it? You're upset he didn't consult you first? But he's feeling under pressure, maybe, and wants to act fast. The date's getting close, is it? Look, I'm not prying, Manse, but is it?'

'If you're under observation—'

'Was the meeting with Aston spotted, you mean? Not a chance, Manse. He rang me at Wankers to fix a place. I don't like that, as you know, but in the circumstances, all right. At least they can't tap a restaurant. I went out the front way again, like with you.'

Mansel climbed into his car.

'And how is mother?' Leckwith asked. 'I do have a fellow feeling, don't I, Manse? Well, as I say, you know I have an elderly mum at home, though in good health to date, thank heaven. Oh, yes, thank heaven. But you and I are very much a pair, Manse. Yes, a pair.'

Chapter 19

Ron Preston was really pleased to see a nice turn-out at Troy Hall for the first night of *Annie Get Your Gun*. These things had to get a good start or the people in it became very disappointed after all that slog and fret about cues, and this could bring a mighty fuck-up to the performances on the next nights. When that happened, you could see it in their hurt faces and feel the misery all round, and he found this very upsetting. He did not want Doris given that sort of pain, or the girl who sang 'There's a place for us' to him. In her special way, Doris was quite sensitive. Yes, in her special way. What you had to remember was this play, *Annie*, was forty years old and a lot of people would say, Stuff it. This was a problem you always had with these old things, plays, books. What use today? If Doris was not in it, or the girl with long legs, would he go himself? Like hell.

Without telling Doris, Preston had bought some extra tickets and sent them to various friends. And, of course, there had been a couple for two nights for Wilf Rudd and the woman he was living with these last few months, a schoolmistress or in the Post Office or something like that, not as brawny as Wilf usually liked them, and a classy dresser. Wilf himself was done up pretty fine, tonight, too – a very brave, ginger suit, the kind dukes had for the shooting season, which would not show mud, and which buttoned very high to stop the pheasants shitting down your country check shirt. Wilf was the sort who might come twice if he thought that was what Preston wanted, so he had a double share.

Looking about, Preston saw that everyone he had supplied with tickets was here, and he offered some big smiles of thanks. This might not turn out to be the best evening's entertainment since the piano lid fell on Liberace's balls, but there was such a thing as duty. Although Preston had to go down to the flat later and make sure Hoppy Short moved in there all right today with Tyrone and Dean for the final week, he would not have dodged out of this *Annie* opening night for anything.

Preston saw Harpur sitting nearby, too, with what had to be his wife. They would be there to give support, just like him, and their kids needed to see them in the audience, lapping it all up on the first night and being what was called supportive by the probation trade. For so many people watching, this was a family night, exactly the same if you were police or anything else. Harpur had a woman interest going on the side, so everyone said, but, when it came to something involving the children, a husband and wife were a team and had to get there together.

This would be another example of those good, old-fashioned ideas, like with Panicking Ralph, and Preston felt happy to see it. Wilf Rudd did not have a wife or children, so he would never understand the situation. All he could do in his usual weak and stupid way was worry about Harpur being in the hall at the same time as him and Preston. Wilf lived all his life in the grip of terror and just to hear the name of a big-time policeman gave him the dreads, let alone seeing one. But police were nothing special, as long as you faced up to it. This was not Peking yet.

Preston saw that Harpur had noticed him looking, and the detective gave a little nod and a grin, for old times. Well, the old times were not too great, but no need to go into all that now. Things had improved since then. There had been victories and next week would be another, no question on that, no question at all. Preston nodded a reply. What harm in a bit of civility? He felt delighted that the terrible, all-over sweating did not come back now. Why the hell should it? Troy was public. *Annie* was for everybody. Harpur's wife looked all right, but maybe a little bit thoughtful and Green Party? There was always something. Of course, Harpur did not qualify as the sweetest thing in the world, or the prettiest.

Grace said, 'Here we go', and the first curtains opened on a big Buffalo Bill poster showing a stage-coach being attacked by Indians, with Bill himself painted at the back of the poster on his chestnut horse, watching it all and looking like he can put it all right soon. A record was playing the overture, which was his tune, 'Buffalo Bill'. Everything seemed great. Grace had not wanted to come, he knew that, although she would never say so.

She would have liked to be with Tyrone. Always she wanted to be with Tyrone, these days. When it hit girls it hit them. All through the thing tonight there would be a bigger signal coming from her alongside him than from all the singing and acting on the stage. It said she wanted to run, a kind of SOS. Anyone could feel it in the stiff way she sat, like she was forcing herself to stay on the chair, and in the way her hands lay in her lap, like dead things. If you had asked her what all the stuff on the stage was about he would bet she could not tell you. But deep down she was a good kid, and she knew about duty and rallying round. Wasn't it bound to be in the blood? She would see it through all right.

Then the main curtains opened and it was around the front porch of a house in the USA. They had been really working on the scenery for months, and it looked grand. Carol, the pretty one who had sung to him, was on stage in the second scene when some Indians were in a railway carriage, which they thought was somewhere to live. The girl was a squaw and she had to pull the springs out of one of the carriage seats and put them on her wrist because she thought they were jewellery. 'Bracelets', she said. It was a laugh. A bit racist, maybe, but nobody worried too much about all that when it was written. She looked tremendous, so it was easy for Preston to stay interested and keep his face alive. Doris was a cow-girl and in the chorus when Annie sang her big numbers. It all moved along quite good and there was a lot of genuine applause.

They had an interval and he went to the little bar in the foyer. Grace stayed in her seat. Maybe she knew that if she moved she would never come back. Harpur was out there, also by himself. 'Ron,' he said, 'grand to see you. Drink?' He bought Preston Scotch and ordered a gin and cider for himself. 'Great show, yes? Guns and more guns. They fascinate people, I don't know why. Annie was real, you know – better shot than Frank Butler, her husband. I hope women don't start getting any ideas. We've got enough trouble on the streets.'

Preston thought he had better say something to that. 'Too true. These days.'

'Doris looks fine in her gear. I've got to stay to the end: my kids are in both acts. By the way, who's the squaw?'

'What?'

'Squaw. The one with the bracelets – and the eyes and legs.'

'In the show?'

'Of course in the show.'

'I didn't notice.'

'You must be joking.'

It offended Preston to find Harpur had been eyeing up a woman's body, even while sitting with his wife and watching his daughters. It didn't seem right, especially that woman. You expected something better from a senior police officer, off duty or on. Somehow it made the thought of the van job seem more right.

'You're looking very fit, Ron. You never age. How's it done? What are you up to these days?'

'Oh, one thing and the other.'

'Yes, I'd heard that.'

'Various business openings.'

'Yes, I'd heard that. I like the sound of it.'

'This area's booming. All sorts of developments and chances.'

'That's terrific, Ron. What sort of things, particularly?'

'Very various. A range.'

'Probably better like that. You don't get bored.'

'That's the thing. Exactly.' He tried to sound as cheerful as he could, but knew the string of questions had brought a nasty frost and made his voice shaky for the moment.

Wilf looked into the bar with his woman, then retreated fast as soon as he saw that Preston was talking to Harpur. Once in a while or oftener, Preston used to wonder how he ever came to be so close to that pathetic, scuttling creature, and it seemed worse now he was in the brilliant suit, like some insect from Africa, or tattooed on Dean's wrists. But Preston did not wonder for long, because there was no real mystery. He knew Wilf because he needed him. Wilf's information created the job. People who traded facts usually had something strange and creepy about them. Think of Aston, too. They were important, all the same.

'And your daughter?' Harpur asked. 'Growing up? They're one hell of a problem, aren't they?'

'She's a good kid, I'm glad to say. No trouble.'

'Lucky. She's very lovely.'

'Still only a kid, really.'

'And still quite willing to go out for the evening with Daddy?'

'Oh, yes. She loves anything to do with the family. That's a very strong side of her.'

'That's great, Ron. Wholesome. Mine? I wouldn't turn my back on them for a minute. Listen, how much did Irving Berlin coin from this number in the next act saying we don't need money because of the sun in the morning and the moon at night?'

'Well, money's not everything.'

'No. I'd heard that.'

A bell rang and the music medley started again. They prepared to go back in.

'The squaw,' Harpur said. 'Is she a regular member of the outfit? As a matter of fact, I've been thinking lately about giving amateur dramatics a go. "Tomorrow on your dressing-room they hang a star" – that sort of thing.'

'Can't help you, Mr Harpur. I don't know what you're talking about.'

'I think I remember you saying something like that to me before, Ron, don't I? But a long time ago.'

'Not that I recall.' The bastard meant interrogation, of course. They were always like that. You could have what seemed to be a pleasant social occasion with them and then, suddenly, it would come out that they were police and you were not. They would hit you over the head with it, nothing subtle. Always, they had to be on top. They were like kids. Well, see what happened next week.

At the end of the show Preston went backstage with Grace to tell Doris how marvellous she had been and take her home. Harpur and his wife were there, picking up their daughters, but Harpur gave no sign of knowing him now. That was supposed to be discretion, probably. Really what it was was the sod had had his little triumph for the night, and he could go home and sleep well.

Grace took Doris to the car and Preston said he thought he had better be polite and find the two stars and the producer and say how great they had been, too. He hung about until he spotted the squaw, in her ordinary clothes now and without her stage make-up. She was with a couple of other women but broke away and came to talk. 'Wasn't Doris great?' she said. 'You must be so proud.'

'You were grand, too.'

'Oh, I was so nervous.'

'It didn't show. You looked grand.'

'Honestly?'

'Of course. Would I say it? When you said, "Bracelets". Great.'

'Are you coming again?'

He was hoping to get away to Devon at the weekend, but said: 'Maybe tomorrow. Are there seats? I'll see.'

'Yes, do try. I mean, if you could bear it again.'

'I really loved the show. This made me think about what you said. You know? Amateur dramatics.'

'You'd be great,' she said.

'I'd like to have a proper talk about it. I mean, Doris knows amateur dramatics, but I'd be, well, sort of embarrassed to talk to her.'

'I know you'd be great. Sometimes I pop out with sandwiches from work at lunchtime in Prince Albert park. A drink first.'

'Yes. That sounds grand.'

'Peter Piper's bar is quiet about twelve-thirty.'

'That's great, Carol,' he said. 'I can't go on calling you Squaw, can I?' And fuck you, Harpur. He went out to the car and drove Doris and Grace back, hearing about the crises with the curtains and props and the pony-tail, and he and Grace told Doris how the singing had really filled the hall. 'It will get better and better the next couple of nights,' he said. 'Bound to. I think I'll come again tomorrow.'

When he dropped them at the house, he told Grace he had to go to the flat and asked her if she wanted to come with him for a very short visit. What the hell? The kid had been good tonight, sitting through all that with real decency and consideration, and if she did not go to see Tyrone now she would get there some other time.

'Oh, Dad, can I?' she said, excited. She leaned forward and kissed him on the nose. Being a father was a complicated thing all right.

When they reached the flat, it all looked pretty good, and Tyrone seemed really pleased to see Grace, really fond and respectful, not just casual, so Preston wondered if he worried about her and him too much. Preston thought he caught a whiff of a different woman in the place, some other scent, some other hair lacquer, which would be Dean's girl, but she did not seem to be there now and he decided to ignore it. What else when he brought his own daughter here, and, anyway, the scent did not seem too cheap and slaggy? There had never been a real chance of keeping girls out if he wanted the two boys to wait around for three weeks, he saw that now.

Hoppy had moved in and the three of them were playing darts when Preston and Grace arrived, no tension he could feel. Darts was better than cards for money from the point of view of violence. The thing about darts, it was all there in front of you on a board, no bluffing or fancy dealing. Hoppy in a card game might not be too sunny.

'I just came down to see everything's all right, lads, because I might be going away for a couple of days Devon way and I want to know everything's in order before I leave.' It was always important to get all the hired people living together the last few days.

'It's all fine,' Dean said. 'As a matter of fact, I had another dream. This one was even greater than the last.'

'A dream?' Preston replied.

'Didn't Manse tell you about the first one?' Dean asked. 'Nelson.'

'Dean's big on dreams,' Tyrone said.

'This is animals,' Dean explained. 'Beautiful animals, some small, such as otters, and others big – elks, llamas.'

To tell it properly, Dean gave up his darts throw and came to stand close to Preston.

'And I've got some good news from tonight,' Preston told them. If there was one thing he hated it was hearing dreams. He believed in thinking things out and doing planning with the mind nice and cool and careful, and then some bugger would come along shouting all this barmy rubbish that trickled into your head from nowhere when you were unconscious. He did not believe a thing about dreams, but he feared them, no matter how cheerful they might seem to be.

Dean said: 'These animals are a community, looking after each other, sauntering about in jungles, no bother. That's how it begins. This is wild foreign country. The tropics, maybe. Well, of course, they cross into a different sort of place. Towns and streets.'

'What you mean, of course?' Hoppy asked. 'What's of course about elks?'

127

'Of course, like in a dream. The way things happen, but no reason, just drifting,' Dean told him. 'These animals, even the small ones, wandering through streets and traffic, but they're quite safe. And then, suddenly—'

'Then what? Suddenly? Police?' Preston said.

'Police?'

'In the dream, with the animals. Is there armament?'

'Police? Armament? No, Ron, what are you talking about? This is a dream, a nice serene dream. There's a wonderful long lake, a mixture of blues and greens.'

'Fucking llamas can't swim,' Hoppy said. 'How could they learn to swim, on them mountains in Tibet?'

'What good news, Ron?' Tyrone asked. He and Hoppy were still playing darts, and Grace marking the board with chalk, her eyes on Tyrone, though, most of the time. Girls were always going to be a problem. Preston felt astonished to see how good Hoppy was at darts. He had a neat, quick style that seemed all wrong – all wrong for someone like Hoppy.

'Grace and I have been to a social occasion, where I happened to bump into the famous Harpur,' Preston replied.

'That Harpur,' Hoppy said. 'I hear tales of him. Keep clear. He knows too much.'

'Sometimes,' Preston replied. 'But he was talking like he had no idea about anything at all. I mean, we knew this already, but tonight it was just a nice little nothing conversation, very pleasant nearly all through. Anyway, how could he know?'

Hoppy had won the darts. Tyrone and Grace came away from the board, while Hoppy practised a few shots on his own. Tyrone said: 'He's only a name to Dean and me, this Harpur.'

'Oh, he's a name, all right,' Hoppy replied. He seemed relaxed with Tyrone, so maybe the crazy fears about him and his glasses had gone.

'Let me finish this dream, where it becomes mainly about leopards and badgers,' Dean said. 'This will give us all a lift, although it's animals.'

'Piss off, Dean, will you?' Hoppy replied.

'I'll be back from Devon on Tuesday, if I go,' Preston said. 'It's not certain I'll go. Something else may have come up, I'm not sure. But it doesn't matter. Tuesday evening whatever happens, the final get-together here. I'll probably do a diagram or two to show the movements. Road plan. You know the score. Everyone here, Manse included. And I'll be issuing the equipment. Then Wednesday, not before, we get cars.'

Tyrone said: 'Sounds ideal. It's running like clockwork and we all know it's thanks to you, Ron. This is a very thoughtful operation.'

'Well, of course. It's my dad organising it,' Grace told him.

Chapter 20

Early in the evening, Harpur sat with Iles in the ACC's Orion watching the Monty club. Harpur would have preferred to be somewhere else, almost anywhere else, and felt a galloping dread at what might happen, but this was very much Iles's outing and, with him in that mood, there had been no real choice. The ACC loved occasionally to be at what he called 'the sharp end' and doing 'the street bit', and for now Panicking Ralph's place was all this.

'Right after what happens here, we go to the Chief,' Iles said. 'At home if he's left the office. Get some healthy havoc into all that Catholic domesticity. Ever been in Lane's house? It's surprisingly high-ceilinged and clean. We'll get permission from him for immediate phone taps. You'll back me in the request, when you've seen what I hope is on view here again this evening. The Chief doesn't care for unsupported suggestions from yours truly. There's a vile, police-like, suspicious streak in him. Well, you can often see it in that poignantly déclassé face, a line to the side of his mouth. I'm his Number Two, Col, and he treats me like Mephistopheles. But, oh, what a good boy am I, bothering to ask him at all about taps. Permission? Jesus, a year or two ago I'd have had them in place by now, and two fingers to Lane. One grows dismally old and compliant, Col.'

Almost frenziedly, he dragged down the sun visor from above Harpur in the passenger seat and leaned across so he could examine himself in the vanity mirror fixed behind it. 'For pity's sake,' he sighed, 'do I have to carry the world's whole mutability burden? How did it happen?' He shoved the visor up again and slumped back in his seat. 'What I have to reconcile myself to, Harpur, is the fact that my son yet unborn will never see me except as riven by decay, a faltering relic.'

'Children regard their parents like that, anyway, sir, regardless of age.'

'Tell me something, Col: have you been aware of its happening?'

'What, sir? This business at the Monty?'

'The Monty? No, for God's sake. How could you know that? No, I mean the way my appearance has begun to disintegrate, and the appalling slide in resolve: this snivelling deference to a superior. Well, to Lane.'

'That's a very small mirror, sir. And the light's not great. If I were you, I wouldn't make too much of it. You've always needed to be viewed in the largest context, like the horses of the Camargue. Anyway, all sorts around your age look much, much tattier. Think of Rictus Williamson, the QC. Or that lad Gordon Chack with the record score of convictions for sucking in public toilets.'

'Yet I've always felt a kind of responsibility to be beautiful, Harpur, like a responsibility to be audible or continent. Now, what the bleeding years are telling me is not only that this responsibility has gone, but that it has already become a thing of the far past. A bitter message and immensely savage. Obviously, it's not something everyone feels as time batters them, since they palpably lacked beauty to begin with. Consider the Chief, or yourself for that matter. I don't think you'll be offended, Col, if I say that – well, I know you won't, you have a fine modesty; as a matter of fact, modesty to the point of disgusting feebleness.'

'Thank you, sir. Are we conspicuous here?'

'I forget these primitive skills.' Iles started the Orion and drove to where they were partly shielded by a parked van, though they could still see the Monty's door and yard. The ACC grew very silent, as if gripped by intense concentration. Perhaps he could listen in to himself getting older and was trying to gauge the pace.

It had been earlier in the day when Iles abruptly decided on this evening's Monty expedition. Harpur had gone to report to the ACC the results of surveillance on the veal cop, Barry Leckwith. For reasons Harpur did not understand then, it was as if the ACC instantly saw a trip to Ralph's as the only possible response to what he heard.

'Erogynous Jones, watching Leckwith, eventually got fed up

with my orders to stay at the back of Wankers and see absolutely nothing, sir,' Harpur had begun.

'A dud, was it, Col? Well, my fault ultimately, I suppose. It was I who fixed on Leckwith as suspect.'

'Erogynous decided to get out of the warehouse and try a watch at the front of the restaurant, even if it meant a risk of being spotted. He'll often do his own thing.'

Iles had been standing at the window, aglow in the morning sun, his features seeming to flicker tellingly under lines of bright light, like a bit of fancy filming from *ET*. Gazing out, he was doing some sort of head swinging exercises to increase or preserve the mobility of his neck muscles. Suddenly, he picked up the optimism in Harpur's tone and turned around to stare at him. 'We're on to something?'

'Something. I'm not sure what.'

'Erogynous was able to tail Leckwith?'

'This was remarkable work, when you remember Leckwith knows all our people and is probably exceptionally wary just now.'

'Yes, of course, of course. Erogynous is the Einstein of gumshoeing, but—'

'What we have, sir, are two observed meetings on different nights. The first is in an old people's home with dear old Mansel Billings, you know, Merry Manse – minor convictions back to the Book of Chronicles.'

Iles said: 'Books of Chronicles.'

'And the second's with . . . well, with someone known to you, sir. Known to you at a remove, at least.' Harpur had spoken the last words with as much gentleness as he could summon.

Iles had at once seen why: 'Aston?'

'Leckwith rendezvoused with him on waste ground behind Old Town Bridge. Erogynous couldn't get close enough in either case to hear what was said, but he had the impression these meetings were on urgent matters. Apparently, there was a girl of about nineteen present with Mansel in the residential home. A difficulty. Erogynous didn't recognise her and we haven't been able to take that any further. We *have* found that Mansel's mother is in the home. He's passably strong on filial feeling. I've hung on to all this for a couple of days, sir, in case Erogynous came up with anything else, but this looks about all we're going to get. I thought we might need to make some sort of move, though I'm not sure what.'

Iles, very upright and slim in one of his unbeatable navy blue suits and some okay rugby tie, had clapped his hands soundlessly in front of his face a couple of times. 'This has capabilities, Col. We might get Aston and a treacherous cop at the same time? Put Aston away? That would be cup runneth over quality, if we're talking Bible.'

'They might only have been arranging a four at badminton.'

The ACC spun the filing carousel in his remarkable brain. 'Billings? Doesn't he work with Planner Preston sometimes?'

'Preston? How does he come into it?'

'*Does* Mansel work with him? I might put you in the picture later.'

'Which picture, sir?'

'Just fucking tell me, will you, Harpur: does Manse work for Preston?'

'Well, yes, possibly he does. We've never managed a conviction on a joint outing. In fact, we haven't managed a catch on Planner of any sort for years. He's become too damn smart a planner. We suspect he's concentrating on nice, modest, manageable hits, based on good information, and infrequent. Not all of them on our patch. It works. We've failed to nail him. Or, there could be another reason we don't get to him. I saw Planner last night at a musical show with his daughter, being very family. He seemed entirely relaxed. Ron's getting on now, sir. Perhaps he's genuinely going straight at last. Retired.'

Enraged, Iles had snarled his reply: 'Planner? He's not much older than I am. Things can't be that bloody bad. I won't have it. Ron Preston's got years of first-class villainy in him yet.'

It had been then that Iles told Harpur to join him for what the ACC called 'a lurk outside the Monty this evening, early'. There was no explanation at first, as if Iles were somehow constrained, though he did not generally suffer like that. Then, just as Harpur was leaving the room, Iles had called him back. 'I'll tell you about Preston, Col.' The ACC went and sat behind the protection of his desk, and, partially shielding his face in his hands, had said: 'I've been up a couple of times lately to watch the Monty from the street, on my own.'

Harpur had felt a wave of coldness start to swallow him. 'Yes, sir?'

Iles dropped his hands and met Harpur's eyes. The ACC snarled: 'Yes, sir, yes, sir, three bags full, sir. Don't smarm me, Harpur. I can live without that.' Then, in one of those schizoid lurches of mood which were his speciality, the ACC went on quietly: 'You get the situation, do you? I'm not proud of it.'

Yes, Harpur got the situation. Iles had spoken of these visits earlier. But Harpur said: 'Watching the Monty, sir? Something irritating to do with Panicking Ralph? Something I don't know about?'

'Harpur, don't piss me around.' Iles had said wearily, the smooth, small-mouthed face full of sadness. 'This is important, not the bloody job.'

'Sarah, sir?'

'Colin, when she goes out sometimes in the evenings I wonder if it really is as over with Aston as I thought it was.'

'You wished to see if she was still meeting him at the club? Couldn't you have asked her straight out?'

'I could. But I might be scared of the answer. Perhaps you don't understand something like that. I see you as crudely sexual and fleshly, Harpur. And, in any case, women tell lies imperturbably, as you know. Anyway, she's entitled to do what she likes. It's just that I want to see.' Iles remained still for a second, then smiled and flicked back his grey hair in that gesture he sometimes described as 'grotesquely Heseltinic': 'But I didn't see her, Col. She wasn't there. On all these occasions I've found her outings were totally innocuous – late-night shopping, bridge, or similar elements in a full, upper-middle-class life. Aerobics. I fear I've been doing her wrong. It made me feel slimy, Col, as you can possibly imagine, yes, possibly: tracking and impugning the woman who's to be mother of my son.'

'I'm glad it turned out all right,' Harpur had said. And then, a bit late, he thought he detected the point of the tale. 'But you saw something else?'

'Aston, yes, as might be expected: it's his haunt. I saw him twice leaving the club. But not with Sarah, thank God. That really is finally, wonderfully closed. No. With the said Planner Preston, deep in what looked like very fascinating converse.

They'd obviously spent time together in the club. Well, I didn't make much of that at the time. Why should I? Monty's is a sink for all the dregs of the region. Two of them talking could be a business partnership, or could be what passes for friendship between that sort. No way of knowing. It seemed of such little significance that I haven't even told the Collator. Oh, I know we're supposed to report all sightings of known criminals to the Collator as routine, but who does? However, now things have changed, haven't they?' Iles became vibrant and heated then. 'All at once, because of that gem, Erogynous, we have some sort of connection between, first, a leaking, grab-all policeman, second, Aston, the well-known link man, and, third and fourth, Planner and his possible sidekick, Billings. You'll understand why I want you to come out there and see Preston and Aston together, and then get Lane to authorise phone taps. There's something magnificently juicy afoot, Col, and we have to find out quickly what the sods are up to, and when. As it stands, we've got something and nothing. And we obviously can't risk any more physical surveillance on Leckwith or the others now. We're sure to get seen and lose the whole operation, whatever it is.'

Except, naturally, for this physical surveillance now, during summer evening daylight, outside the Monty in Iles's well-known car. Harpur had already twice suggested they abandon it, but the ACC would not listen.

'Of course, I know what you want to ask, Harpur.'

'Sir?'

'Suppose it had been Sarah he was with, not Preston. How would I have reacted?'

'No, sir, I—'

'Suppose, snooping about here in that contemptible way, I had seen what I was here to see: Aston and Sarah together still – pregnant or not.'

'Well, no, sir. I was thinking of the implications from the job point of view only, as a matter of fact. As I see it—'

'Even then, in those circumstances, I'd still be certain that child is mine, Colin.'

'I'm sure, sir.'

'Even then, I would have been certain that things between Sarah and me would sort themselves out once the child came, and there would be a proper, happy, secure family. I know this

135

is the future, Col, know it and need it. Oh, yes, need it.' He was almost chanting.

'I know it, too, sir. Yes.'

'How?' Iles grunted.

'How what, sir?'

'How the hell can you know it, Harpur, when you're doing your best to mess up two families, your own and Cotton's?'

'Sir, I don't regard it like that. I—'

'You're taking risks with Cotton, in my view. A man can only put up with so much, and this man has a lot of other punishment to take, and this man also knows how to shoot.' Iles flapped a hand. 'But, leave it. Yes, it would have hurt to see Sarah and him together, but hurt me within bearable limits. I want to know, that's all.'

'Entirely reasonable, sir.'

'Oh, I keep on about a son, but that's trite and rubbishy – picked up from dynastic tales, I should think, or the Asians. A girl would be lovely. But do I need to tell you?'

'This looks like Aston now, sir.'

He came out from the Monty and for a moment seemed to be alone, fair-haired, fresh-faced, wearing a cardigan and white trousers, looking about twenty. No wonder Iles grieved about his age. Then Aston glanced back, as if waiting for someone. It was not Preston who followed, though, but Panicking Ralph himself, in shirtsleeves. They stood chatting animatedly for a while.

'Ralphy in on it, too, whatever it is?' Iles muttered. 'This gets better and better. We can put them all away.'

'Wait a minute, sir.'

Ralph moved aside, to let someone else out through the door, but still not Preston. It was Sarah. Harpur heard Iles give a tiny, broken groan. His wife was carefully made up and groomed, and must have been tending her face while Aston waited. She looked happy and lovely and not yet very obviously pregnant. Now, the three of them moved into the yard and Ralph waved the pair off, then made for his Montego, as if going to fetch something. Sarah and Aston walked towards a Fiesta.

Harpur said: 'Christ, I'm really sorry, Des.'

'Des?' Iles replied, turning from the wheel to stare at him. 'Who the fuck are you talking to, Harpur?' The ACC drove out of the street before the Fiesta could pass them. 'The way I see it, someone as bright as Sarah is not going to get accidentally pregnant by some villain's runner, is she?'

The ACC waited for an answer and Harpur said: 'Hardly, sir.'

'So you're going to ask, what if she actually wanted this jerk's child, not my child, but a child by this piece of peroxided, messenger-boy rubbish, and did it calculatedly?'

'No, sir, I—'

'Out of the question, Harpur.' Iles was whispering now, but the words sounded fairly steady, not the near-shriek that could occasionally come from him when in pain over Sarah. After a while he reverted to normal voice. 'You were afraid of something like this happening tonight? I could feel the tension. But, then, you're not a marriage man, are you, Col, don't believe these outside connections can ever be really switched off, or should ever be?' Harpur did not answer and this time Iles seemed ready to let the question die. 'Ever considered that someone could watch you, as I've watched him and Sarah, Col? Life has its parallels. But your someone knows firearms and can hit a gnat in the dark and might still be unhinged. Do I keep on about it?' Harpur let this one alone, too.

Iles called the office and found Mark Lane had left, so they drove to his house on Baron's Hill, looking out over the city. It was a grey stone ex-rectory, almost a mansion, in wide grounds and with a paddock and decently long, tree-lined drive.

'I'm sure he deserves it,' Iles said, as they approached. 'This is a man who's come from deepest nowhere, with a great hulking, seamstress wife in tow, and a totally quaint university background, yet is still at the top. I used to think he was a Warwick student, but that turned out wrong. Somewhere entirely on a par, though. I sent Hubert Scott up to Warwick to dig dirt on Lane, when I was trying to stop his appointment here, you know, but not the place at all. Poor old Hubert. Poor us. I suppose everyone can see now that Lane should never have come here, even you. I'm one of those funny folk who prize foresight above hindsight.'

'The Chief has some fine points, sir.'

'That so? What's the sod promised you, Harpur?'

When Lane opened the door to them, Iles said: 'This is a gross liberty, sir, infringing so late, and disturbing a period of mental replenishment. I hope we'll be able to make our apologies to Sally.'

Lane could not have been home long and was still in one of the suits that Iles said were made by Zairean convicts in place of mailbags. The Chief led them into a big, light sitting-room with country scene water-colours on the walls and some framed, photograph portraits of what must be relations. Iles hurried to look at these.

'May I? Ah!' he cried. 'Ah! One sees the recurrent family qualities here. It would only embarrass you if I listed them but suffice to say that these pictures must provide a magnificent encouragement to you, daily, sir. You are reminded of the traditions you must keep up, are proud to keep up. Col Harpur here wants a phone tap on one of our people, Barry Leckwith, whom we've been watching, and an old bent friend, Ron Preston. Colin makes a very persuasive case, sir, extremely valid. As a matter of fact, I myself spotted Preston in interesting circumstances while I was outside the Monty club. Twice.'

They sat down, and Harpur watched Lane's normally benign and cheerful face grow increasingly uneasy. All sorts of faces went that way when Iles was on form.

The ACC said: 'Colin feels he might have stumbled on something, but at this stage hasn't any real notion what it is. Would that be a fair summary of the state of play, Col?'

'Pretty much, yes.'

Lane asked uneasily: 'Does all this come from one of your grasses, Colin? I do hate that kind of information.'

'No, sir.' He wished more of what they knew had come from such sources. If material originated with, say, Jack Lamb, that supreme, infallible tipster who sometimes fed Harpur, he might have felt a good deal more sure of things.

Lane said: 'Leckwith? If we're keeping one of our own people under observation I feel I should have known about it earlier, Desmond. This is a grave matter, potentially.'

Iles took up the last parts of the sentence and repeated them as two separate elements: 'Grave matter. Potentially. Grave matter. Potentially.' Savouring chosen words aloud and sometimes making notes of them was one of the ACC's techniques when dealing with Lane. 'I'd certainly accept what you say, sir. All I'd venture in self-defence is that when we began this it was only the very slightest of hunches – that's so, isn't it, Col? Leckwith had been asking questions of one of our marksmen, that's all. The

138

potentiality couldn't have been more distant, as it were, and the gravity very problematical.'

Lane said: 'Even so, Desmond, where possible corruption of an officer is involved, I do think—'

'On reflection, I'd have no hesitation in saying you are right, sir,' Iles acknowledged emphatically. 'Mea mucha culpa.'

Lane leaned forward in his armchair. 'What I fail to understand – forgive me, I might be missing something – but I don't know how we came to make the connection between Preston and Leckwith. You saw Preston when you were twice waiting outside the Monty? I don't follow this. Have you missed out a link? What had taken you there, Desmond? Have I got this right?'

'My wife, sir,' Iles said, without a tremor. 'I wanted to see if she was inside, with a club member called Ian Aston. In fact, Aston left with Planner Preston, and, from elsewhere, we have a proven connection between Aston and Leckwith. Detective work is so often like this, sir, isn't it, the fitting together of the otherwise inconsequential.'

Lane remained crouched forward, a little stricken, trying to take it all in and fitting together his own morsels of information. 'I see. Forgive me, Desmond: I don't wish to pry, but this Aston – this is the man who . . . ?'

'Aston, yes, sir. A very close acquaintance of Sarah. She casts a wide net.'

The Chief pulled back in his chair. 'Yes. Again, you must pardon me, but I do hear things, rumour in the air and—'

'Inevitable, sir.'

'I understood all that might be finished – this misguided, well, friendship, if I may say so. But perhaps it is. I gather from what you report that she was not at the club with him, in fact, on these occasions.'

Iles paused for a second and then obviously decided to say nothing about tonight. 'That's right, sir.'

'It must have been a great relief.'

'Indeed, sir. Harpur has just been saying the same.'

'I'm glad for you, Desmond. Every man needs stability at home. This is the secret of everything good in life. Sometimes these things do sort themselves out. The worthwhile, the solid, will assert themselves. They have their own fine power.'

'Thank you, sir. Very kind.'

'And we have the information about Preston by accident, as it were, then?'

'Exactly, sir.'

The door opened and Mrs Lane appeared, pushing a drinks trolley made of some gleaming, gold-coloured, tin-like metal. Iles gazed at it seemingly enraptured for a few moment before standing. 'Sally,' he said, 'grand to see you again.'

'Is this man's talk?' she replied. 'I won't stay.'

'Oh,' Iles mourned. 'Don't say that. Worse than man's talk, shop talk. But we can dispose of it very quickly. Something we had to call about immediately, I fear. But a formality, entirely that.'

'How is Sarah?'

'Wonderful.'

'I heard the lovely news.'

'Yes, isn't it splendid?'

'And she's looking after herself?' Sally Lane asked. 'She must, these early months. I know Sarah liked to get about, but she must take it easy.'

'Yes, she does like to get about,' Iles remarked. 'That's exactly what she likes to do. But I'm going to keep on at her to do less.'

'And Megan?' she asked Harpur.

'Fine.'

'And the girls?'

'Fine, too,' Harpur said. The methodical inventorying of family reminded him of the way airline pilots did a spoken check on all cockpit equipment before taking off. As Iles had said, Sally was very burly, but she poured and distributed the drinks with surprising lightness of touch. She did not take one herself and left them soon afterwards, to fierce protests from Iles.

'Leckwith was asking questions of which marksman?' Lane asked.

'Sergeant Cotton, sir,' Iles said.

Again Lane looked disturbed. 'This is Cotton the husband of—'

'Robert Cotton, sir,' Iles told him. 'Possibly our best man with a handgun. He had Ditto Repeato when we took Mellick at the bank.'

Lane gazed into his glass of sherry. 'Desmond, I can't really go forward with a phone tap request on this basis, can I?'

'Sir?'

'Again, check that I have this right, will you, but it appears to me that both our main pieces of information rest on – involve sources who are connected to the two of you in markedly unfortunate ways. This has to be said. I mean, extra-professional ways. I have to give detailed reasons to justify any phone tap, as you know. The onus is very much on me, and I'm liable to be closely questioned. Do you see what I mean? How do I explain why my Assistant Chief was hanging about the Monty, Desmond? And then, how did we discover that Leckwith had been quizzing Cotton? Does that come via Mrs Cotton to Harpur? Excuse me, but I have to say this.'

'It comes from Cotton direct to both of us,' Iles said.

'Does it, Desmond?'

'Yes.'

'Does it? Well, perhaps it does.'

'But I'm telling you it does,' Iles said.

'Yes, you are, Desmond.'

'Jesus,' Iles muttered.

'There are some matters I don't want to get involved in, however distantly. Personal matters. I won't get involved in them,' Lane replied.

Iles said: 'This information is—'

'How do I explain, if I'm asked, why you were outside some recidivists' drinking club night after night? I have the Force to think of, Desmond.'

'But do we have to disclose where information comes from, sir?' Harpur asked. 'I didn't think so. If you say you're satisfied taps are necessary, don't they accept your word?'

'Yes, they might,' Lane said.

'So, you're not satisfied, is that it?' Iles asked.

'It's flimsy and – I have to say this – it's tainted, Desmond. I simply don't have confidence in the brief you're giving me. Not at this stage.'

'It could be too late very soon,' Iles said.

'And what's the purpose of the phone taps, anyway?'

'We want to know where they're going to pull a job, so we can be there and get them over the pavement,' Iles replied. 'What else?'

'I see the point of that, of course. But, really, we've absolutely

141

nothing saying unambiguously that any job is going to take place
– no names, locations, times, nothing.'

'This is why I see it as a classic case for tapping, sir,' Iles replied.

'I'd suggest more surveillance, Desmond. I'd like to see what
are at present little more than intuitions given a trifle more sub-
stance. Then I might feel more comfortable.'

'We'll be spotted, sir, if we try further surveillance. These are
professional people, one of them a cop,' Iles replied. 'Naturally,
we'd all like more surveillance. It's impossible.'

Lane shook his head. 'And I have to ask myself about the
whole *raison d'être*.'

'*Raison* fucking *d'être*, sir?' Iles inquired.

'You're talking about an ambush, presumably with firearms as
possibles? Yes? Do we want that? Would I be right to sanction a
shoot-out in the streets?'

'It might not come to that, sir, if we're quick and in numbers
and right on the spot at the proper time,' Harpur said.

'Do we want to take them or not?' Iles asked.

Lane said: 'Oh, of course we want them.'

Iles said: 'Well, sir—'

'But you see my dilemma?' Lane said.

'Sir, we—'

'Do I let a dangerous crime go ahead so we can bring off a
catch? We might well have gunplay threatening all sorts, including
the general public. It's not a new problem, but it does exist.'

'What choice, sir?' Iles replied. 'We can't take them in on
suspicion before it's happened. We've absolutely no evidence.'

For the first time in Harpur's memory, Lane suddenly allowed a
look to come on his face which suggested he had routed the ACC.
The usual amiability slid somehow into wiliness and resolve, as
if the Chief could understand, for a moment at least, why he
was Number One. Coyly, he gathered the rough-and-tumble suit
jacket closer around him, like a woman with a shawl. In a way
it did Harpur good to see Lane so happy, even if he probably
had it all disastrously wrong. The Chief murmured: 'Desmond,
exactly my point about the phone taps, isn't it? Totally inadequate
acceptable evidence. How could I substantiate the request? I'm
sorry. Not on. Of course, we could prevent their operation easily
enough, whatever it is, by openly showing we're very interested
in Leckwith or Preston or Billings. Planner would ditch it at once.

But I certainly don't say we should behave like that and utterly abandon all chance of a catch. No, indeed. Just let's get some more information.'

'If we try for more information, except through taps, we *will* be openly showing we know something,' Iles said. 'Erogynous has gone as far as he can.'

Lane ignored it and stood up: 'Now, while you're here I must show you the gardens. You're really going to love this. They're all Sally's work, I might say.'

'Gardens in the plural, did you get that?' Iles said as they drove back. 'Like Chatsworth.'

'Or the Books of Chronicles.'

'Remember this, Harpur: ask for something, you invite the answer, No. Especially from a craven cipher like Lane. Never ask. Take. Take.'

'He used to be great, sir.'

'I've heard.'

'It's the job.'

'Do you think he actually still gets aboard that green-fingered piece of freight who served the drinks?'

Iles dropped him at headquarters but instead of going straight home, Harpur decided to see if he could catch the end of this evening's *Annie Get Your Gun* at Troy Hall. For a few minutes he did try getting in touch with Jack Lamb to see whether he had any useful whispers. Jack was almost always worth a check call. Harpur telephoned from a box twice, but each time the line was busy. It might be Jack fixing up one of his deals, or Helen, the young punk girl he lived with these days, talking to some of her friends. Anyway, Harpur let the idea slide and decided he would go to see *Annie*, or what was left of it tonight, instead.

There was no pressing reason, and anything but a general, irresistible urge to rewatch the musical itself, but he knew he would enjoy seeing the young squaw woman again and confirming that she was as good-looking and leggy as he remembered. There had been enough frustrating work today and he needed an interlude: perhaps that lad at Megan's literary evening had it right, after all, about the way life was a thing of pointless digressions, errors, madly illogical decisions, and altogether a random sequence. Or could there be a bit more to it? Now and again lately he felt that Ruth Cotton might ditch him and settle down fully to married life, just as Iles wanted Sarah to, and if that ever happened Harpur would urgently need something to soak up the pain. Two or three times, Ruth had proposed they finish, and on each occasion he had frantically argued her out of it, and on each occasion, too, had felt himself near breakdown at the prospect. How much longer could he hold on to her? No doubt someone like Sally Lane would say there should be no pain at all for him in such a split, and, if there was, that he should look for any consolation he needed in his marriage, not from yet another woman. These days, Iles would probably say the same. Harpur did not believe it would work, though.

Tonight, his daughters were being taken home by a neighbour, so there might be a chance to hang about at the end and work a conversation with the squaw. From the back, he stood and watched the closing scenes, bored to the bone by the bouncy music and story, but glad for the kids' sake to see the hall once more almost full. Glancing around the audience, he was astonished to spot Planner Preston there again, awake, though apparently on his own tonight. This really was noble backing for his wife. Did Harpur have it right, after all, when he suggested that, in his dotage, Preston for one had finally decided to sink into the safe contentments of family life? Perhaps. All the same, as a routine, Harpur would feed this sighting and the previous one of Planner to the Collator.

After the show, Harpur went backstage and talked for a few moments with his daughters and the neighbour who was taking them and her own children home. While Harpur was still too heavily involved with them, the squaw passed on her way out and when he hurried into the car park a few minutes later she seemed to have left. At least, though, he had discovered from both sides of the footlights that she was as attractive as he had thought. Her name would be easily discoverable from the cast list. He did not see Preston again and felt a strange, stupid kind of relief: this dusty old musical was a worthy, community event, a happy series of evenings, and Harpur did not want to put a repeat chill on Planner, who had obviously made himself so much a decent part of it.

144

Chapter 21

Mid-morning Ron Preston drove out to the country again, alone this time, to do some more shooting, and feeling as troubled as ever about the weight of a full holster on his shoulder. Although the way he performed when Hoppy Short came had been all right, all right could be a wreath. God forbid it should turn into a gun battle next Thursday, but if it did there would be no time for near misses, not with people like Ambrose Rowles, Synott and Robert Cotton.

Preston also wanted to see whether he could get more used to the countryside. Carol, the girl from *Annie Get Your Gun*, liked countryside a lot, including trees and buzzards – everything out there, really. She had told him this yesterday at their meeting in her lunch hour. They had a drink at Peter Piper's and then some sandwiches in Prince Albert park nearby. She often went to the park at lunchtime and knew trees and flowers, but said she liked them better in nature, meaning country. This was a nice outing and, in the evening, he had been able to see her again on stage, and then briefly in the Troy Hall car park after the show. He spotted Harpur there once more at the back of the hall, probably supporting his kids. Family was a strong thing, a wonderful thing, really. Carol said he could not ring her at work, but he had her home number now. She was a very sweet kid, not just the legs and so on. Because of her, he was thinking of not going to Devon this weekend, after all. There might be another chance to see her. She had real warmth this girl and was interested in everything, himself included, which rated.

Strolling with Carol in Prince Albert park he had pretended he loved country, too. You had to make an effort. But he would never like the idea of all those animals hidden away in holes and woods, watching secretly and waiting to come out. That crazy

145

animal dream of Dean had chilled him, though he did not let it show.

He pulled on his rubber boots and with the Beretta in his pocket and another carrier bag of target cans picked his way carefully down into the quarry. Funny to think a tip from some little nobody like Wilf Rudd produced all this work and effort. The shooting could be important not just on account of the opposition. Since meeting this girl, Carol, he had started to think along lines which could turn out very costly. Whatever happened with her, he would still look after Doris and Grace properly, of course, and Devon. If you had responsibilities you had responsibilities and they did not go because something else turned up. That could mean money to dish out three ways, so the van and its very juicy pay-off had become important. Matters had to go right, including the shooting if it did come to that.

Jesus, he had started doing what he always used to make fun of and fear. He had noticed that before. Yes, suddenly, he was looking for 'the big one', the special, super-size job supposed to solve all problems at once and put everything right to the end of time. Never mind: it was youngsters who usually thought like that, and, with Carol in the frame, he felt happy to be guilty of something youthful.

He spent an hour practising and did better this time. No gun existed that he could like when it was actually firing, but this Beretta gave him less offence than any other weapon he had ever known. In his hand, it felt right and looked right. He gathered up the cans and shells and made his way back towards the car.

Thinking he might bump into Carol at lunchtime around the Peter Piper or at the park, he drove down there and waited between the two for a while in the street, but did not see her. She must have been having her meal somewhere else today. In a way he was not sorry. He would have disliked walking with her while this pistol was tucked in under his shoulder still smelling of use. He hung about for half an hour and then, when he saw a patrolling policewoman sauntering in his direction, moved off. That bulge under the jacket did make him nervy.

Chapter 22

Iles rang Harpur at home on Saturday morning and asked affably enough if he would mind coming into headquarters immediately: 'Sorry to spoil the weekend, but a thing of passing urgency, Col. Lavish regards to Megan and the family. Or is Megan away?' When Harpur arrived, he found Iles at his desk radiating special assertiveness, with a piece of print-out paper in front of him.

'From the Collator, Harpur. It concerns Planner Preston. The interesting bit originates with a patrol car officer. I asked for all sightings of Preston after the Monty business, and this one from her could be of high significance. But, of course, we also have a Collator note here of two observations from you—'

'Yes, I saw him at *Annie Get Your Gun*. My children are in it.'

'So you have to make *two* visits? Twice to Cornsville? Is fatherhood such a burden? Am I destined for such a future? You are a saint, Col.'

'Planner likewise, but he's backing his wife.'

'Wonderful institution, marriage, its inescapable compulsions and duties. All sorts can be going on around, but Preston still gets in there and watches *Annie Get Your Gun* night after night out of fierce, admirable loyalty to his missus. And you, too: family calls. Or, on the other hand, any high-calibre spare cunt in the show?'

'I wouldn't really have noticed, sir.'

'Ah. So there is, is there? Notorious in amateur dramatics, of course. Women seeking means of self-expression and yearning to "find themselves", as the phrase goes. Yes, yearning to find themselves under the local Romeo.'

'I don't think he's in *Annie Get Your Gun*, sir.'

Iles picked up the print-out. 'And then, from yesterday lunchtime, this sighting of Planner in the street near Prince Albert park,

147

alone, gazing about as if on a survey. This comes to the Collator from our lady patrol car constable, Peta Cade.'

' "As if on a survey"?'

'Her words. She means as if planning a job – casing somewhere, running the eye over, presumably in preparation for an operation.'

'Bit imaginative? It could be entirely innocent, couldn't it, sir? He might have been waiting for someone. Doris. Or he has a daughter.'

'Nobody showed. But perhaps you're right. But perhaps, too – listen, Harpur, you do know how detection works, do you? One grabs at anything, and every now and then, or much rarer than that, the anything turns out to be something. I'm in this job and you're in that one because I have a higher proportion of somethings to nothings. It's called flair. Think about this, would you: there are two banks on Prince Albert Street, Barclays main branch and Bank of Ireland.' Iles threw the piece of paper across the table. 'You resent landing a workload at the weekend? Were you and a friend hoping to have an outing? Incidentally, on that subject, it looks as if we'll be needing Robert Cotton to stand by very soon, plus Synott and Laissez Faire Rowles. All the Earps.'

'No, I was going to be around, anyway.'

'Good. Good. I can be thoughtless, I know that. Sarah's weekending away, as a matter of fact. A school class reunion?' He winced. 'Yes. Well, it's not impossible.'

'Women go in a lot for that sort of thing. I don't think I could take it. All those grey moustaches and purple veins on faces one remembers as sunny kids. But perhaps it's different with women.'

Iles, himself looking somehow slightly gone to seed today in an East of Suez drill suit, nodded towards the print-out. 'This could be the link we wanted, Col. We knew Preston was into something. Now, maybe, we know what. Well, almost. One or other of the two banks. And, the point is, we can easily put an ambush in place that will cover both. Viva Peta Cade.'

Harpur read the report.

Iles said: 'You'll see the girl did a very good job. She left the car and walked back. Preston was still around. I've spoken to her. She reckons Preston stayed there or thereabouts for at least twenty minutes from the time first spotted, and God knows for how long before that. Planner was giving something a thorough examination. Cade had the idea Preston might be tooled up – a shoulder holster. She couldn't be totally sure because he moved away before she was close. She almost challenged him there and then, but used her head and thought there might be something really big in this.'

'Why would he go armed just to case a bank? Preston hates guns, as far as I remember.'

'Intend niggling over every fucking point, Harpur? Get this, will you: if I'm in here on a Saturday and my wife's away having it off with some youthful, blond slob, I follow up every tip that might lead to deep change. We can't put Preston under surveillance, because he'd spot it and call everything off. We're dependent on lucky sightings like this, and have to make the most of them. All right, the pistol bulge is Cade's impression only, though she's pretty sharp. But what's altogether more than impression is that Preston hung about there, apparently doing nothing, for as long as I said.'

Harpur did not cave in. 'Quite, sir. It's conspicuous for an old hand like Planner. Would he do it like that? And right in the middle of the city? Planner usually works on the outskirts, and rarely with banks.'

Iles nibbled a finger. 'Nothing's more certain than that my home problems will sort themselves out, Col. One thing about age, it brings patience, the longer view. All these griefs will be removed.'

'I know it, sir.'

'But, for the moment, I'll come in myself on a Saturday for something to do – a distraction – and then I tend to forget that other people might like a day off. Lane and his wife, for instance, are at Cowes. Imagine. He was talking of getting a striped blazer. He'd look like a knickerbocker-glory. I'll say this for the bugger, though, he doesn't mind being seen with Sally anywhere at all. There's a definite gentlemanly taint in the Chief. Why was Preston lurking about, you ask. Possibly noting traffic levels in the street for approach and getaway, and taking note of numbers in and out of the bank. Time spent on reconnaissance is never wasted. Conspicuous? Christ, Harpur, he's not there with a crew, is he? This is someone on his own at an innocent and crowded part of the day. It's his sort of job, yes?

149

He does wages and cash deliveries and, despite what you say, we think he raided a bank at least once, don't we, a few years ago, though unproved – some small-town place for two pounds fifty and a couple of HB pencils? All right, this would be on a grander scale. But you've made the point yourself, and there's validity to it, some validity, that Preston's of a certain age. I'm not saying he's old or thinking of quitting. None of that crap. But he could be doing some strategic thinking about his eventual pension. He might want a bonanza outing. Remember the extra commitments in Devon. A big Barclays or even Bank of Ireland on a good day could look like a happy future for him. We can get our people into buildings round there and block off the street at least from the park end once it's all under way.'

'Cade was in uniform?'

'Of course.'

'And Preston moves off as she approaches?'

'Cade thinks that was coincidence. She doesn't believe Planner had spotted her.'

'No?'

Iles stared at him but said nothing.

'This is Planner Preston we're talking about, sir,' Harpur went on, 'not some kid too young for Borstal.'

'The prospect of big bucks can numb the functions of even the very finest minds, Harpur. We'd never make a major arrest, otherwise.' Iles stood and walked to the long looking glass, meant for checking his uniform. He seemed to gaze past himself into an immeasurable distance. 'Where might they go, Col?'

'Preston and his people, before a job?'

'Sarah. And will she come back? That's what you want to ask, is it?'

'From the class reunion?'

'That's right, from the class reunion.'

'Well, of course she will, sir.'

Iles did not answer at once. Then he spoke crisply: 'Of course she will, Harpur. She'll be here on Monday. Soon it will be a new life, in all senses.'

'Absolutely. The child.'

'Absolutely. So, I want you to get a party together, Harpur, for the banks. This is going to be a difficult operation. We've got a location, but no date. Our crew has to stay in place in constant readiness at least during daylight until it happens. That means shifts, change-overs, meals, hygiene. Secrecy isn't going to be easy. I don't mean just at street level.'

'Leckwith?'

'Leaksmith. It would be great if we could lock the sod up, or send him today to help policing in the Falklands. We can't. If we touch him in any way, he's alerted and the job's off. You know Planner. So, somehow you've got to stop Leckwith getting a whiff.'

'I'll try. Will the Chief let it go ahead, sir? This is potentially a shoot bang fire ambush in a central street, possibly during a busy lunch hour in summer weather.'

'The Chief's a problem, obviously. By no means gutless, but limp with high quality angst, and a frozen prey to politics. Yes, he's got all the qualities for rapid advancement. Yet he's a cop, Col, made like us, with the same beaky-nosed, helmeted guardian angels present at his birth. He wants to catch people and there's a cutting edge under all that moral stodge: a razor blade in a cream cake. On this job, we're certain to catch people, or knock a hole in them. Worry not, I'll be able to put a case to Lane. Get good people together, Col. People with the delicate touch: humane, naturally, and yet positive. Fire-power above all. You're still not convinced?'

'I'm convinced there's something. I'm not sure this is it.'

'Get me whatever's more likely, then. But, in the meantime, cater for this one, will you?' He smiled. 'Oh, you're right, of course, it's quite possible that Sarah actually is at a class reunion.'

'Of course, sir. She went to a very good school, didn't she? They like to keep an eye on each other's lifestyles.'

'I wonder if she admits to being married to the fuzz?'

Harpur went back to his own room and began telephoning around to arrange the trap at the banks. In the middle of it, he had a call himself.

'Busy today, Col? And a Saturday? I rang your home and then haven't been able to get through to you here, either. Yet I need to.'

Cheerful, mellow, triumphant as ever, the tones were Jack Lamb's, and Harpur always gave the most unwavering attention to them. Every detective worth his pay and prospects

151

had confidential voices who whispered facts or half-facts or non-facts or outright lies to him from somewhere beyond the strict boundaries of respectability, and even of legality. There were harsh names for these people – grasses, touts, narks, snouts – but without them the battle against the darkness would be lost before it started. As well as harsh names, there were harsh fates for them, too, if they put a foot wrong. Lamb never put a foot wrong, and never relayed a bum fact. Harpur would have bet that no other detective anywhere had a tipster quite in this category and when Lamb spoke, you listened and you'd better believe it.

Unfortunately, Jack rarely spoke beyond the very basics on the telephone, and especially not on a police telephone. That caution was not particular to him, though, but a feature of the trade. If you spent much of your life, and earned some of your income or other privileges, infringing on other people's private information you took care it did not happen to you.

'I tried to reach you, Jack.'

'Never mind, I'm reaching you. A coming together? Monday afternoon, fourish down among the goddesses, Col?'

'Right. Among the goddesses.'

'That's it. You like a bit of class.'

Chapter 23

As the day for a job came nearer, Mansel Billings liked to keep himself occupied, not with anything too grave, and not by desperately flea-combing every detail like Planner, but through a bit of minor checking and giving another polish to morale and welfare if they were using youngsters. This way he could usually stay pretty bouncy and remain on top of things. When you had slabs of cell time in your life story, this was important. Otherwise, you might get to feel doomed and that could sadly fuck up poise.

He called a taxi again and went and had another long loiter near Planner's house on the Ernest Bevin estate, just to make certain there was still no surveillance. What Leckwith had said about possibly being watched must have gone bone deep. And then, even without that, there would always be worries about leakage when you were working on information from someone like Wilf Rudd. Ron put up with him, but the trouble with Wilf was he was a mouth and nothing else, and mouths could spout their stuff in any direction, no loyalties, just the best pay-off, or a personal immunity deal if things got harsh.

Why Preston stayed living in a pissy little council house all these years Mansel did not understand. But Ron had gone ahead and bought this box when the Conservatives offered them to sitting tenants. For the classy, individual touch he had put a big brass coach-light by the front door lately, in case he wanted to get his whip out one night and drive the place away to Christmas card land. The thing about the estate was – this was the first area police came looking when any meaty crime happened in a radius of twenty miles. Without a doubt, Ron could have owned a nice, sweetly inflationary property hidden away in a private road, with deodorised neighbours, but he hung on here for some reason.

Whoever Ernest Bevin was in history he never had so many mentions in the paper as he did now, through addresses in woundings and thievings.

Of course, Mansel had still not mentioned to Preston that he might be under watch, and would not mention it. Keeping an eye on his home like this had always to be strictly confidential. If Planner suspected even a hint of surveillance the job would be ditched, no matter how near the date now. There had already been enough of those scares, what with Grace and her gorgeous fret about Tyrone. Love is the sweetest thing, but also a purple pain, sometimes. Thank God, Barry Leckwith's few well-chosen words still seemed to be working there.

Mansel saw nobody on observation at Preston's and afterwards went home and picked up his car. He drove first to visit his mother, then went down to the flat again, keen to make sure that Hoppy's arrival had still not caused any problems. Last time, the three of them seemed to be getting along as well as you could hope, but as the pressures grew things might become sticky there, what with being cooped up, and Dean's loony dreams and slip-on shoes and the girls. Hoppy could be as right as rain if you were careful with him, but these other two might not bother, because they thought they ran the universe. One thing Ron definitely had right was trying to keep lads in a waiting situation away from women, but it was no good being right if you could not do it, and nobody could do it. Harness pussy power for the nation and you wouldn't need nuclear. Ron could not even keep his own daughter away. Mansel himself, he had tried to stay clear of girls since 1986 when Sharon took off with an electrician while he was inside, only for eight months. Sharon had been great, and even now he would not think evil of her, but you could not go on letting yourself get torn like that. This was another thing that would smash poise. The doctor said he would be starting ulcers.

When Mansel arrived at the flat he found just the three men, no sign of girls, and he was glad of that because it meant they could talk without any problems. Tyrone let him in and the other two were sitting in the lounge, Hoppy looking at television and Dean playing five-stones alone. They all seemed fine, not too much tension, no more than you would expect, really, now the time was moving on, and yet he had the feeling straight away of something wrong. He stood in the middle of the room, gazing about, not knowing where this idea had come from and not knowing, either, what he was looking for. None of them had cuts or fight marks, and he could not read anything in the faces. Tyrone and Dean were too clever for that, and Hoppy's face did not change much whatever went on, it could not keep pace. If they ever got him in the electric chair he would probably take the lot without a twitch.

Somehow, Mansel felt excluded here, as if these three were their own little cliquey team, made special by something he could not know. Well, that might be natural. In fact, if they did not fight one another, it was almost bound to happen. They were stuck in here, pretty much sealed off, so of course they turned into a partnership. That was why Ron had put them together, and why he told Hoppy to move in. But although Mansel could see how it would come about, this sensation of being shut out from something still worried him, and scared him. The team had to be everybody, not just this trio.

The funny thing was they did not look at one another much today these three, so although there was a way they seemed more bound together and partners, it was also like they were more separate, as if something had gone on that made a dark barrier between them. What, though? Nothing must go wrong and bad here. That was his job to look after this end, he had decided it for himself. These were hire kids, but Ron and he and the job needed them, even Hoppy.

Tyrone opened some mock-wood double doors leading to the dining area. 'Come here, Manse, will you?'

It was said all right, friendly, not an order, but Mansel felt even more troubled. He waited a moment, then grinned and went through the doors. Taking a few steps might break that feeling of numbness and unexplained dread. God, none of this was like him – not the stupid panic, not defeat by the feeling of mystery all around. Wasn't he the laughing boy, Merry Manse? Tyrone had gone ahead of him and when they were in the dining part he swung one of the doors back so Billings could see a large piece of lined paper fixed with drawing pins to the other side. Somebody had sketched what looked like a street map on it with pencil. There were arrows and places marked with crosses.

'Recognise this?' Tyrone asked.

Dean came through, too, but Hoppy stayed with the television.

'This is done from memory and only a couple of visits, so I don't know if I've got it dead accurate, Manse,' Tyrone said. 'But you can put us right. I think it's good enough to work from.' The words were humble, but the way his voice was he made it sound like the best piece of drawing since something in an art gallery.

'We've been thinking out moves,' Dean said, pointing at a couple of the arrows. When he stretched his arm forward, it gave a good view of one of those bloody ugly insect tattoos on his wrists, some technicolour louse. 'All right? This cross here is yours truly. And this is you, Manse. Sorry it doesn't do justice to your complexion.'

Tyrone said in a whisper, glancing towards the other room: 'What still bothers us, Manse, is Hoppy. Where do we mark him in? What's his rôle?'

'This is the job?' Mansel asked, staring at the sheet, horrified.

'Can't be that bad, then,' Tyrone replied, speaking normally again. 'At least you recognised it. Here's Brand's and that waste container and the gatehouse and Acre Street, and the van done at the point where we hit it.'

'Yes, but to stick it up here, I mean, in full view,' Mansel said. 'Ron would have a stroke.'

'Well, obviously, we're not going to show it to the sod, are we, Manse?' Dean said. 'Are we crazy?'

'Something to while away the hours, that's all, Manse. Plus familiarising. Bound to be a help,' Tyrone remarked.

'Tuesday, Ron will be down here himself with a proper map and all the moves, covering every eventuality,' Mansel told them. 'How he always does it. This is leadership. These are Ron's skills.' He did some pointing himself now. 'These arrows? How do you know that's the sort of moves he wants? This could be running entirely contrary. And Ron doesn't like anything on paper till the last moment. I agree. In the past, things have gone wrong through whispers. There's got to be security.'

'I know, I know,' Tyrone replied. 'So when he gets here with his stuff we act as if this is the first time we've seen a sketch of the site, naturally. Ron can have his *gloire*, never fear. It's still his operation. This is only preparatory.'

'A bit of homework,' Dean said. 'You should be pleased, Manse. We're not idling, drinking Coke and playing cards. And then another thing. All right, for the moment everything looks great with Ron, but this is in case he chickens out, finally.'

Tyrone pushed the doors back, so they were almost closed and glanced again towards where Hoppy sat. Dean now took to whispering.

'Manse, we've got to have a fall-back, in case. There've been a couple of bad scares, now haven't there? Suppose, come Tuesday, Planner says No again. A final no. He tells us something's happened which, in his opinion, changes the whole situation, such as a general election in Malawi or the price of zinc's sunk. Suddenly, we're high and dry. Locked up here for God knows how long, and then no job, no earnings. We've got to be able to slot something in, Manse, and handle it without him. No good waiting until that moment, is it? We'd have two days to set the whole thing up from scratch, and it couldn't be done, not to give any chance of a win.'

'That's not going to happen,' Mansel said. 'Ron's made his decision. Before a decision, yes, it could be variable. Options open, sure. Not once it's done. Never. That's not Ron.'

'Manse, we know it,' Tyrone replied. 'I mean, I'm fond of him. Of course I am. I'm with Grace, aren't I, and Ron's her dad. I see him in two lights. We're sure he's going to do it, no question. We depend on him, don't we? Where's the armament, for instance, without Ron?'

'Insurance,' Dean said, passing his hand over the map. 'Like the people of Hong Kong. The six million don't all want to move in with us, but just in case.'

Hoppy called from in front of the television: 'You ought to see this. How they make roofing felt.'

'That with Harrison Ford in?' Dean replied. 'I caught it in the cinema.'

Mansel went close to the map. It was as good as it needed to be. Anyone with a bit of local knowledge could work out the place as Acre Street in The Pill.

'So show us Hoppy, Manse,' Tyrone whispered. He held out a pencil for Billings to mark him in.

Billings said: 'Ron will have a part for him, don't worry. These arrows you've got here, supposed to show our movements, mine, Ron's, even Dean's to the gatehouse, they could be all balls. That might not be how he sees it in the least. So where Hoppy goes nobody can say, not till Ron comes down here on Tuesday and gives all the detail. I think all this is out of turn, this map, Tyrone. I've got to say that.'

Dean, still whispering, leaned closer to Billings. 'Hoppy's going to have weaponry, we know that, don't we? So he's got to be up here with the two of you doing the van, yes? Do we mark him in here, Manse?' He pointed a pencil at a spot where the van was drawn, just an oblong, really, with three circles in it for the crew.

Mansel knew what they were asking. They wanted to discover whether Hoppy would actually be getting his fingers on cash right from the start of the job, and especially Dean would be interested. Everything about the take and how it was handled mesmerised that bugger. It did not make a blind bit of difference who lifted the money. Nobody was going to run off on his own with a sack of it or stick a handful of tenners down his trousers. Did they really think there would be time for anything like that? They drew their clever fucking map with the arrows and crosses like the D-day landings, but did they have any sense at all? This is what it meant, dealing with infants. Did they know how a job like this went, the speed, the din, the chaos?

So, they were anxious about Hoppy because he came in late and he was local and Ron knew him pretty well, which to Dean and Tyrone meant three home-grown people who might group if there was any trouble, two of them armed, leaving these outsiders as another group, with one pistol between them. That's how these two saw it. Right from the start they had been full of questions and doubts, especially Dean. They spent half their time looking for a double-cross and the other half trying to work out their own little double-cross. They were loners and troublemakers and could not understand the way organisations had to function. Bloody freelances. What they were badly low on was what was known as corporate feeling.

'If someone followed me here and then they break in and find that map, where are we?' Mansel said. 'For once they wouldn't need to stitch us up. They've got it on a plate.'

Tyrone behind those big, stockbroker glasses purred away: 'Nobody could follow you, not without you knowing it, Manse. You're the old pro.'

'Why talk about being followed?' Dean asked. He sounded more jumpy.

'I just want you to think about it – see the perils. No, I haven't got a tail and I'd know it if I did, but it's a scenario.'

'Crazy,' Dean said. 'Why play games, Manse? I can take a joke, but I hate people who play games. They can start fooling about with the important things. I can never trust people who play games.'

'Well, fuck you, Dean,' Mansel told him. 'Tender little you. Painful to be so raw? I'm not playing games. I'm showing how something could go wrong.'

'Manse has to think of every possibility,' Tyrone told Dean. 'That's habit, and a good habit. That's the way of a thinker, not some shit-or-bust merchant. We ought to be grateful.'

'Well, yes, but talking about being followed, that's not funny. I mean, how could it happen?'

'It hasn't happened,' Tyrone said. 'It was an idea, just an idea, can't you get that?'

'That's right,' Mansel said. 'There's no cop anywhere who could do it, I told you. Jesus, how many times does it all have to be spelled out?' If things were not so edgy, he could probably get to like Tyrone. That kid was still a kid, but he had a brain, regardless. He could understand a situation, and he knew about people and could be sensitive. He could see Mansel did some thinking, and was not just that jolly idiot Ron considered him. This appealed to Mansel, and standing by the map, he found himself thinking that Tyrone might have a point, after all. He was sure the whole notion of the map and a reserve plan was Tyrone's. Dean could only tag along. When you thought about it, you could not expect a kid to just take whatever was coming from an oldie like Ron, and especially not a bright kid like Tyrone with so much confidence it was coming out of his earholes.

Of course, they made mistakes, kids like that, but what they would not do was knuckle under to any old orders, like a butler. If Ron did do another turnaround, it could be right there ought to be a second scheme ready. A thought that had come to Mansel earlier sneaked back – that in a way it was a privilege to be welcomed into the plan these two had worked out for themselves because it meant they looked at him like somebody young enough to be in their special team, not just a worn-out, nobody side-kick for balding Ron.

If you really examined it, it was not a bad map, especially when

159

it had been done from only a couple of views of the scene. The arrows and crosses, they could be wrong, but they could be right. You never really knew what was going to work until you were doing it. Tuesday, Ron would be down here with his drawings and plans but the real point was it could all turn out almost anyhow, and you made it up as you went along. That was why having a lot of hope and morale mattered, which he always concentrated on. You did not expect to be standing outside Brand's in Acre Street reading from a book of instructions. When you considered it, these kids had just as much chance of getting it right as Ron did. Dean had dreams, but Tyrone could think.

All the same, Mansel still knew it was wrong to have this map on public view, and it still worried part of him that these people seemed to be setting up their own operation, like the competition. 'What about the girls?' he asked. 'They might see this map. Grace might tell Ron. And then the other one – Debbie Simms was it? Dean, your girl, the one with Trivial Pursuit and the arse, and the parents and the clever friend called Helen.'

'Such a memory, Manse,' Dean said.

'Things like that stick, don't they? These are people she might talk to, the parents, and Helen, the friend. Where are they, the two girls? How can you be sure this girl, Debbie, doesn't look at that map and put two and two together? She might gossip to Mum and Dad and Helen outside? Who is she? Have you thought of that?'

'We take the map down when Grace is around,' Tyrone said. 'I always know when she's coming, don't I? Myself, I don't think she'd say a word to Ron, I think she'd understand we had to have a reserve, but she doesn't see it anyway. I only put it up today because I had an idea you might show, Manse.'

'And the other one? Debbie?' Mansel asked.

'She's not here now, either,' Tyrone said.

'Don't worry about Debbie,' Dean told him.

'So, where is she?' Mansel asked.

'Like I told you, Debbie Simms lives not so very far away,' Dean replied. 'She's got parents. And friends, yes. Helen, and others, I suppose. Now and then Debbie wants to go home. It keeps everybody happy.'

'And that's where she is now?' Mansel asked.

'Don't worry about Debbie Simms, Manse,' Dean replied.

'She could talk,' Mansel said. 'Not about the map, maybe, if she hasn't seen it, but—'

'Now you sound like Planner,' Dean told him. 'Relax.'

Hoppy pushed the double doors open and came in. 'What's the big conference? Don't I get to hear?'

'Oh, only Debbie Simms,' Mansel said.

'What?' Hoppy asked. He turned to Dean, quickly: 'What's he—'

Tyrone said: 'Manse was just asking if we were sure she wasn't a talker, that's all.'

'A talker?' Hoppy asked.

'Security,' Tyrone said.

'Why?' Hoppy asked.

'Why what?' Mansel said.

But Hoppy only shrugged and the other two did not help, either. Mansel noticed they were not looking at one another again. All at once he felt he might be getting the very beginnings of a glimpse of what was wrong here, but only the beginnings and still nothing clear. There had been a few moments when he thought it must have been their secret reserve plan and the map that made him sense something not too healthy, but now he could not be sure.

'Why were you asking about her?' Hoppy replied.

'Where is she?' Mansel said.

'We told you, home at present,' Dean replied.

Hoppy paused for a second: 'Yes, that's right.'

'When you say home, where?' Mansel asked.

'In the area, but I haven't got an address,' Dean replied. 'It'll surprise you, Manse, but I haven't been asked to meet the parents.'

'Not asked to meet the parents,' Hoppy shouted, with a big laugh.

Chapter 24

By Sunday evening, Harpur had put his ambush party together and on Monday spent lunchtime with them watching the two banks in Prince Albert Street. He did not believe in it, but tried his best to, because it had to be done, regardless. That's what chain of command meant, at least if Iles was well up in it. As to timing, Harpur had to work blind, but he calculated that if Preston did his observations at this part of the day it must be the likeliest. Harpur carried a Smith and Wesson magnum himself and also put two of his three best marksmen on this shift, Cotton and Sid Synott.

They had a spot behind venetian blinds in a first-floor office suite belonging to accountants, Lentle, Lentle and Burt, opposite the banks, more or less ideal except for the time it would take them to get downstairs if anything happened. Just out of sight, were a couple of unmarked cars on radio call and three hired vans ready to block off the park end of the road. It was as neat as it could be: as neat as it could be without telling the banks and putting men inside to give a welcome. The drawback was that Harpur had no way of knowing which day the targets would be especially ripe with cash, or when money deliveries might take place. Quite possibly Preston was better briefed, and had timed the raid to suit. Harpur wanted the banks ignorant, all the same. Preston was supreme on information and could easily have a tipster in the one he meant to hit.

That was, if he did mean to hit either. Harpur's doubts were deep, although he agreed with Iles that enough pointers said Planner had some operation brewing. Whether it would turn out to be one of these banks was another question.

Harpur found it unnerving to be sealed off in this setting with Robert Cotton. Normally, Harpur tried to avoid any long or close contact. Normally, too, if he knew Cotton was certain to be incarcerated on an operation he would do his best to see Ruth then. Now, he waited, incarcerated with him. They had become partners. There was something macabre about it. Was work taking over? At one point today, around noon, he and Cotton kept vigil together from the same window. They gazed down into the sunny, thronged street, bright with women's summer clothes and glowing skin, but looked for boiler suits and balaclavas. Harpur felt decency required him to talk. Yet what kind of chit-chat did you give someone whose wife was your long-time lover, probably to his knowledge or half-knowledge: someone you might be relying on at any moment to protect your life, or, at least, not to take it?

It was Cotton who opened the talking, though. 'The counsellor told me after Ditto Repeato I should never go back to firearms. Even at the time, I mean, right after Ditto's death, I knew that was shit.'

'You would have been a hell of a loss.'

'I hear I've got to thank you for helping me back. Well, then, thanks.'

'Self-interest.'

'Yes?'

'People like you are scarce, and getting scarcer.'

'Yes, people crack and turn in their ticket. Good people. They shoot someone, someone who had to be shot, and then can't take the media storm and the MP storm and the Home Office storm and the storm from the villain's mates and family, who say he was a harmless, misunderstood darling, really, always reading *Winnie The Pooh* to underprivileged children, and would never have fired the loaded sawn-off he happened to have with him and pointing at the copper's guts. I see all that turmoil as natural enough. Of course there has to be a fuss. This is someone dead and guns on the street. A serious episode. It's right there should be questions. They can be dealt with, though. And the anon phone calls full of froth and cursing are a giggle. All they do is show you've hit them where it hurts. Would I let myself go to pieces over someone like Ditto? There's too much mystification and self-indulgence about guns. Once in a while I cave in to all that myself, but it's a weakness. You've got to root it out. I use a gun within all the rules and I'm not ashamed. I get support. You. Mr Iles. My kids know I do it and, of course, my wife. Yes, I'd be nowhere without the backing of my wife.'

He kept staring down from the window when he mentioned her and his voice did not waver. Perhaps he could not bring himself to say her name to Harpur, though, just her status. People were often sensitive about names and how they addressed others: Harpur could not remember Cotton ever calling him sir.

Harpur said: 'You were bound to recover – and quickly.'

'No, I don't think so. It was a lot of will. I'm not all that bright. I won't get much further. But on will I'm tops. Always have been. I will things to come right.'

'Yes?'

'Things of all sorts.'

'Yes? It's a very big plus.'

'Yes, it's a plus. I can look as if I'm doing real badly, in some situation, but I'll turn it around, if it can be done, if it's at all possible. And it will be done more by will than skill.'

'I've seen you shoot. I wouldn't ever run down your skill.'

'Oh, shooting. That's a trade, like a motor mechanic. It's bugger all. Did you understand what I was talking about?' He had turned from the window and looked along the slats of the venetian blind at Harpur. Cotton was thin and athletic and a lot more intelligent than he said. Fair-skinned and blue-eyed, he used to throb with enthusiasm for the job, though Harpur thought that some of this had gone since the Ditto shooting, despite his words just now. 'I'm not sure whether you get what I mean.'

Yes, Harpur did. He knew that Cotton had been talking about Ruth and his marriage and saying, as Iles sometimes said, that it would come right because he meant to make it come right. But Harpur replied: 'Wider things – will-power generally, you mean? Not something that can be taught.'

Cotton gave what could have been a suppressed snarl, or even a groan, and resumed watching the street. 'All right, you dodge out of it. You do know what I mean, though. I can crack it.' And then he muttered something which Harpur was not sure he heard properly, either, but which seemed to echo a word Iles had used recently, 'One flew over the cuckold's nest.' Harpur decided against querying it.

At that moment, Sid Synott came into the room, anyway. Sid was first class when things started but not so good at waiting.

Harpur could smell sweat off him now. 'This a dud, sir?' Sid said. 'I have that feeling.'

So you set one man's intuitions against another's. Since one of the men was Iles, though, the contest had to be uneven. Sid, forty, nervy-looking, and as thin as Cotton, knew the streets, knew about banks, knew about Planner and Mansel, but Iles knew all those things as well, and also knew how to manage a career. So, the ambush stayed. But the signs had to be against.

Harpur knew, as Sid would know, that this kind of raid needed more people than just Ron Preston and Mansel Billings, especially as Manse stayed gun-chaste. They would have to be talented and/or experienced assistants, too. So, where was the rest of the team? Did it exist? Harpur had run a check and found that most of the boys Planner led in the past were either locked up, or too old, or too drunk, or strutting about tanned in Malaga, or any combination of the last three. A lad called Brian – Hoppy – Short seemed the only one not accounted for. Hoppy was the sort of dim, freelance, rough material Planner did not like, but Harpur suspected he used him now and then. Apparently Hoppy had left his place a few days ago, nobody knew for where. Harpur had a call out for sightings, though Preston would probably make sure he stayed hidden if a job was close.

On the other hand, if Planner had brought in outside people they would have to be accommodated somewhere, and almost certainly not in his own place or Mansel's, because that would be noticeable. It would be rooms or, more likely, a flat. Strange faces moving into a street, all of them men, often attracted attention, yet there had been no reports.

Harpur could see no evidence that anything as major as a main street bank raid was planned, no evidence beyond the fact that Preston loitered for a spell at a street corner. Both these edifices were huge, cocky places, built in big stone blocks at the time of the city's first prosperity, and now water-cleansed and glistening to echo a new local boom. The job looked too much for Preston, way above his weight, with or without a team. Planner was a miniaturist, his motto, 'Think small.' He took nourishment like a bird, little and often. Harpur feared that although they might be right to wait and watch, they ought to be waiting and watching somewhere else. But he would admit he had no suggestions to make and that Iles's speculation was the best around. Once the ACC had accepted that Preston could have been on reconnaissance when spotted by Cade there was no alternative to laying the ambush. Anything else would look like neglect, and screaming neglect if the raid actually happened. Iles must be relying on that kind of logic to pressure Lane into keeping the trap in place. Of course, if Planner did his job somewhere else while they were all tucked-up, waiting here for him it would not look too brilliant, either.

As soon as the banks shut at three-thirty, Harpur left them. Synott said, as Harpur went out the back way: 'Didn't I tell you, sir? A non-starter.'

'There's a lot more days, Sid.'

'God, are there?'

Harpur made his way to the lawn furniture section of a garden centre at the edge of the city and waited contentedly among large urns, teak benches and statuettes that Lamb had told him at other confidential meetings here were classical goddesses. Harpur would not have minded a stone goddess or two for his own garden but had an idea Megan would regard them as pretentious, a pathetic attempt to mimic the grounds of stately homes. Like many raised in good, upper-middle-class households, Megan lived in terror of pretentiousness, always scared of seeming to want to climb, because most of them did want to.

He was sure she would have especially hated the statue he liked most: a nice snub-nosed young girl dressed in billowing, clinging things and carrying a rich armful of wheat sheaves. He felt almost certain it was a very famous classical figure, and displaying this one would be not only pretentious but trite. Megan feared the trite almost as much as the pretentious, and his daughters were very anti-triteness, too. A fair bit of what he said to them they declared trite, or less.

Lamb, vast and as affable-looking as ever, in white trousers and a white sweat-shirt, bearing in red italic the motif, 'Bring Back Attlee', arrived at a rush just after four. He was with Helen, the teenage, one-time punk girl he lived with these days.

'Here's a delight, Col,' Lamb cried. 'One of our too rare reunions. Why this distance between us so often? That's what I ask myself. As a matter of fact, it's Helen who's called this meeting. Concern about a friend, Col. Helen's a worrier. I'm only link-man.'

'How long have you two been back from Italy?' Harpur said. Now and then, Lamb, like any other voice, had to get far away quickly for a time, and take all those he loved and feared for with him.

'You make the streets safe for us, Col. I reckoned it would be all right to come back, now.'

'We missed home so much,' Helen said. 'And friends. Perhaps me more than Jack. I found myself dreaming of Darien's long, lovely rooms and springy floors and the Aga. I feel like a renegade staying away. But I come back to – well to bad anxiety.'

'Yes?' Harpur said. He felt he had been brought here by deception. If Jack telephoned it was usually because he had something good to tell him.

'A friend of Helen gone missing, Col. Don't know her myself.'

Punk seemed over. Now apparently into severity, Helen wore a very simple, dark silk suit, her hair longer than Harpur had ever seen it, and swept back on one side. According to Jack, she knew about *l'art fang* and advised him in some of his picture deals. Such deals helped pay for Jack's beautiful manor house, Darien, behind its stone wall near Chase Woods. A proportion of these transactions were definitely above board, but, just the same, Harpur tried not to know anything much about Jack's business. In this kind of traditional, delicate relationship between policeman and informant you closed your eyes in some directions so they could be opened in others. Like most great commercial and moral decisions it was a matter of striking a useful balance, and, as Megan used to say, the symbol of justice was a pair of scales: Megan loved irony.

'This is a girl called Debbie Simms,' Helen explained. 'I'm worried, and her parents.'

'Yes?' Harpur said. 'What age?'

'Nineteen,' Helen replied.

'Girls do take off sometimes then.' They stood grouped around the girl with sheaves, like a small harvest festival.

Helen turned her bright, coarse features towards Harpur. 'Can I say something to you straight out first? Jack, don't listen if it embarrasses you. It's this: naturally, some part of me suspects police, and I wouldn't usually approach them with my troubles.'

Lamb tut-tutted loudly and held up a vast hand in apology. 'She's phrasing it badly, Col, that's all.'

'But you, Colin, I don't think of you as police.'

'No?' Harpur replied.

'Col, what she means is not you're not police, obviously, because of course you are, and full of distinction and achievement, not to mention total integrity, of course, but—'

'This friend of mine, Debbie Simms, has dropped out of sight, Colin. She's a girl who went her own way in many respects, if you know what I mean, and yet keeping in touch with parents, also. I'd go over there and see them for a chat. She was there off and on up to last week, but . . . Maybe she's a kid liable to get things not quite right – some of her acquaintances and so on, and men, especially that – but no real harm in her at all.'

They went and sat on a couple of the garden benches facing each other, Harpur and Helen on one, Jack Lamb opposite, now like passengers in a railway carriage.

'I'm into a biggish thing just now,' Harpur said. 'An Iles thing,' he told Lamb. 'I can't possibly take on anything else.'

'You're not offended by what she said about you, Col? I know you're bigger than that. Helen has to say her piece. It's youth, isn't it? Look, I told her you were obviously at full stretch. Saturday working and so on. She wanted to come and see you earlier. I demurred. Helen can be very intense. It's appealing, I think, generally.'

Harpur said: 'If this girl, Debbie, has been gone a while you could report it officially, Helen. Or the parents can. They'd listen to you at a police station, even though you don't usually talk to police. Police are used to people who don't talk to police until they need something.'

'Col, as I understand it, this is a girl who would be around off and on, free spirit, take off for a little while, but then shows up again. Lately, she hasn't showed up again,' Lamb told him.

'Could be anything,' Harpur said. 'She fallen for someone seriously. She might go off with him.'

'She said a couple of things before she disappeared. I thought they might be up your street.'

'Except I'm busy, Jack. I'd help, but I'm not just busy in the usual way. I'm tied up on something that's almost sure to turn out a dead loss and I've got to be ready to salvage something when it does or we're going to look very stupid.'

168

Helen stood up. 'He's not even listening, Jack. Let's forget it. He's decided Debbie's a slag and old enough to take care of her own perils. This one has shut off.'

Harpur stood, too, glad at the prospect of being rid of her. Lamb stayed where he was and said: 'Debbie would chat away nineteen to the dozen about some things, apparently, and mentioned to Helen and her parents that she'd met a couple of interesting lads who'd come to work here from outside. What work, she couldn't sort out, or so she said. They had a flat. There was another girl, called Grace. No second name.'

Harpur said: 'Lovely name. It's sure to come back in, after Grace Jones.'

'Right. Then a couple more men came into the picture, off and on, apparently, one she didn't think much of. Col, she said he was called Hoppy. Dim? Again, no second name. Helen got the idea Debbie was scared of him.'

Harpur revived: 'Where was this?'

'And then another figure who seems to drift in and out, a visitor. Someone nicer, older, named Mansel.'

'But where was all this happening? Drifted in and out where?' Harpur asked.

Lamb said: 'These two names, Hoppy, Mansel – it's why I said it would be okay for Helen to come and see you.'

Helen sat down. 'Jack said he thought he recognised these names, and you would, too, Colin.'

'You know Hoppy's not around, Col, do you?'

'Where? Where are these people?' Harpur asked.

'That we haven't got,' Lamb replied. 'These names just came out in chat, Hoppy, Mansel – Debbie having a bit of a gossip, yes, Helen?'

'And the other two men?' Harpur asked.

'No,' Helen replied. 'She never said. It was like she had some idea she shouldn't – not about those two names. They were special. Or the place. Yes, now and then I got the idea she had become a bit scared, like being into something she was beginning to understand and didn't like much.'

'It means something to you, Col? What?' Lamb asked.

But Jack was for giving information, not receiving. That little line of demarcation always had to be carefully preserved. Harpur turned to Helen: 'She never said anything at all to give even half or half a hint where this flat might be. I mean, in the city? Outside? No district?'

Helen thought and her face became even more like a troubled child's. Then she shook her head. 'I don't think she wanted her parents to know too much. Well, she never did, about anything. You know how people like that are.'

'People like that?'

'Well, parents.'

'Oh, them.'

'What is it, Col?' Lamb asked.

'I'll put out some feelers,' Harpur replied.

When they broke up, he drove back to Prince Albert Street. He had intended ringing Ruth after the meeting, but felt the need now to see the men in the ambush. It looked as if Iles almost certainly had things right after all. So, there was in fact a team lying in wait somewhere: two outsiders, plus Hoppy Short, with Mansel Billings looking in from time to time to see if they were all right. Some called him Merry Mansel, some Mother Mansel. He did fuss. And then there was Grace, who must be Grace Preston. At first, Harpur had wondered whether this meant they were all in Planner's place on the Ernest Bevin. He doubted that now, though. There had been no mention, apparently, of Preston himself or Doris. It sounded as if Grace might fancy one of the outsiders, with the second girl, Debbie Simms, for the other. Yes, there would be a transit camp somewhere, with Grace and Mansel and Debbie calling in now and then. So, what had happened to her?

At the moment, he could not give that much thought. He needed above all to make sure that none of the scepticism he had felt about the trap had rubbed off on the people waiting. He must get Sid Synott to stop thinking of it as a dud.

The shift was changing as he arrived, a much scaled down operation for the night. Nothing would take place while the banks were closed. He took Sid and Cotton into a side room. 'This raid is certainly going to happen,' he said. 'Could be tomorrow, could be any day. This will be one of the sweetest over-the-pavement jobs we've ever had. There'll be total surprise for us. We're lucky to be on it.'

'You know something extra, sir?' Synott asked.

'Something.'

'So, who are they? Who are we going to be meeting, beside Planner and Mansel? It helps to know. I mean, the original briefing stopped bloody short, you've got to agree, sir,' Synott said. 'How many? What category? Armament? Yes, of course, armament. What? Have they got a history? Handguns? Sawn-offs? Stuff they'll really use, or carried as frighteners only?' His face was contorted with nerves and his voice shook as he pumped out the questions. It was hard to credit that in a shooting situation he became like ice.

'I'm working on it,' Harpur replied.

'They're all much of a muchness, anyway,' Cotton said. 'Dross on a day out. If they want to play deadly, that's how it has to be. Now, can we go home? I want to see the family. And Sid needs a shower.'

Chapter 25

Preston drove down to the flat on Tuesday with a suitcase containing the boiler suits and balaclavas and Bulldog pistols, and with his diagrams and street maps in a document folder. This would be the last briefing and he would make clear to Tyrone and Dean which kind of cars to take next day and where to leave them overnight. You had to cover the details. These young buggers were so sure everything would work the way they wanted they would probably leave the vehicles outside the flat if he did not tell them. And it might be all right if they did. People like those two often had the luck, which was one reason he picked them. Preston did believe in luck, but he believed in work and carefulness more, and they were a habit right through him like veins now.

He always enjoyed giving a team the final talk. It meant there were no more doubts over whether the job would happen. They really could not turn back. Although he was a worrier and a perfectionist, there came a moment when he felt relieved to pass beyond all the preparation and go into the launching count-down. It was the warm, that's-it feeling, like taking a couple of heavy drinks again after a long lay-off.

And another thing he had a lift from was that this last meeting always seemed to fit with his notion of what a leader should be and had to be. A leader was someone who came to his boys with all the moves worked out for them and done with good clarity on paper. This was their safety and their earnings he would be talking about. It was worth the sweat. In the folder were five diagrams giving alternative schemes for the operation, depending on how the early moves went – what was known as contingencies. Useless having only one diagram. That would not be planning but mad, lazy, hope-for-the-best thinking, the kind Manse might use if he ever got to lead an outfit, which he wouldn't. Manse was great, great at number two.

Even five possible schemes might not be enough. The thing was, you had to keep it down to as many as someone like Hoppy could hold in his handsome, dumbo head. But anybody who thought about it for ten minutes could see God knew how many ways a raid like this might turn out. If there could be one extra man aboard the van, there could be more than one. There might be a doubling up in the gatehouse. Wilf Rudd's information could only go so far.

Obviously, nobody could forecast how the traffic would be near the gates. Then, there might be some idiot, have-a-go member of the public around, someone full of fucking guts and nuisance. Always Preston lived in horror of this. What was in it for people like that, throwing their lives away? Or timing could be altered for some reason. And, lastly, there could be police waiting. He wished he did not have to talk about this one, because it could knock all the fight out of the boys before they started. He had one street diagram for that possibility, though, and he would show it. They had to take it into account. It would be another failure of leadership to pretend nothing like that could happen. When Eisenhower laid on D-day he did not tell the troops there would only be shrimps on the beach.

You could not talk as if everything was sure to go exactly right. Five diagrams or five hundred – it didn't necessarily mean a thing. The real leader did all that preparation, of course, but he also told his group, even a group with some dope like Hoppy in it, that they had to be ready to use their brains in case something unexpected came out of nowhere. If you gave them good plans and it made them feel better, this was half the battle. What you did not want, though, was a team that turned to ashes if the plans took a knock or two when the time came on the street. In boxing they talked about someone training so much he left it all in the gym. He did not want it all left in the gym. In one way you could say he and Manse had been in training since Wilf Rudd first rolled up with the word about the van all that time ago. The others, Tyrone, Dean and Hoppy did not start until later, Hoppy much later.

When Preston arrived today, the three were all ready for him, Tyrone, Dean and Hoppy, but Mansel had not shown yet. This was strange. Manse liked to be early so he could set the scene, prepare the way. Wasn't that one of his special jobs? Preston could see it worried Tyrone and Dean, too, that Manse was not there. They were kids and they would be edgy anyway as the day came close. On top of that, there were the changes and scares, so nobody could be sure if it was going through or not. Preston would not have minded betting they had their own ideas of how to run this thing, in case he pulled out. And now it would look to them like Mother Manse had pulled out, instead. They might think he had some information or just his bottle went. They would have trouble coping with that idea. He could hardly cope with it himself. Where the hell was he? No Manse, no job, that was certain. So, all at once, these two, Dean and Tyrone, probably saw the job going down the tube again, and if it did, and they still thought of handling it on their own, they would really be on their own now, no Preston, but no Manse, either. Maybe Hoppy, yes. They might not be sure whether that was good or bad, though. Even someone as perky as Dean would wonder whether two or three of them could pull this one off.

Preston would not start the briefing without Mansel but he did what he could to talk and take some of the jumpiness away. That was not usually his line, because it was always down to Manse, and Preston knew he himself would not make much of a go at it. He dredged out some chat about old jobs that had gone sweetly, and the way people spent their slice of the take, but he could see he was not getting through to them. Even without this worry about Manse, Preston had the feeling there was something wrong here, something that went beyond just nerviness about the job. There was a special tension that touched even Hoppy, a sense of something dark and hidden which they would not allow him to share or understand. Almost overwhelmingly the bloody dread that had eaten at him from the start came back, the one that said this outing was jinxed and double-jinxed and he ought to get out.

And then the bell of the flat went with Mansel's special ring and Tyrone and Dean grinned and relaxed a fraction, and so did Hoppy when he saw the others were pleased. For a second, Preston felt a rush of regret and he realised that all his good spirits on the way here in the car had gone and he was looking for an excuse to quit. There could not have been a better one than Manse not turning up. He made sure he grinned like the rest of them, though. The street door opened direct into a little hall, which was part of the open-plan room, and when Dean went to answer they found that Mansel was not alone. Two men pushed in hurriedly past Dean and Preston saw at once that the other was Barry Leckwith. Although it was a hot and sunny afternoon Leckwith wore a raincoat buttoned right up to the neck, and he must have sneaked away from duty somehow and still had his uniform on.

Preston felt appalled. What the hell was Mansel doing bringing that heap of hazard here? And the others could spot right off from the coat and black trousers and black shoes he was police. Hoppy might even have recognised him from the wrong side of a pair of handcuffs somewhere in his past. They all stood like hypnotised.

Mansel said: 'I had to bring him, Ron, had to.'

'You gone fucking mad?' Preston answered. 'You realise after this we can't—'

'Listen to what he's got to say,' Mansel replied. 'All of you.'

'You bring a cop here?' Dean whispered. 'Manse, you've shopped us? Where's the rest of them then?' He started to screech. 'Ron, is there armament in that bag? Quick.' He made a move towards the case. He had some fight, then, after all, this one.

'There's no others. He's alone,' Mansel said.

'It's all right, Dean,' Preston muttered.

'All right? A cop?' He did not try to open the case, though.

'But why, Manse?' Preston asked.

'Barry came to my place.' Manse beamed like an idiot. 'This is the best news you've ever heard, any of you.'

'What, he's bent, is he? All right?' Tyrone asked. 'You both know him?'

'Barry keeps us in the picture, that's all,' Mansel said. 'Nothing extreme. We don't need words like "bent". It's just a kindly service.'

'What great news?' Preston asked.

'So, tell them, Barry,' Mansel said. 'Sit down. Everybody sit down, right? Try and relax.'

They took seats. Leckwith undid the top of his coat and they saw the silver insignia. To Preston's amazement, this tiny glimpse sent his mind sliding back to when he was a child and fascinated and delighted by the police and their uniform. When did all that go?

Leckwith said: 'Harpur and the rest have set up an ambush.'

'Jesus,' Preston muttered. 'I knew it.'

'Ron, he's teasing. Cut it out, Barry. They're on edge. Give them the good news,' Mansel said.

'It's in the wrong place,' Leckwith told them.

'In the wrong place. An ambush in the wrong sodding place,' Mansel said. 'This is the great Harpur all adrift.'

'This is at Prince Albert Street. The banks,' Leckwith said.

'Banks?' Tyrone asked. 'Are they kidding.'

'Prince Albert Street? Why?' Preston said.

'You were spotted there,' Leckwith replied. 'A routine report to the Collator. Were you in that area, Planner?'

'What?' At first, he did not even recall waiting for the *Annie* girl there. 'I might. By the park?'

'By the banks,' Leckwith said.

'Ron, they're watching the banks. They think we're going to hit them,' Mansel told him.

'Now, look, this is supposed to be two hundred per cent secret,' Leckwith said. 'They've gone security mad. Harpur personally responsible for secrecy. But a lot of men involved, and catering and so on. With that number, things still leak, if you know where to look. I do. I had the whisper only last night, though. So, the rush.'

'Barry wanted to tell you himself, Ron,' Mansel said. 'It's why we're here. I know it's not right, a breach of rules. But he insisted on the chief hearing it face to face.'

'Well, of course,' Leckwith said. 'This is very big information, Planner. I have to be certain it's going to the top.'

'Thanks,' Preston said.

'Yes,' Leckwith added. 'I thought I'd done well for you before this, with other news, but this is really something else, yes? It's taken a hell of a lot of getting.'

Preston said: 'Well, sure, if it's—'

'At first, all I heard was they were placing an ambush, so I thought there must be some genuine tip and they would be moving in up near Brand's at Acre Street. Listen, I even went up there and had a quiet look around. Nothing, of course. But I like to be thorough. This is your lives, yes? Then, later – this is last night – I get the location. Prince Albert Street. They're in a couple of offices opposite, twenty-four-hour survey, maximum readiness around lunchtime, because that was when you were spotted. You can bank on this, Planner.'

'Bank on it,' Dean said, giggling. 'Have you been down there? Seen them down there?'

'No need. It's a fact, old son. I've had it from two sources.' Leckwith did his coat up again. 'I can't hang about. I'm working today. Look, Planner, obviously, this has to be very good terms. Very, very good terms. You won't ever get information like this again. I'm sticking my neck right out for you, you realise that, the security being the way it is? Well, just coming here like this, for one thing.' He tugged at the collar of the raincoat, to show what he meant. 'You've got a free hand up there for the raid, haven't you? You know now you can rely on max leisure – all the time in the world to clean out the van, every sackful. No need for violence. No need at all. I hope you remember that. I don't want any part in violence. Just terrorise the crew – threats only – and go to work. This has to be ten per cent information, even fifteen. You want figures? All right. I hear it's a bumper crop this time. So, I think I'm looking at, say, thirty grand for this, Planner. Twenty-eight at the least. Why I needed to see you face to face. You've got to okay this kind of payment from the top, I realise that. This is a boardroom decision. All right, so they'll tumble to the fact they've made a cock-up once the alarms come in about the van raid, but think how long it will take them to adjust. This won't be like getting a hit team out at speed from headquarters – what they're practising all the time. This is first a call to headquarters and then the checking, because they've been told it's all supposed to happen at Prince Albert, and they'll go on believing it, and then eventually getting the message down to the ambush boys and telling them to drop everything there and get somewhere else, people pissed off about the error, a scramble to the cars, and no close knowledge of the terrain. All the marksmen and Harpur himself are down there, as I hear it. You should be miles away or home doing the garden by the time they get their act together, Planner.'

Hoppy was laughing all over his face and halfway down his back: 'Miles away, miles away,' he crooned.

'Of course, they'll call and see you afterwards, Ron, and you,

Manse,' Leckwith went on. 'They would have done, anyway. You're on the books. But they'll have nothing to go on. In a way, the Prince Albert thing is a kind of alibi! That's where they think you should be. It's beautiful.'

Tyrone said: 'Yes, it's beautiful, Ron. You're a genius.'

Leckwith looked puzzled. 'What? What's that mean?'

'What?' Tyrone replied.

'A genius. You've got some good luck, that's a fact. But genius?'

'Oh, obviously, he did this deliberately, didn't you, Ron? Hanging about near the banks, knowing they'd pick it up for the Collator? My God, and I thought you might be . . . well, might be getting on a bit. All right, getting on a bit and past it. I've got to admit, we even had an alternative, I mean, a possible alternative. It's so bloody laughable now. Grace is right: you're great, Ron, a real mind. We're useless babes alongside you. As if we could have handled this!'

Leckwith was still a bit dazed. Maybe he could feel some of his fee slipping. 'You intentionally decoyed them, Planner?'

'Of course he did. That's obvious, isn't it?' Tyrone replied. 'Why the hell else is he hanging about a street corner in full view? This is someone thinking at full throttle.'

'Christ, that would be bloody brilliant, even for you, Planner. I don't believe it,' Leckwith said.

'I wasn't sure it would work,' Preston answered. 'Why I didn't mention it, lads.' He did not know whether Tyrone really believed all that or had just thought very fast, the way Tyrone could, to keep Leckwith's share down. It was worth following, though.

Dean came and patted Preston happily on the back. 'If Ron set all this up, planned it, well, obviously that's going to have some effect on costing for the tip, isn't it? You didn't realise Ron had planned it, did you?' he asked Leckwith. 'You thought you were telling us something we didn't know, didn't have any idea of. But, really, Ron knew it could be on the cards all the time. You see what I mean?'

Leckwith stared across the room at him. 'Who's this little fucker with spots then, Manse?'

'You're like pigeon post when we've had it by fax machine,' Dean said, laughing. 'Yes, pigeon post. But you've got shit all over your feathers.'

'Listen, jerk, I'm taking risks,' Leckwith muttered.

'Oh, I like that, *you're* taking risks,' Dean replied.

'No need for aggro,' Mansel said.

'None at all,' Preston told them. The atmosphere here was rough all of a sudden. Dean did not take his eyes off Leckwith.

'I'm due a boon payment here, Planner,' the policeman said.

'And he's got a proper name, you know, copper,' Dean told him. 'He's Ron. Planner this, Planner that. It's rude. It's like police.'

'Listen, Planner,' Leckwith replied, 'now come on. This is balls. You were shocked when I told you all that – the ambush, and then the location. Don't ask me to believe you were expecting it. I saw your face. This was news to you, and you thought bad news when I started.'

'Because he's clever, of course,' Tyrone told him. 'He's working away all the time on the quiet. That's how Ron is. He's not going to plaster everything he thinks and feels across his face, is he? That's how·people get ten years. He plays us all along, you as well.'

'Too clever for your lot,' Dean said. 'Always has been.'

'Are you going down there again, Ron?' Tyrone asked. 'There's time. I suppose you'll make a real show around the banks. Keep them on the boil?'

'I've thought of it. I might.' It would be a good idea, as long as he could make sure the girl from *Annie*, out having lunch, did not come and join him. They might guess then why he was there in the first place.

'It's a great idea, Ron,' Dean told him. 'Clinch it.'

Leckwith stood up, that big, bony face very angry. 'I'm going back. It's dangerous. Once or twice lately I thought maybe I had a tail.'

'What?' Mansel yelled. 'You didn't tell me that. Why should you have a tail? They're on to you? If they're on to you, they're on to us.'

'I told you before. I don't know. But not today. I went all round the nick building and then a bit more before coming out. I know I'm clear. And, Planner, you and Manse are clear, too. I heard they're afraid to put anyone on you in case you spot it and cancel. We're all all right. Cool down, for God's sake. So, listen now, Planner, I've got to have your word. Now.

This is ten per cent or thirty grand. Take your pick. But say it now.'

'This bastard has to be joking,' Dean said. 'Maybe he leads people here and—'

'This bastard knows too much to joke,' Leckwith replied. 'Nobody's been led here. Planner, if you want the job, you say yes to the payment and you say it before I go. I'll trust you. I wouldn't say the same to any of your crew, but you've got a name, Planner. I can believe in it.'

'Tell him to get stuffed, Ron,' Dean said. 'What's he mean "if you want the job"? What can he do about it?'

'There can be leaks two ways, sonny boy,' Leckwith told him. 'Planner knows that. If I'm not paid, and paid what I'm due, you could find Cotton and Sid Synott and Laissez Faire plus Harpur all waiting for you in the right place on Thursday. Or they could be around here before. They might receive one of those anon calls.'

'Christ.' Dean suddenly stood up and, stepping across the room, reached for the case again. 'You hear that, Ron? Who knows he's here? We can deal with this one.' Hoppy jumped up, too.

Tyrone grabbed Dean's arm and pulled him back. 'That's enough. There's been enough of that. This is a cop, you fool. We'll have the wrath of God here.'

Dean struggled for a moment, but Tyrone held him. Hoppy sat down again.

'One kick and I could have broken your little-boy wrist then,' Leckwith told Dean. 'But I realised you could be needed on Thursday. What for it's hard to think. Serving the tea?'

Preston said: 'Tyrone's right. This isn't the time for trouble.'

'I'm making a reasonable point, Planner. You can see that, I know,' Leckwith told him.

'Yes, reasonable enough.'

'Ten per cent or thirty grand, then?' Leckwith asked.

'I'll say thirty grand.'

'Done. I've settled cheap, have I? Never mind, I'm like that. But I know what I need for the restaurant.' Leckwith turned to Dean, who had sat down again. 'You: do this job and then disappear from here. Don't ever come into these parts again or you're fucked. Understand? With this money, I could be out of the Force by then, but I'll still make sure you're very adequately seen to. You're marked, and I don't mean the tattoos.'

When Leckwith had gone, Preston did his briefing and shared out the gear. 'What did you mean, Tyrone, talking to Dean, when you said "there's been enough of that"?'

Tyrone became like he was baffled, a real thorough job of it. 'Well, enough excitement from him. Enough tough stuff. That's all.'

'That's all? It sounded like . . . Sounded like something else had happened already. Should I know?' Preston saw Mansel was gazing at Tyrone for the answer, like he had wanted to ask the same question.

'What something else, Ron?'

'What I'm asking you.'

'Nothing else. What something else could it be, Ron? It just seemed so unnecessary – Dean's attitude.'

Preston waited a second, and saw he would not get anything more. 'All right. Good. Yes, it was unnecessary.'

'Yes, out of order. It's just we're all a bit high-strung just now,' Mansel said.

'There's going to be nothing left in this take, the way it's being carved in advance,' Dean grunted.

'There'll be more for you than you've ever seen,' Preston told him, 'even though you've possibly just fractured one of the best communication lines we ever had, you realise that?'

He handed out the gear and the pistols and ammunition to Dean and Hoppy. When it was people like that, he would have liked to hold on to the guns until the day of the job, but they had to have a chance to get accustomed. As an outing came nearer you always found you did not have many choices left. It started as just an idea when someone like Wilf Rudd turned up with the tip, and at that time there were a million choices – do it, don't do it, do it this way, do it that way, do it this week, do it next, do it with weaponry, do it without. And then, gradually, the thing itself would take over and you discovered you could do it one way, and only that way. This was why you had to be so thorough and careful at the beginning.

Look at what had happened here this morning. Everyone on a high because Leckwith said the ambush would be in the wrong spot. Great. But why would it? Because somebody had seen Preston in the street. So, they had one thing right and one wrong. The thing they had right was that he had a job in mind. How did they know that? Of course, Harpur would always expect him to have a job in mind, because he had a past. But would they expect it enough to set up a big, top-quality waiting party in Prince Albert Street, or was there some extra information? If so, where from? What else did they know? He even thought about Hoppy's doubts over Tyrone.

In the flat, the others were still giggling and chattering and trying on the gear and Dean and Hoppy did gunplay tricks with the Bulldogs. The niggle with Leckwith was forgotten as soon as he left. They were talking triumph, even Tyrone. Usually, this was the sort of mood you had to work like hell to get them into before a job. Now, it had all come just like that. They did not seem able to see behind this great piece of news about Prince Albert Street. They were already spending the cash. That was what Preston meant about a job taking over. It began at nearly nothing with Wilf and then picked up its own pace from somewhere and was unstoppable, like a ride on the switchback. Or like getting ready for D-day. He realised he was thinking about D-day a lot lately, that big childhood memory.

At home, Grace told Preston that a Veronica Carter from the car hire firm had rung, which meant Maggie from Devon in the code they used if she wanted to telephone the house. That was a call he had been expecting. She would want to know why he did not get down there at the weekend as promised, and he would have to think up something very wholesome and unknockable. Maybe he should have rung first and said he would not be able to get there because of business, but she always made such a fuss. He had put it off and put it off until it was too late. You could understand her getting a bit ungovernable now and then, stuck down somewhere like Devon with a kid.

He waited a couple of hours and then drove around until he found a phone box that worked and gave her a call. He hoped she might be in a sulk by now and would not answer. When she did, he put a pound in on top of the ten pence and said: 'Maggie, at last. I've been trying to get you.'

'Like hell you have.' Her voice sounded dead.

'Friday. At the weekend. Something wrong with the line. Is your phone all right? I wanted to say I couldn't get down. It was a business thing. You know how it goes. But next weekend, definitely.'

'No.'

'Are you away then?'

'Just don't bother.'

'Maggie, I know it was—'

'I'm not taking any more of it, Ron. You just roll up when you feel like it. I've had enough.'

Through the glass walls of the box he could watch almost all round. Leckwith had it right. There was no tail.

'Something came up, that's all,' he said. 'Maggie, I'll be there, Friday or Saturday.'

'And I'm getting out of this house. It costs too much. I've found somewhere.'

'That's crazy. I've got plenty.'

'I told you, I'm not taking any more of it, and that means money. I'm in line for a job.'

'A job? How can you do a job? There's Fiona.'

'A minder. You can see Fiona whenever you like. We'll make arrangements. It's over, Ron.'

'On the phone, in five minutes?'

'We'll talk again if you want, but it will still be over.'

'I need you. I need you both, Maggie.'

'No you don't. You need some comfort and extra family now and then, that's all. Well, just cuddle up to Doris, or whoever.'

He thought for a second. 'There's somebody, is there? There's some bugger down there in Devon? You're moving to his place? All I've spent down there. I mean, it's not I'm thinking just about money, but that's like another home to me.'

'I can't go on like it. Simple as that, Ron. It's not fair on Fiona. You've got to let me be strong.'

'I can't let you. Don't you realise?'

'Well, I'm going to be.'

'Is it age?' he said. 'Is that it? I know the hair treatment's not going to change my birth certificate, but— Are you there?'

He was getting the tone that said the line had been broken, although the meter showed he still had forty pence to go. He put in another pound and dialled again and heard the unobtainable. When the operator tried she said the receiver was off, and perhaps the subscriber had accidentally failed to put it back properly. Yes, perhaps the subscriber had.

It would be all right. He would try again tomorrow or just turn up there this weekend. By then he would be super-loaded even after taking care of things at home and they could go out to the smart shops and get stuff for Maggie and the child. He liked a bit of temper and backbone in a woman.

For a couple of seconds, he considered ringing up Carol, the girl from *Annie*. He needed something to take his mind off things, not just off Devon but the job. One of the great points about Carol was she had no idea how he made his living. She thought some sort of trading, and he had talked nice and vague when she asked. Then he decided it would be pretty rotten to contact her now. Come off the phone from one woman and call another. Degraded. Of course, the thing was, at his age, there were not many chances left and you had to grab whatever decent you could get, but you still had to think about behaviour and what was suitable, too. Carol was a sweet girl, pretty and warm and interested – that counted a hell of a lot, interested. Hadn't that bastard Harpur spotted her straight off? But Maggie and the child, this was serious. He had to act in a way that proved they mattered, which they definitely did.

They mattered and Doris mattered, too, in a different way. He would go home to her now. Perhaps he would be in touch some other day soon with Carol, but definitely not until after the job. She was a long way from that side of his life, and it would be better if it stayed like that. Even if he went strolling by Prince Albert park doing the decoy he must make sure she did not see him. Before leaving the box, he telephoned Devon twice again, but the receiver was still accidentally off.

Chapter 26

Iles wanted to go down and see the ambush in place, so Harpur drew a magnum from the armoury and drove him there. In the car, the ACC, speaking in a gentle, strangely vulnerable tone, said almost at once: 'That unpleasant incident we witnessed – Sarah and Aston together outside the Monty, Col – could have been the last. An end-it-all farewell.'

'Good, sir.'

'Don't fucking patronise me, Harpur,' he snarled. 'I'm putting you in the picture, that's all. A courtesy.'

'Right, sir.'

'If you think about it, they did look as if they had come to an end of something. The body language. They were seeing to the formalities.'

Harpur could not be sure whether he was supposed to comment and, if so, what. He said: 'Now you mention it, sir, there was that impression.'

'Plainly valedictory.'

'I'd say so.'

'I can't object. She's a reasonable woman and in many ways a considerate woman. They're not going to split apart, just like that. She would want to do things sensitively.'

'To her credit, and it probably means the break is permanent.'

'It is indeed to her credit. I'm glad to say she's around the house much more now. A different woman. Well, you'll see for yourself tonight at the long service awards for Erogynous and the others.'

The Chief liked to make an all-ranks social occasion of the awards ceremony, at the club. On *esprit de corps*, and recognition for his people and loyalty to them, Lane was unbeatable.

'Have you asked her, sir?'

'What?'

'Whether she and Aston have finished.'

'Does one ask a woman one respects something like that?'

'Perhaps not, sir.'

'But you would? Yes, I suppose you might. You've got your own way of handling things, homespun yet possibly perfectly valid. In fact, sometimes I envy you your arrant crudity, Col. It's inherent, not a thing that can be learned. A different woman in what way, you'll ask. Well, suddenly it's as if she lives there, not just using Rougemont Place as a camp. The pregnancy would almost certainly account for that. She's noticing things – dirty windows, empty store cupboard, rubbish shoved under cushions. I'm not saying she's gone house-proud, and I wouldn't want it, but she seems to recognise all at once that we've been up to our eyes in muck these last months.'

'Cleanliness is a plus, but it can be overdone.'

'God, Harpur, are you trying to fill the gap left by A. J. Ayer?'

To avoid any sudden increase in traffic around the ambush nest at the accountants' offices, the drill was to leave cars at a good distance. Harpur and Iles walked through side streets and then Prince Albert park towards the rear of the building. The ACC asked: 'Nothing new?'

'Nothing, sir. We still have to assume it's one of these banks, and at any time now. We're not tailing anyone. We can't – not even Leckwith any longer, in case we're spotted and they eject. I've pulled Erogynous and the rest off. And no phone taps, as you know.'

'So we wait.'

'Some of the lads are down in the mouth a bit. Sid Synott.'

'I'll change that, Col.'

'We're very fortunate you could come, sir.'

'Leave irony for your betters, Harpur, and for queers and dons. I say, look at this.'

'I know her.'

'Really?'

Harpur left the park path and approached a lovely, dark-haired, long-legged girl in a lime-green dress who was eating her lunch sandwiches on the grass. She glanced up at him without recognition.

'Excuse me, but didn't I see you tearing a train seat to pieces

186

recently?' Harpur asked. 'This is a squaw of my acquaintance,' he told Iles.

The girl smiled suddenly. 'You were at *Annie Get Your Gun?*'

'Regularly.'

'Of course. Your children took part. Megan's husband. Sorry, I didn't recognise you.'

'*Annie Get Your Gun!*' Iles cried. 'Wonderful thing!'

'You know it?' the girl asked.

'He knows everything,' Harpur said.

Iles began to sing 'Who Do You Love, I Hope'. The others joined in the first verse, but Iles went right through, in a small, mild, wheedling voice. 'Glorious. So many of these old, popular works get to the root of things. "Love is my middle name." This your regular lunch spot?'

'Often.'

'Nice.'

'Am I remembering this right?' she asked Harpur. 'Didn't someone say you're police? Sort of plain clothes and big deal? Are you working in this area? Something afoot?'

'Us. Just a stroll,' he said.

'We often do,' the ACC told her, 'alone or together, mulling matters over. We might bump into you again, who knows?'

He and Harpur walked on.

'Yes, I might take a lunchtime saunter up here one day soon,' Iles continued. 'I suppose you might, too, though? But, Christ, Harpur, how barefaced can you get? She's familiar with your children, for heaven's sake. I'd have loved to see her ripping upholstery apart and tugging the springs out. Visceral. Why the hell didn't I hear about that show?'

'Preston's wife had a part, too. Doris. Very community and across the spectrum. Here we are, sir.'

Immediately, Harpur was aware of a different mood from yesterday's among the ambush team. All signs of boredom and disbelief had gone: the men seemed tense and stood grouped around the windows, watching the street. Sid Synott was holding a pistol in his hand, pointed to the floor. He looked utterly composed now, his head quite motionless as he stared towards the banks.

Turning for a moment, Cotton said excitedly: 'Preston's out there.'

In a corner of the room a sergeant talked continuously by radio to waiting vehicles, relaying what he was told from the men at the window. Harpur and Iles joined them. Planner was walking slowly past the banks, gazing up at the swing doors of Barclays, his face intent.

'Christ, he's looking seedy,' Iles said happily. 'Yet Planner's not much older than I.'

'So far we haven't identified any back-up with him,' Cotton told them.

'We think probably a final reconnaissance,' Synott said. 'You know Planner. Every detail and do it himself. It looks like Barclays, not the Bank of Ireland.'

Preston walked on until he was more or less directly beneath them, then turned and went back at the same leisurely pace, still with his eyes towards Barclays. He disappeared around a corner and they did not see him again.

'Tomorrow or the day after, I'd say,' Synott muttered. 'But it's real. Oh, yes.' He put the pistol into a belt holster, leaving the flat open.

Chappell, the shift inspector, said: 'We need timing. Still no information on cash deliveries, is there, sir?'

'Can't be done,' Harpur replied. 'As we said at the briefing.'

After an hour, the men relaxed and the radio told all vehicles that it would probably not be today. Iles and Harpur waited a further hour and then walked back through the park to Harpur's Viva. The girl and other lunchers had gone.

'Shall I hang about while you sniff the grass where she sat, Harpur? That parade in front of the banks just now: a bit obvious for Planner, don't you think? We know he's thorough, but to make a display? Now you see me, now you still see me.'

'I expected him to get a sketch pad out. He posed under our window.'

'He knows we're there? Jesus. How? Leckwith's found out and tipped him?'

'It's possible.'

'My God, you were supposed to keep it close, Harpur.'

'I tried.'

'So, Preston's conning us? Keeping us there while he's setting something up elsewhere? Planner clever enough for that? Doggedness is his long suit, I thought, not subtlety.'

'He could be getting smart advice, sir. There might be people from outside.'

'Marvellous: all our boys crowing and ready, and nowhere near where it's going to happen. The Chief could grow intemperate if it turned out like that. Can we think of other possible venues?'

'Any bank on the patch, sir, if he's really up to doing big banks. Or anywhere there's a money delivery or collection – that's banks again, factories, football grounds, pop concerts.'

'Yes, hopeless trying to forecast. So, tell me, would Planner know the squaw, as well, through *Annie*? I mean, could that possibly be why he's up here? Perhaps he's heard about her lunch hours, too. Planner's keen on fanny, isn't he? Devon.'

'He was here today to look at banks, sir. And maybe to get us to look at him looking at banks. He's at least twenty years too old for that girl.'

'Up yours, Harpur.'

He took Iles back to headquarters and then went out to a pay phone and called Ruth Cotton. On the special shifts the ambush were doing, her husband would be tied up until six o'clock. Ruth's number was busy and he stepped outside the booth and for a moment considered abandoning the call. Was it somehow especially treacherous and calculating to cash in on the ambush? Perhaps, but adultery operated like that; stupid to imagine there was a clean way. He tried her number again and this time it rang. Before he could say anything her voice screamed at him, enraged and desperate, through the headpiece: 'Leave me alone, can't you? Can't you, for God's sake? Just fuck off. We've beaten you – beaten you, don't you understand?'

'Ruth?'

There was silence for a second. 'Colin?'

'What's happened?'

She managed a giggle. 'I just had one of those calls. I thought you were another.'

'A call about—'

'The usual. About Robert. About the shooting. Ditto Repeato's death and the single-double wound. Threats. The children – naming all the children. Yes, the delightfully usual.'

'Well, you're right. We beat them.'

She giggled again. 'I didn't think fast enough to say that when they rang. It's what Rob told me to tell them. But only you got that slice of the message.'

'It's true, all the same. Come out? It will do you good.'

'I'd take the phone off, but . . . Well, there's you, and the children. And Rob. He's on something special, isn't he? There could be news.'

'He's fine, Ruth. Come out. You need the break.'

He picked her up on a street corner and they drove to the edge of the city and parked. He could not wander far today: the ambush might look like rubbish, but he would have to get back fast if a call came, all the same. There were streets all around them and traffic, so there could be no love-making. He felt almost relieved, as if the treachery would be less.

'I'm all right now,' she said. Her eyes were puffed up, though, through crying.

As happened sometimes, he felt that men might have it easy. Rob Cotton could come through the Ditto shooting well enough to want to work with guns again. He had a philosophy that gave him all the strength he needed, and thank God for it: policing would not exist otherwise. So, this afternoon, Cotton was back in the stand-by position, keen to have a go at them again, and as thrilled and ready as any man on the ambush. Meanwhile, his wife took the evil calls and did the fretting. Cotton wanted her to tell these callers and the people behind them that they were beaten. Could she really believe it? Were they ever beaten?

And, when he considered the way men somehow came out on the bright side as often as not, Harpur knew he had to include himself. Crisis in Prince Albert Street could be turned to opportunity. And while he chatted up a girl in the park, Ruth was at home, wondering who would be at the end of the phone next time.

'I hear Rob spoke to you,' she said.

'Yes. It was all right.'

'Be careful, Col. He's not like he was. I never know what he's thinking.'

'He seems to have everything under control.'

Ruth laughed. 'Yes. He can still shoot straight.' Then she said: 'Look, Harpur, if we've got an extra afternoon I want you in me.'

'Yes?'

190

'Well, of course.'

'We're in the wrong place.' They were words that hounded him today.

'Well move. St Peter's Common. There's a bit of a wood at the edge. We've been there before.'

'In the dark.'

'Are you refusing me?'

He drove to the common and they left the car and picked their way into the middle of the small clump of trees. He was carrying a radio handset and, when they lay down, he took off his jacket and the shoulder holster with his magnum still in it.

'God,' she said, 'is this love or a demonstration of police hardware?' In a while she muttered: 'All right, it's both.'

In the evening, Ruth, wearing a grand black and white polka dot silk suit, and accompanied by Robert Cotton, was at the long service awards party for Erogynous Jones and a few others. Cotton, like Harpur himself, would be on call to the ambush and, also like Harpur, would have his pistol with him. Harpur managed a smile and nod across the room to Ruth, which would be about as far as things could go here. That, also, was the nature of adultery.

Megan had agreed to come with him, though after a lot of niggling argument, and on condition they did not hang about. She disapproved of police social functions that were also compulsory turn-outs, and often said no. Harpur was able to talk her into it tonight. He did not know exactly how but, like almost everyone, she was fond of Erogynous. Also, she preferred this sort of all-rank affair to those for senior officers only, where she claimed the zombie conversation gave her vertigo. In the past he had mentioned this to Iles who said: 'You've got a fine, perceptive girl there, Harpur, a girl of taste. I don't understand why you have to go shagging everything in sight. Grow up, sixties man.'

Iles was reading the citations tonight, while the Chief presented the plaques and shook the hands. Watching them, Harpur could almost understand why Iles seemed certain always to remain an ACC, while Lane had made it to the top. The Chief was wonderful at this kind of occasion, radiating geniality, knowledge of his men and women and complete loyalty to them, and, above all, unflagging pride in the outfit. Iles also possessed this pride and loyalty, and knew everything worth knowing about all members of the Force, but he had difficulty radiating anything, except a brain power three or four times Lane's and six times most other people's, and which scared many of those who arranged promotions. You had the feeling as Iles performed his duties tonight that he would have preferred to be somewhere else, like Megan: but Megan did not yearn to be a Chief Constable, and had no need to display enthusiasm.

After the little ceremony, she wandered off to congratulate Erogynous. Harpur spotted Sarah Iles alone at the bar, and went to buy her a drink. Slim, fair-haired, combative-looking, she had on a blue trouser suit Harpur had seen before and liked. 'I heard the good news about the baby,' he said. 'Nice work.'

'You can't notice yet?' she asked.

'No.'

'Pity. I want it proclaimed.'

'It is, by your husband.'

'I'd like it obvious. I want to be made someone different.'

'The ACC said you were.'

'Poor Des.'

'He's very happy.'

'Well, it's time. I watch him get old, Col.'

'Yes, but what about you?'

'Ageing, you mean? I suppose so. Where do you see it?'

'No, I was talking about happiness.'

'More than one way to it, I'm told. So I'm trying the baby. As calculated as that. And, then, you? Are you very happy?'

'Of course.'

'It's a laugh, isn't it?'

'What?'

She stared into the crowd of guests, her eyes hard and sad. 'Oh, I look about here and see couples, and one knows that behind it all . . . But Lane and Sally seem content.'

'It can certainly be done.'

'What did you think you saw when you were with Des outside the Monty the other evening?'

'You spotted us?'

'I did. Ian, no.'

'Your husband thinks it was a leave-taking.'

'And you?'

'I agreed with him. But it wasn't? I don't follow. You were talking about—'

'Becoming somebody different? Yes, I know, but do people really do that?'

'Do what?' Megan asked, joining them.

'Change basically all of a sudden,' Sarah said.

'Saul of Tarsus,' Megan replied.

'But he'd been kicking against the pricks,' Sarah said. 'I've never wanted to do that.'

'You ought to circulate, Colin,' Megan said. 'Meet some of your people.'

He strolled away to where Leckwith stood holding a beer. 'Barry,' Harpur said. 'Isn't it good to hear Erogynous announced by his full, formal names.'

'Jeremy Stanislaus,' Leckwith replied. 'A mouthful.'

'Twenty-five years of tailing. Strange way to make a living.'

'Well, he ought to be good at it by now, sir.'

'The best.'

'I think so,' Leckwith replied. 'We're lucky to have him.'

And it sounded as if he genuinely meant it.

Harpur said: 'I often wonder whether I'd spot him if he got behind me one day. I might ask him to try it. Things are so quiet.'

'Yes, they are, aren't they, sir. Totally, abysmally quiet.'

'Could I borrow Colin a moment?' the Chief interrupted. Mark Lane had Maurice Tobin, chairman of the police committee, with him. The three of them edged away from Leckwith. 'Councillor Tobin has something to say, Colin.'

Egomaniac, strong-faced, and deceptively wholesome-looking, Tobin declared vehemently: 'Well, yes: I'm in the Gents and a man, presumably one of your people, takes off his jacket and is wearing a pistol holster. Chief, it's like something out of *The fucking Godfather*.'

'That will be Robert Cotton,' Harpur said.

'But can it be necessary? At a very pleasant social occasion? It seems – barbaric.'

'We've an operation running. As a matter of fact, I'm tooled up myself.'

'My God,' Tobin said. Agitatedly, he turned to Lane, his voice cracking. 'I don't like it, Chief. What sort of Force are we running here? A lot of drinking tonight. Suppose a couple of your armed people turned nasty with each other.'

'They're trained men, councillor. And why should they turn nasty with each other?' He looked across the room. 'There's Rob Cotton now with his lovely wife in the polka dots. They look happy enough, surely. Wouldn't you say? I don't think he's going to start blazing away, do you?'

Tobin did not reply.

'Wouldn't you say he seems content, Colin?'

'Yes, indeed, sir.'

Tobin said: 'Anyway, Chief, as you well know, I hate this whole idea of guns on the streets. So many mistakes. I thought you hated it, too.' He spoke as if Lane had committed a betrayal.

'We all hate it, councillor,' the Chief replied.

'Increasingly, one wonders whether in the last resort it's worth while,' Tobin continued.

'Now and then it becomes inevitable,' Lane said.

'So I'm told, so I'm told. But the committee and I, personally—'

'Yes, inevitable, regrettably,' the Chief said, and Tobin drifted away to talk to someone else.

'I have to admit I don't know whether this particular operation really is worth while, sir,' Harpur told Lane. 'You weren't very keen on it originally yourself. I've thought of cancelling. The ACC would probably agree now. It's possible we're being systematically deceived. And we could be at a disadvantage deployed where we are.'

'What?' Lane's round, normally friendly, sallow face grew almost fierce. 'No. Stick with it now. All right, I wasn't happy about it, but I'm not having my people pushed around by some greasy politician.'

'Tobin wouldn't know whether we'd taken any notice of him or not, sir. He's not aware of the actual operation.'

'No, but *you'd* know, Colin. Do I want you or any of our people thinking I'm in the pocket of some pontificating left-wing fart-arse? I'm responsible to him and his sort, yes, but more so to you and your sort. It's known as leadership.'

'Right, sir.'

Lane picked up his usual lighter tone again: 'No likelihood of what he suggested – you and Cotton opening up on each other, I take it?'

Half an hour afterwards, Megan wanted to leave. Erogynous came up to Harpur while she was saying her goodbyes. 'Get anything out of Leckwith, sir? I saw you talking.'

'Only he thinks you're the greatest.'

'Oh, that. Interrogation's supposed to produce stuff we didn't know before, sir.'

Chapter 27

On Wednesday evening as it was getting dark Mansel decided he had better go down to the flat for a last check that the boys were still in good shape. All right, this was Mother Mansel doing her fussy bit again and acting soft. He knew it was for the best, just the same, especially when things had seemed so dark and tense there last time.

Mansel found he had fallen into a kind of routine for these visits now and took the taxi again first up to the Ernest Bevin estate for a spell outside Ron's place, to make sure Planner still had no observers. These anxieties were not like him, but he knew some of them came from being so involved with this leaking sodding copper, Leckwith. Mansel had never really got over that shiver when he saw him feeding his mother in the home. That had to be wrong and bad. There could not be any link between those two. Although he had dealt with Leckwith before this job, things were different now. The contact was too close, too deep.

It looked safe again up there and he went back for his own Renault, as before, and then drove to the flat. At least there were no unusual, big-engined cars outside. They must have listened to Planner's advice. Even big-headed kids like Tyrone and Dean realised they could learn something from Ron. Say what you like, Planner had leadership. This outing tomorrow would be all right. Almost all the old optimism came flooding back to Mansel after the sessions of doubt.

He could not make anyone hear at the front door and walked around to the rear entrance of the flats in the service lane. What looked to him in the darkness like a Vauxhall Carlton was parked a distance up the lane at the back door and, for a moment, he thought this was their solution for at least one of the vehicles, the stupids sods, as if putting it here was much better than in front.

Then he saw that the lid of the car's boot had been raised and after a moment something bulky and wrapped in a big cloth, or perhaps a carpet, was brought out through the lane door and manhandled into the boot by two men, probably Hoppy and Dean.

An instinct told him he should not be seeing what was happening here, and another instinct said it was tied up somehow with that sense of something hidden and wrong the last time he called. Mansel stepped back from the lane into the street out of sight, and after a moment heard the boot lid go down. Shortly afterwards the car's engine started and he looked briefly into the lane and saw it being driven out of the other end. Mansel went around to the front again and when he knocked this time Tyrone opened the door and welcomed him inside. Grace was drinking coffee in the sitting-room.

'Dean and Hoppy are just trying out the second car,' Tyrone said. 'They won't be long. We've got a Granada and a Carlton. They'll do the business. Decent acceleration.'

'How's Hoppy?' Mansel asked.

'Fine.'

'He can be difficult.'

'No problems at all.'

'It's going to be fine, isn't it, Tyrone?' Grace said. Her voice was full of confidence, and maybe too full, like a boxer with no chance. 'Isn't it, Manse?'

'Of course it is,' Mansel replied. He felt shocked to find her here tonight, so near to the job, and obviously knowing it was next day. But there had been changes in the way things were run, and if he was going to work with youngsters he had better get used to it. Ron must have got used to it, too. Until a week or two ago Mansel had thought of Grace as not much more than a child, still – the big, dark, wondering eyes, and the dim ideas. Well, she was growing up, and her eyes looked very wary this evening, and all her body nervier.

'We're going to have a really great holiday, Tyrone and I, soon,' Grace said, a bit too loud.

'Where?'

'Somewhere I've always wanted to see,' Grace replied. 'Guess, Manse. Exotic.'

'Not bloody Spain.'

'Spain! For the little people,' she said. 'This is exotic, I told you.'

'Sounds great,' Mansel replied. He would have liked to take a look around and see if any of the carpets were gone. Dean's girl, Debbie, still seemed to be absent and Mansel thought of asking about her, but then decided to wait.

'You'll never guess,' Grace said. 'This is too much for you, Manse. You're still stuck in Blackpool, aren't you?' She came over and whispered in his ear. He smelled some really good, grown-up perfume, something you knew was there but which did not grab you by the throat. 'I'm talking about Hawaii,' she told him.

'Get away! Hoola-hoola skirts,' Mansel cried.

'Right.' She did a little swaying dance and then went and sat near Tyrone.

'Dorothy Lamour,' Mansel said.

'Who?' Grace asked. 'This will be a full month, just the two of us.'

'Grand.'

'Well, Tyrone deserves it after being stuck in here so long. Palm trees and cold drinks. He's going to need sun and building up.'

'Grand,' Mansel said.

'This is not just talk, you know, Manse,' she went on. 'Not like Dean's dreams. This is the flight booked and the hotel. Tickets in the post. Deposit paid. We'll be giving them the rest as soon as — As soon as it's all finalised. That's right, isn't it, Tyrone?'

'Sure.'

'I wish I was coming,' Mansel said.

She had a smile. 'Someone to bring? You might feel a bit spare, otherwise, that's all, Manse,' Grace told him. 'No offence. You know what I mean. This is erotic as well as exotic.'

'Anyway, I've got to stay – my mother,' Mansel told her.

'You're good to her, Manse,' Grace said.

'I'm the only one she's got.'

Tyrone said: 'I wish to God I had some armament. Sitting in a fucking car while you boys are doing your bit. I'm wide open, Manse.' He was crouched forward in an armchair, denim jacket undone, some fashion shirt underneath, and the eyes behind those bloody glasses looking really frantic, not his usual big-time cool at all, and the Adam's apple sticking out like housemaid's knee. This clever one was taking it a lot worse than the tattoo boy.

'I won't be carrying anything either,' Mansel replied.

'Yes, that's your choice. Me, I need to be able to look after myself. Manse, things could go wrong. Suppose I'm suddenly on my own.'

'No, it's better, Tyrone,' Grace said. 'That way, you're not a target. Those police, they see a gun, they're entitled to shoot. They've got their rules after all these mistakes, and they can't fire if there's no danger. This is a fact.'

'What do you mean, on your own?' Mansel asked. 'Are we going to desert you? You're part of the outfit. That doesn't happen. Anyway, you're our way out, for God's sake, our way out twice – first car, then the change.'

'Separated,' Tyrone replied. 'If we were all separated. Suppose you couldn't get back to the car.'

'Oh, God, thanks,' Mansel said. 'This is the disaster script.'

'This guy, what's his name – Robert Cotton? And I'm just sitting there for him.'

'That's what I mean, Tyrone,' Grace told him. 'If you're not holding something he can't fire. Not allowed. That bastard can be as good as he likes but if you're not a target – this is obvious. Dad says the other one, the one who was shot—'

'Ditto Repeato,' Mansel said.

'Ditto had it coming to him. He was waving a gun about, and would have fired. Anyway, stop talking like this. Think about Hawaii.'

'What's Dean doing after the job?' Mansel asked. 'Are he and the other girl, Debbie, thinking about something like that? A good break.'

They did not answer at once. Then Tyrone said: 'Oh, Dean? Who knows what he'll do? He's on his own is Dean.'

'On his own?' Mansel asked.

'I mean, he does what he likes. He doesn't talk about things.'

'They're back,' Grace said, and Hoppy and Dean came running up the stairs and into the room. 'Manse,' Dean yelled, 'this is great. All keyed up and ready?'

'Had any good dreams?' Mansel replied.

'I just said you've been trying the Carlton,' Tyrone said.

'Right,' Hoppy replied. 'Trying the Carlton.'

'It'll do,' Dean said.

'Where did you go?' Mansel asked.

'Just around,' Dean said. 'To get the pace.'

'What about Tyrone?' Mansel asked.

'What?' Dean said.

'Well, he's the driver,' Mansel said.

'I know what he's looking for,' Dean replied. 'A car's a car. If I say it's all right, Tyrone knows it's all right.'

'Sure,' Tyrone said.

'Questions. Can't we try the car for him? What you here for, anyway, Manse?' Hoppy asked.

'Christ, don't be so friendly,' Grace said.

'Why's he here?' Hoppy asked.

'Seeing everything's all right, that's all,' Mansel said.

'Of course it is,' Hoppy told him. 'Why not?'

'It's good of him to come again,' Tyrone said.

'Is it? Oh, all right,' Hoppy replied. 'Good of you to come down, Manse.'

'It seems better here now,' Mansel said. 'Like more – oh, I don't know, like more relaxed.'

'So what was wrong before?' Dean asked.

'Yes, what, Manse?' Hoppy said.

'I don't know. Something a bit unusual.'

'Unusual?' Dean asked.

'What's unusual mean, Manse?' Hoppy said.

'Search me, but I felt it.'

'Just the waiting's nearly over now,' Grace suggested.

'Could be that,' Manse said.

'I should think so,' Tyrone added.

'What are you saying was wrong before, Manse?' Hoppy asked. 'Why are you down here?'

'Christ, he's told you,' Tyrone said.

'Nothing wrong,' Mansel replied. 'Nothing I could put my finger on.'

'Put your finger on? What's that supposed to fucking mean?' Hoppy asked. 'Look, what's he getting at, Tyrone? I don't like this.'

'I told you, it's better now,' Mansel said.

'Better than what?' Hoppy asked. 'Because we've been out in that car? Is that it?'

'Out in the car?' Mansel replied. 'What's that got to do with it?'

'Is that why you think it's better – because we've been out in the car?' Hoppy said. 'Did he know we'd gone out in the car?' he asked Tyrone.

'I told him you were trying out the car,' Tyrone replied. 'Calm down.'

'Just trying out the car?' Hoppy said.

'Of course. Manse knows a car has to be given a run.'

'That's it, giving a car a run,' Hoppy said. 'So, why does giving a car a run make everything here seem different?'

'I didn't say that.'

'Yes you did – like something been moved out, or something like that, and making things better because it's gone,' Hoppy said.

'Has something been moved out?' Mansel asked. 'What?'

'Of course not. What would there be?' Grace replied.

'Of course not,' Hoppy said. 'What was there to move out?'

'Exactly,' Dean added.

'I don't know how the hell we got into all this,' Mansel said, laughing. 'All I say is it's great here now and suddenly Hoppy is saying what was wrong with last time, like I'm making some accusation.'

'What accusation?' Hoppy asked.

'Oh, Jesus,' Mansel said.

'It's all right, Hoppy. All. Right. Got it?'

'I don't like suggestions, that's all,' Hoppy replied.

'What suggestions?' Mansel asked.

'We won't start it all over again, all right?' Tyrone said.

'All right by me,' Mansel replied.

Hoppy said: 'If I'm doing the dirty work, I don't want no suggestions. This could be just the start, that's what I've got to think. Something go wrong, and this bastard Mansel is making suggestions somewhere else, like in an interview-room with Harpur.'

'Hoppy, we're all doing the dirty work,' Dean told him.

'There's going to be no interview-rooms,' Tyrone said. 'There's going to be a nice simple clean-up and a nice healthy take and a nice healthy share-out.'

'And Hawaii,' Grace murmured.

'Grand,' Mansel said.

On the way home, he called in on his mother. 'How are you?' he said.

'That's what I was going to ask. How are you?'

'I'm all right. How are you?'

'Yes, how are you?'

'You'll be all right,' he said. 'I might not be in tomorrow night. But soon. I'll be back to see you very soon.'

'How are you?'

Chapter 28

The evening before a job, Ron Preston liked to go out somewhere pleasant with Doris for a meal and wine, a respectable place, not too full, not too empty, though, so there were people to look at and an atmosphere of happy chat. All that could help. He needed to feel nice and normal – normal at the right level, with a suit and a decent bit of money, to make him welcome in this sort of place. If he stayed home, he knew he would be messing about with the Beretta, checking the action, and wondering again about Hoppy Short holding a gun tomorrow. That was no good now. It could wear down your nerves.

In the old days they might have taken Grace out with them, but she was not around this evening. She would be over at the flat with Tyrone, which Preston did not like at all. How could he stop it, though? These kids did what they wanted, even a girl who had always been so good and thoughtful as Grace. Love alias sex was a very powerful element. It had to be, probably, or where was the human race? We would be swamped by nature and the animals, which was still a real danger, in his opinion. Think of the swans landing on that pool when he was out with Hoppy, as if it belonged to the bastards. He wondered if Tyrone had told her it was tomorrow. That would be stupid and would set her worrying, but it could happen.

Another reason he liked to get out, he wanted nobody talking to him about the job tonight. That could unsettle him. Wilf Rudd was round the house every couple of days this last week, supposed to be handing out new little bits of information, but all of it less than fucking useless, and just his way of reminding again he was part of the team and on the payroll, although not part of the team that actually had to hit the street. Wilf he could do without seeing tonight.

Again in the old days, Manse would sometimes look in on the night before a job, too. That would be to check Preston felt all right and had not suddenly gone Rampton barmy under the stress. Manse fancied himself as a bit of a psychiatrist, full of comfort for the worried soul. He was a lovely guy and meant well but Preston had to tell him a couple of times long ago that his soul did not get worried, and Manse eventually gave up making his calls, except if he decided a job was really tricky. He might think that about the van, though, and Preston would rather go through another post-mortem on *Annie Get Your Gun* with Doris than listen to Manse dishing out calm and hope.

They went to a restaurant called Seconds, which no question had a lot of bent money in it, from the Noisy Graham and Leonard Carl Dimber outfit, but which Doris liked because the walls were decorated with theatre stuff – programmes and signatures and pictures of old actors – and the cloths looked spotless. The head waiter always used to say to her, 'You like the table under the tree, don't you, madam?' which Preston found was a kind of joke, meaning an actor in the past called Tree whose picture hung on the wall, letting go in some big part in one of the plays of that era. Doris would have a giggle about this and said, yes it was her favourite spot, which put another couple of quid on the tip, but never mind if she was happy.

Obviously, Preston would never take her to a shit-heap like Panicking Ralph's Monty. That would be degrading. You could not have your wife sitting on the same upholstery as some of the women Ralph let in. And they kept clear of Wankers, too, not just because Mansel's police contact, Barry Leckwith, worked there, but on account it was a rip-off for jerks. They did the bill accurate in Seconds and gave you a fair feed, with more helpings if you wanted, which was what the name meant. In fact, Preston still had not worked out where the fiddle came. It could be the wine. Maybe Noisy and Dimber were into the labels game, although you needed a lot of turnover to make that add up to more than peanuts. Or it might be just two sets of books, one for real, one for tax. There must be something. Quite a few lads from the wrong side put money into restaurants, like Leo Tacette with Chaff. That was another one Harpur caught up with.

It did Preston good to sit opposite Doris and talk about all sorts on a night like this, none of it to do with the business.

Dealing with these other topics could remind him that life was not just about pouncing on a sack of cash tomorrow like a dog on a rat. There was more to existence. There was Morgon wine and acting and saddle of lamb, not to mention harmless conversation. He always liked being out with Doris. She looked very reasonable for her age and was getting through all the hot flushes stuff without a hell of a lot of bother, because of hormones from the medics. Sex gave her personal problems, which was only natural at her age, but that did not matter too much because there was still Devon, probably, and maybe this girl from *Annie* now.

When Doris talked about something that really interested her her face became wonderfully excited and lively. She had always been like that. It was not just the theatre. Tonight, she did talk for a while about *Annie* and then about the chances for a production of *West Side Story*. He took notice then, after what Carol had said about seeing if he could get a part. Later, Doris spoke about problems on the motorways, which concerned her quite a bit, and also something she had read in a magazine to do with making pianos. It all quietened him down just right.

Then she said suddenly: 'The Wilf Rudd job's tomorrow, is it? You're going through with it?'

'What? Why do you say that?'

'We're out to dinner.'

'Doris, we're often here for dinner, love.'

'I still think it's tomorrow. You're tense. Look, don't worry. I'm not going to dial 999, am I?'

He did not tell her, yes, it was tomorrow, but she knew for certain, he could see. Noisy Graham was at the till, up near the kitchens, counting. Some of these lads had good ears.

'What's going to happen to Grace if this boy, Tyrone, just clears off afterwards? That would really knock her, Ron.'

'Maybe he won't. Didn't I hear something about Hawaii?'

'That's the talk. But an outsider? Nothing to keep him here, is there? Won't he want to put distance between himself and people like Harpur?'

'There aren't people like Harpur, thank Christ, only Harpur. Hawaii is distance. But, yes, could be Tyrone will want to evaporate. I warned Grace.'

'Just the same, what happens to her?'

He watched a couple he knew come in and take a table at the

other end of the room. The man, very big and heavy, nodded to him. It was Jack Lamb and the girl kid he lived with these days in that bloody big manor house behind a wall and gates out near Chase Woods. It was grubby, really, the age difference, though she had a great body, supple. Lamb did a lot of trade in superior art. This was genuine material with proper, foreign signatures from way back in history, such as Italian – not the rosebud with a drop of rain on it – and he made a beautiful living. Jack took heavy risks, but they all said he had good protection, somewhere near the very top.

'What happens to Grace, Ron, if it's goodbye for ever to-morrow?' Doris repeated.

'Don't say it like that, for God's sake.'

'What?'

'"Goodbye for ever".'

'You know what I mean. The way these kids take off.'

'I can't stop him, Doris.'

'You could talk to him, couldn't you? Say how much she cares. He's used to slags, probably – girls who know they're around for as long as it takes and no longer. Grace is not like that. She's committed, I can tell. This is our daughter, Ron.'

'Well, yes, maybe I'll talk to him, afterwards.' He wanted to avoid an argument or any edge tonight if he could.

'You've got control of the share-out, haven't you?' Doris asked.

'I have to pay him, love. That could be bloody dangerous. These kids look young, but they're pros.'

'What I'm saying, it's a way of pressure, that's all. She's really put a lot into this relationship, if you understand what I mean. I know you don't like it, the two of them. She told me. But he's the one she wants, Ron. We've got to let her know her own mind.'

'Yes. I will talk to him afterwards.'

'Ron, I knew you would. You're a good man.'

'I don't say it will work.'

'I think you can make it work.' She leaned across and squeezed his hand.

That sodding Tyrone. Only days ago, Preston had been worrying about whether he was two-timing him, after what Hoppy said. Hoppy was wrong, he felt sure, but now Preston had to fret in case Tyrone two-timed Grace. Lovely.

One of the other good things about Seconds was it had a pay phone that could not be seen from the tables and when they were into the coffee he went out to the Gents and tried a call to Devon. He had rung a few times since that difficulty the other night, without success. The failure to reach her might begin to unsettle him and he could do without that tonight, too. This was not just the matter of a woman. A child was involved here, after all. Again he could get no answer, though. He would have to go down there and see what was what as soon as the job finished. But that would not do anything for his uneasiness now. Doris sat waiting for him at the table, yet he still felt deserted and somehow on his own. In search of a little extra comfort right away, he telephoned Carol, the *Annie Get Your Gun* squaw, instead, even though he had promised himself to keep clear of her until after the outing. And Carol did reply and sounded really pleased to hear him.

'I just wanted to call,' he said. 'I'm busy for a few days, but maybe we could meet next week?'

'That would be great.'

'You mean it?'

'I thought I might see you these last few days. I took my lunch in the park a couple of times.'

'No, I've been very tied up. And I am tomorrow again.'

'I won't go to the park, then. All sorts up there.'

'What? Trying to chat you up?'

'It's a pest, Ron. Smarmy creeps.'

'Disgusting. Can't a woman relax without bother like that? I'm sorry I couldn't make it. But definitely next week. I'm on a deal tomorrow and then I've got to go to Devon on other pressing business. But Monday or Tuesday.'

'Great.'

When he left the booth, Jack Lamb was standing outside. 'Ron,' he said, 'grand to see you. I just happened to spot you and took the opportunity.'

'Well, Doris is waiting.'

'Really, only a moment. My companion, Helen, lovely kid, but she's very anxious about a friend. This is a girl called Debbie. Dropped off the face of the earth suddenly.'

'Do I know her?'

'I'm not sure, Ron. Do you? From what I gather, she knows Mansel and someone called Hoppy.'

'Mansel? Don't see much of him these days.' He tried to recall the name of the other girl who had been around the lads' flat with Grace. Had he ever known it? Was it Debbie? 'You mean Hoppy Short?'

'Could be.'

'Doesn't mean anything to me, Jack.'

'You're sure?'

Lamb was a menacing bugger but he did keep a smile going and his voice stayed friendly.

'Don't know her, Jack.' And that was true. What the hell had happened to her, if it should be that girl? Maybe it had been a mistake, after all, to put Hoppy in the flat.

Lamb said: 'Of course, I didn't tell Helen you might know her, or she could come down and make a scene in the restaurant, and Noisy wouldn't approve.'

'Well, thanks. But I don't know her, anyway. Have you been to the police?' Christ, that could be awkward if they started looking for Mansel and Hoppy.

'Not so far. We know what they'll say – she's old enough to take care of herself. But, if you hear anything, Ron . . . '

'I'll be in touch, Jack. I've got the name.'

When he returned to the table, Doris asked: 'Am I doing the alibi tomorrow, Ron?'

Usually, he would not tell her something like that until he was actually leaving for a job. That had been a drill for a long time. There did not seem any point in holding back now, though. 'I thought we could be doing some decorating together in the little bedroom. I'll pull some wallpaper off before I go,' he said. 'It could do with it.'

Chapter 29

Before dawn on Thursday morning Harpur had a call at home to say the nude body of an unidentified woman in her early twenties had been washed up on the foreshore just east of Valencia Esplanade. Death appeared to be by strangulation: the neck was badly marked and might even be broken. It did not look as if the corpse had been in the water long.

The ringing woke Harpur's daughters, though not Megan, who had learned a long time ago to shut out such interruptions. As he was putting on his shoes downstairs, Hazel appeared in her school raincoat as dressing gown, on her way to make tea. 'What a life,' he said.

'Don't give me that. You love it,' she replied. 'It makes you feel indispensable. Mr Thin Blue Line. What's happened, anyway? Someone's tax disc out of date?'

He telephoned Iles before leaving and told him: the ACC liked to be kept in touch. Harpur said: 'Go back to sleep, sir. I'm sorry to have disturbed you.'

'It's all right. We're up. Sarah's got morning sickness.'

'Congratulations again.'

'My own mother was a martyr to it. You might say her body must have sensed what was on the way. But I see it as a definite proof of lineage.'

'I think I can hear Sarah in the background, sir. Yes, it sounds very Iles.'

'I'll join you down there in due course, Col. Another dark harvest of the sands.'

'Sir?' Harpur knew what he meant, but fuck phraseology at this time of morning.

'Detective Sergeant Avery, ponce.'

'Ah, yes.' A few years ago Ruth's first husband had been

found dead on the foreshore, killed by one of the gangs.

Early light was sneaking through the overcast when Harpur arrived on Valencia Esplanade and picked out a cluster of people at high tide line, some moving about, obviously searching. He walked down. Here and there trails of thin, damp mist hung low on the beach and made the skin of his face cold. The body lay on its back uncovered, amid wreaths of seaweed, nappy liners and a couple of ancient, splintering rail sleepers. He saw what they meant about her not having been in the sea long: anyone could still tell that she had been pretty, and except for the neck marks and a little grazing on her legs from the shingle, her skin seemed undamaged. She was dark, small and thin, with a neat, short nose, and good teeth, exposed now in a horribly over-wide grin. Perhaps she was younger than had been suggested: more like eighteen or nineteen than in her twenties.

Francis Garland was there, lording it in a green tweed suit, which must be his body-on-the-beach gear. 'Found by someone digging for bait, sir,' he said. 'No possible connection.'

Harpur bent down to look at the neck scars.

'I thought manual rather than a ligature,' Garland said.

'Yes? Has the doctor been?'

'We're waiting for him.'

'No sign of clothes?'

'We're searching now it's properly light.'

'Or anything she might have been wrapped in.'

'There's a carpet along the beach. It doesn't look old enough to be ditched.'

'I might take it home later, then.' Harpur stood up.

'They come in about here either from a boat or if they're thrown in from the pier head. Think of Avery.'

'I do.'

'We'll start checking on any missing whores as soon as the day gets under way. She has that sort of figure.'

'Yes? Have you had a look at her underside?'

'I thought wait for the doc, sir.'

'Is he sleeping at home lately? Could be anywhere.' Harpur bent down and with two hands turned the body over. 'No tattoos and no other wounds.' He put her back as she was. 'Let's cover her now, shall we?'

'I'll just wait a moment. Here's the ACC, sir.'

Iles squelched towards them over the mixture of mud and sand wearing gum boots, old jeans and one of his fine, London-made, double-breasted lightweight cream blazers with a rosebud in the buttonhole. He gazed down for a while at the corpse. 'How many lovely young kids have I seen so, Harpur, Garland?'

The ACC liked his questions answered. 'Enough, sir, indeed,' Harpur replied.

'Do you wonder that I would prefer my child to be a son? These beautiful destroyed girls, everything open to the viewer and wild life. But you'll say, what about Avery? I still maintain women bear the brunt.'

'Oh, yes, I heard you and your wife were to be congratulated, sir,' Garland said.

'Just keep out of it, will you,' Iles snarled. 'I've got enough to think about.' Before Aston, Sarah had had a long and fairly well publicised run-out with Francis Garland. Iles bent forward and looked at the neck: 'This is either rope or flex.'

'Flex,' Harpur said.

'Yes. The sort of precocious kid who goes missing and nobody reports it because her parents and friends think she's off somewhere enjoying herself, and well able to survive,' Iles went on.

'Right,' Harpur said.

'So putting a name is hell. That's what I mean about girls: mothers and fathers don't have a clue what's going on inside their heads.' With thumb and finger he tried to close the awful smile, but it was too late. Straightening, Iles went on: 'Col, you'll contradict me about daughters, I'm sure.'

'No, I don't know what's going on inside their heads.'

Iles said: 'Oh, look, I didn't mean—'

'Francis thinks this girl could be a whore,' Harpur said.

'Tentatively,' Garland muttered.

'I knew a whore of that build,' Iles said.

'What I meant, sir,' Garland told him.

'Mind, some like fat whores only. What do you think, Col?'

'I think her name could be Debbie,' Harpur replied.

'You know this whore?' Iles asked.

'I wouldn't say she's a whore.'

'But you know her? Is this someone else out of *Annie Get Your Gun*?'

'I had some information,' Harpur said.

Iles became silent for a while. 'This is information from a source that—'

'I can easily augment it. Find an address, and so on.'

Iles said: 'Listen, Harpur, I know you have your own methods, but we're out here on Sewage Strand at six in the morning and—'

'If I've got the right girl, she could be connected with the Planner Preston business,' Harpur went on. 'She knew Mansel and Hoppy Short. Possibly the others. My feeling is – well, her death could mean it's very close, sir. They've silenced her.'

'If it is Debbie,' Garland objected.

'For Christ's sake get wise, Garland, will you?' Iles replied. 'If he says it's Debbie it's Debbie. What in God's name did Sarah ever see in you?' Iles bent down again and brushed some sand off the girl's shoulders. 'Don't rush the identification, Col. Once you get it we'll have to talk to Mansel and Hoppy, even Planner, and that would stop the job. I want them on the street. I want them in front of Sid Synott and Ambrose Rowles and Cotton. I don't necessarily want them dead there, but I want them on the street and ready to be taken.'

'Yes, but which street?' Harpur replied.

'There is that. But, if they killed this girl, they're acting out of pattern, Col. That's not the old Planner. He could be under unusual pressure. So, maybe he was out of pattern when he cased the banks at Prince Albert Street, too. We could be in the right place after all.'

'If Planner knows about this,' Harpur said, nodding down towards the girl.

'Stay with the banks. It's all we've got. I'll probably come down myself later to see how things are going.'

'I expect you'll come via the park, about lunchtime.'

'What? I might.'

Harpur said: 'The Chief says stay with the banks, too.'

'Does he? I wish you hadn't told me that. It can't be right.'

Garland could make the immediate moves about the girl. Harpur decided he would get in touch with Jack Lamb and Helen later in the day to start his own investigation. Perhaps he had it all wrong. A girl was missing and then a girl's body around the right age turned up on the foreshore: had he jumped too fast to make the connection?

After a canteen breakfast, he went to see the bank party again. It had become a kind of reflex, an absurdity. The ambush was imposing conditions just by being there. Harpur remained certain it was not in the right place, yet he automatically set out to join the men. Iles was probably no better: his brain and knowledge told him it was rot, but he forced himself to believe it could be right. At least the Chief did not enter that kind of duplicity. He backed the Prince Albert Street operation not out of conviction or contrived conviction or automaton habit but to prove to himself and the Force he took no orders from councillor Maurice Tobin. None of it was logical, but the Chief's brand of irrationality was special to him.

At the ambush he found Synott and Cotton and the rest still full of enthusiasm and belief in the operation, flak jackets on, the window watch continuous and tense, all armed men with their holsters open. Harpur tried to act up to the high spirits. That was leadership.

Chapter 30

Another aspect of the ritual was that, on the morning of a job, Ron Preston liked to sit down to a proper breakfast with Doris and Grace. This was part of things, just like the outing the night before. He did not eat much at breakfast, not after the restaurant dinner, but it was important they were all together, chatting away, plenty of tea, no rush. This could help make the two women feel everything would turn out fine and that was important if they had an idea the job was going to be that day, like Doris did now. You had to look after their morale. This was leadership. All right, it was only home life, but it was still leadership. Breakfast time, they could be uninterrupted. Not even Will Rudd came round at that hour.

Preston could not make out whether Doris had told Grace it was today. Probably Doris would not, because Grace could get all sorts of worries if she knew that. But then, Tyrone might have told her, anyway. In the old days, the worries might have been about Preston. He knew they would not be now. They would be about Tyrone in the street today, and then about herself and what happened afterwards. It hurt him, especially when the man was someone like Tyrone, who had nothing to him except a bit of a brain and lawlessness. Like Doris said, though, girls went their own way and the only thing to do was let them get on with it. He made sure he talked a lot to Grace at breakfast today – all kinds of general matters, such as cars and her studies and how the bloody bolshy doctors are kicking up about the National Health. Doris was good, too, munching away at that filthy fibre cereal like normal, and absolutely no sign, in case Grace did not know. They fretted about their bowels. It was a thing with women.

Chapter 31

Mid-morning Harpur had a telephone call at the ambush asking him to ring home. His younger daughter, Jill, answered. She was skipping school to do exam revision.

'There's a man here to see you, Dad.'

'Who?'

'He won't tell me. Just he's got to see you.'

Harpur heard a man's voice in the background say: 'Urgent. Very urgent.'

'Urgent. Very urgent,' Jill said. She sounded fairly calm.

'He's in the house? You let him in?'

'He said it was urgent.'

'Where's Mum?'

'Out.'

Harpur was aware of a sudden rush of people around him and saw that all the ambush had moved to the windows. He picked up the telephone base and went and looked down with them. An armoured van had just pulled up at Barclays.

'This could be it,' Synott said.

'This *is* it,' Cotton muttered.

Harpur moved back. 'Jill, put him on the phone, will you, love?'

He heard her say something and, in the distance, a man reply.

'No, he won't. He says "face to face". Dad, can't you come? Please?'

'What's he look like?'

'Well . . .'

'You can't say, because he's there?'

'That's right.'

'Tall?'

'No.'

Far back in Harpur's police head had been the thought, the

215

noble hope, that Barry Leckwith might have remembered late in the day where his loyalties ought to be, and wanted to come clean. But no, not Leckwith.

'Jill, I'm tied up just now, but I'm going to tell the office to send the nearest patrol car. It will be there in a couple of minutes. Try to stay close to the telephone.'

He rang off, called headquarters and gave the instruction. 'Tell them to go very carefully,' he said. Then he went back to the window. He hardly understood his own thinking. It sprang from the crazy hold this ambush or any other operation would exert once it was in place. He still did not believe anything would happen here, yet felt it completely impossible to leave now, when the men thought the hit imminent. Whether it took place or not was immaterial: if he went they would assume his nerve had crumbled at the possibility. Cometh the hour, ducketh out the brass. Christ, Ruth's husband would see, and talk about it to her and everyone else for ever. Nothing could explain it away properly afterwards.

So, while his daughter of thirteen tried to deal alone with an unknown visitor until help arrived, Harpur stayed stoutly with his lads and mimicked their excitement at this dud. It was a matter of leadership.

Chapter 32

Mansel Billings left his house at just after eleven-thirty a.m. and drove out to the big Asda supermarket car park at Trieve, on the western rim of the city. Preston would be on his way there, too, and they were both going to leave their cars anonymous among the massed vehicles of shoppers. Tyrone, Dean and Hoppy would pick Preston and him up there in the Carlton at twelve twenty, which would give a good hour before they were due to hit the van at Brand's, around one thirty. They must not reach the area too early because five men waiting in a car was neon.

After the raid they would drive four miles and switch to the Granada in a side street, go another three miles to some waste ground and make the share-out in the car. Mansel hoped that would be over as quick as Ron thought. With Dean and Hoppy, it could be a problem. After the cut, it was back to Asda, and Mansel and Preston would leave in their own vehicles. Tyrone and Dean were sticking with the Granada to get back to wherever they wanted, London probably. Mansel did not want to know. Nobody was sure of Hoppy's plans. If he liked, he could go with Tyrone and Dean. They were not mad about it, but said they would take him, and it might not be a bad idea for him to disappear for a while somewhere else. In fact, it would be a bloody good idea. That silly sod would be flashing money no matter how much you told him no, so distance would help. Or Mansel might give him a lift home. Whatever happened, Mansel and Preston had to get back fast. They would be high on the police calling list as soon as the job was known, and they needed to be ready to receive guests, pulse nice and slow and looking very idle and washed-up and unwealthy.

Mansel would visit his mother on the way home and leave his share, Preston's, Wilf Rudd's and Leckwith's in her clothes

217

locker, for which he had a key. It was a risk, but not as big as taking the money to the house today, or trusting it to the mail in that old-style, self-addressed package ploy. Too many fucking postmen had read about that way of shedding gains, and the gains could get shed for keeps. Mansel hoped the police questions and aggro would be finished by evening, so he could slip down to the home and recover the parcels. Ron was going to ditch the Beretta and spare ammunition in the river on his way home. Being Planner, he had made sure the tide would be right.

Mansel parked at Asda and saw Preston arrive soon afterwards. They stayed clear of each other for the moment. After another five minutes the Carlton turned up, Tyrone at the wheel and Dean and Hoppy in the back. Mansel joined them and Preston climbed into the front. At a nice gentle pace they pulled out of the car park and turned towards the job. Mansel saw Preston immediately check the petrol gauge and then he turned and glanced down to see that the boiler suits and balaclavas were ready on the floor at Dean's feet, plus the carrier bags for the shares.

'Like clockwork, Ron,' Mansel said.

'Is there any more information?' Dean asked.

'What information?' Preston replied.

'The take.'

'Just like we heard – maybe three times up on the usual.'

Ron still made it sound like it was a mad sin to be thinking about so much. He had a nice dark suit on and a narrow striped tie, such as the air force or some college with extensive grounds. Planner always had to look good when he was going to work, even if it would all be covered. It made him feel good, an important factor.

'And they're still waiting down at the banks – this Harpur and the killer, Cotton? Staking out nothing?' Dean asked.

'That's the intelligence,' Preston replied.

'Questions,' Hoppy said. 'Stop frothing. Let's just do the bastard, right? And no more fucking dreams, either.'

'Nerves,' Mansel said. 'It's natural. No harm. Better like that. Gets the adrenalin going.'

Preston said: 'You cleaned up the flat?'

'Nearly all the morning doing every surface,' Tyrone replied. 'There won't be prints. We paid cash, and I had gloves on for the notes. And no identity bracelets left behind.'

218

Hoppy liked that and had a laugh. 'No identity bracelets!'

'Where are you boys heading for straight afterwards?' Ron asked Tyrone. 'What I mean, can we get in touch?'

'We can get in touch with you, Ron,' Tyrone replied.

Preston did not seem too pleased with that. Maybe he was thinking about Grace. But he did not push it.

Chapter 33

Harpur watched the armoured van draw away from Barclays.

'False alarm,' Sid Synott said.

People drifted back from the windows, leaving only the look-out detail. Excitement and tension died.

'We on a fiasco here, sir?' Synott asked.

'We do what we can, Sid. Policing's not an exact science.'

Harpur immediately telephoned his house and after an agonising couple of seconds Jill answered. 'They're here,' she said. 'Your heavies. But he won't talk to them. Can't you come?' She fell into a whisper. 'They're getting rough. He's only a little man, Dad. Very twitchy.' Her voice fell. 'One of your finks?'

'Could you bring an officer to the phone, Jill?'

It was someone from Traffic. Harpur did not know him.

'We'll shake an identity out of this object soon, sir,' the man said. 'Sorry about the delay. He's saying he'll talk only to you, and if there are no police about. What's he think you are?'

'Bring him to Prince Albert park. I'll wait there. Tell him we'll be private.'

God, in his situation it was half farce and half dereliction to be thinking of the girl from *Annie*, yet he was determined to be in the park at lunchtime, in case Iles took the chance to smarm his way ahead with her. Sex did not rest. Harpur knew that from his own state, but could have discovered it anyway thinking of the ACC: Iles fretted over Sarah, and pined for family solidarity, but also kept his eyes and options ceaselessly open.

Harpur strolled past where she had eaten her sandwiches but could not spot the squaw today. In a moment, the patrol car pulled up at the park gates and he saw a small, deeply scruffy but nimble-looking man with a baby face get out and come swiftly forward, as if desperate to be clear of the police vehicle. Harpur did not recognise him. They approached each other.

'You wanted to talk to me? I'm Harpur.'

'Well, I know that, don't I?'

'Do you? How?'

'It's like my business to know. Information: I specialise.' He seemed to grow confused. 'But what are you doing here, Mr Harpur?' he asked intently. 'I thought you'd be with the ambush now. You haven't got long. Why I went to your house so early. As to finding your house? My business to know that, too.'

'Who are you? What are you talking about, an ambush?' Jill was right: the man seemed almost overwhelmed by nerves, yet he certainly had the power to alarm.

'But I suppose you've got your good men on it, Mr Harpur – that Cotton, and Sid Synott etcetera, etcetera – so you don't need to be there.'

'Who are you?' Harpur asked. 'What ambush?'

'Come on now, Mr Harpur. You know what ambush, and who I am. Why I'm here, isn't it, and why I went to your house? But you should have come yourself, not sent uniforms. Think it's safe for me to be seen with uniforms, for God's sake? This is peril, even being with you here.' He looked at his watch. 'Three-quarters of an hour.'

'Let's sit on the grass.'

He glanced down at it suspiciously. 'Grass on the grass. You can guess, I suppose – I'm here to do a deal, Mr Harpur. Are you going to say, Too late? Don't. On, please.' He reached out and Harpur thought he was going to grip his hand, but the man seemed to reconsider and pulled back. Though the sun blazed today, he drew his old blue anorak around him more closely, like some sort of cover. 'Look, you know most of it, of course, obviously. But I can give you more pointers. There's still time. Definitely still time. You'd be in touch with your boys on radio. Obviously, I can tell you the armament. Cotton and the others will like to know what they're up against, yes? And I can give you names you might not have. This is valuable, isn't it? There's enough to be worth a deal between us?'

They sat down, near where the girl had been the other day.

'What deal?' Harpur asked.

221

'Well, immunity. That's obvious. You do that sometimes, don't you – for information. I've read about it.'

'Some information. What information?'

'And, then, could be a reward? You see people all right, don't you, Mr Harpur? What I heard. Or a golden thank-you from elsewhere. Think – I'm going to be saving someone a hell of a lot of money. This is a triple load.'

'What information?'

'I told you. Pointers. Who's tooled up, who's not, for instance, and what with. Also, the contingencies for the hit. You know that word? I keep my ears open. But I wouldn't have to go to court, grass in court, would I? That would make me a dead man.'

'Start it from the beginning, just so we can be perfectly clear.' Harpur still had no idea what he might hear but knew he had better not show it.

'All I am is the tipster for them, Mr Harpur. I'm just lucky enough to work for Safemove, aren't I? So, a couple of little leaks? That's the total, honest to God. I'm not big time, not really part of the operation at all. Frankly, I'm not worth your trouble. Well, you see that, don't you? Don't you?'

'Of course.'

'I just let them know about the van and the load and the crew – the increase in the crew – that's all. And the timing, obviously. When they reach Acre Street and Brand's. You know – all the stuff you must have found out for yourself already.'

'In three-quarters of an hour at Brand's?' Jesus, how authentic was this? Did this little grubby wreck look like truth? And how long would it take to switch the ambush up to The Pill?

'A bit less now, isn't it, Mr Harpur?'

'Right.'

'Your boys up at Brand's will be getting tense. You going to be with them?'

'I hope so.'

'I left it late coming to see you, Mr Harpur.'

'You have.' Bloody late.

'All right, I'll tell you straight out, I wasn't going to come. I thought they might still get away with it. I was going to lie low and take my cut, keep right out of it. Well, except for the cut, obviously. And then it was something that happened last night.'

222

'Yes?'

'At Seconds. That restaurant?'

'Yes? Noisy Graham's place?'

'Yes, I know a lot of people. I talk to Noisy now and then. We have little bits of information for each other once in a while, nothing too grand.'

Harpur said urgently: 'So what about it?'

'He told me Planner was in there last night, and Jack Lamb. Now, that really struck me.'

'Jack Lamb? The art dealer?' Harpur wondered whether he could bother to listen any more. Shouldn't he be moving himself and his gun party to Acre Street and Brand's immediately? But how did he judge whether this strange, gabbling figure in the shattered anorak had things right? There was a ripe chance of creating a second useless ambush.

'You can trust me, Mr Harpur, but, look, I've heard gossip re Jack Lamb.' He whispered and pushed his head closer to Harpur's: 'This is, that you use him.'

'Use?'

'What I'm trying to say, and no wish to be disrespectful or intrusive, but he's a source for you, yes? This is a business relationship, you two. Mutual? These things happen, I know. He's in the restaurant because he's watching Planner for you? Am I right, or am I right? Well, of course.'

Harpur tried to sort out what the hell this mystery creature was talking about and gave up. He kept listening, though.

The man began to talk faster, with fewer hesitations. 'Look, I heard this from Noisy Graham and right off all sorts of other things started to make sense. Falling into place? I suddenly saw it. I realised you've been watching Planner non-stop, haven't you? You know just what he's up to. I mean, you're down at *Annie Get Your Gun* – you, personal, down there twice, tailing him. What would you be doing twice at some diabolical punishment like that? So, you've got kids in it, but going twice? This has to be work for you, hasn't it? And then, nearly every time I go to see Ron Preston at his house there's a taxi hanging about and someone keeping down in the back, but watching, really watching. That's you or your boys, too. I usually go in and out the back way at Ron's, but I have a good look around everywhere. Habit. Naturally. So, am I right or am I right? This is surveillance. This is thoroughness. Wilf

Rudd's not stupid. On top, there's this big lad I know for a fact is a cop, know it from way back, name of Leckwith? Barry? He's been up there around Brand's for you, feeling out the ground, hasn't he, fixing the ambush site? Wilf spotted him, too. These old eyes, they see, they know. Where are your boys, Mr Harpur, hidden in Brand's, or one of the old yards in the street, waiting with the reception? Yes, I saw Leckwith there, myself, while I was doing some checking for Planner.

'So, look, Mr Harpur, I hear this from Noisy Graham last night, and suddenly it all goes into place. You know about this operation. You and your boys, such as Cotton and Sid and Laissez Faire Rowles, are expecting it. Well, you see my situation? Do I want to be a part of that? This is like suicide? You know, or you can work it out, where their tip came from, and I'm suddenly looking at eight years as an accessory. I'm clean to date, and I'm proud of that. I don't want anything changing it. So, I say to myself, Get down to Mr Harpur's house right away and put yourself right, Wilf – tell him all the little bits he doesn't know and he'll come to an arrangement, because that's the sort of decent officer he is. I'm not crawling, Mr Harpur, that's how you're regarded, definitely. You're known as someone open to negotiations.'

Wilf Rudd? The name meant nothing to Harpur. If he had no record, it wouldn't. This man's panicky, grab-all mind had misread a handful of signs and finished up with as big an error as the Prince Albert operation. Lamb by total fluke at the restaurant, Harpur girling at the musical a second time, Leckwith probably casing Acre Street for Preston to see it was clear of ambush preparations: all heard about or observed by this quivering lad and distorted, thank God. Yes, thank God. What the recurrent taxi might be outside Preston's house, Harpur did not know, but it had helped, too: certainly no part of police surveillance, but perhaps one of Planner's own people keeping a bit of watch, just to check there was no observation. Mansel? The ever faithful Mansel? Could be. God, Wilf's disclosures and ramblings made Harpur recall for a moment that literary night at home when the speaker sounded off about life's seeming mistakes and part mistakes and digressions and nonsense reasons for decisions, and the importance of getting them into stories. They could all add up, eventually. Chance mattered.

'Yes, I might be able to think about an agreement, Wilf. Co-operation with us always pays.'

'Trouble is, it's so fucking dangerous.'

'So, what extra, Wilf?'

He leaned forward and whispered again, though there was nobody near them on the grass. 'Ron Preston, a Beretta. Hoppy Short and a new boy, Dean Tait, Charter Bulldogs. That neat little thing, five-shot cylinder? Did you know Hoppy was part of it, or this new kid, Dean? And then another new lad, Tyrone Gullen, Wheels.'

'I wondered about Hoppy.'

'He's a head-case and he's got weaponry, plus spare ammo. That's got to be valuable knowledge for you, Mr Harpur. Your boys will want to deal with him early.'

'What sort of cars are we looking for?'

His childlike face folded, as if the whole bargaining apparatus had suddenly come apart, and for a moment Harpur thought he would weep. 'I didn't get the cars. Couldn't. I knew it was important, but they only took them yesterday. If I—'

'Don't worry, Wilf. You can't know everything.'

'Thanks, Mr Harpur. I want to do my best for you, honestly. But five men in a car, three recognisable to your boys? Should be all right, shouldn't it? Look, you can get up to Brand's now and tell your lads what's on the menu, can't you? Or let them know on radio.'

'I'll go myself. Thanks Wilf. You've done damn well.' But he would never know how well: the location and the time.

'Depends whose side you see it from. Planner's not going to back me for a knighthood if he hears I talked to you. Take them all, Mr Harpur. I don't want people around looking for me afterwards.'

Harpur stood and began to run towards his car, speaking on the handset as he went. He was just pulling out in the Viva when he saw Iles, beautifully dressed in his navy blue, inner-Cabinet, pin-stripe suit, making for the park gates and starting to stare about earnestly in his search for the squaw.

Fear closed hard around Harpur as he drove, weighty, intelligent, well-informed, thoughtful fear, based on numbers. If Wilf had it right, they would be three to one up in fire-power, and Harpur did not pride himself as a shot. He was certain to arrive

225

first, before the ambush party could be re-deployed, or whoever was available from headquarters. Why the hell couldn't Rudd have cracked a bit earlier?

The dossier said Preston was a marksman but had never opened fire on a job. Maybe it would stay like that, or maybe not. Maybe he had never needed to until today. It was Harpur's job now to make him need to. Then, Hoppy: to think of Hoppy armed was – was as Wilf said. And, after that, the new man. Dean? His skills and temperament remained unknown, but Preston did not recruit passengers.

Planner was split down the middle. He carried a gun but did not want to use it. He liked his operations to run without violence, but enlisted people who dealt in violence and knew about little else. He prized control and foresight, but brought in help like Hoppy, and maybe these other two, who had no idea of control and foresight, and who were always liable to run riot. If they ran riot today it would be Harpur who was liable to get trampled. As a whizz-kid career continued to unfold fairly nicely, one fate he would not care for was to be killed or wheel-chaired by some nobody thicko like Hoppy Short. If you had to get shot it ought to be by someone who rated.

Chapter 34

They came into Acre Street spot on for time, about fifteen minutes before the van was due, and Tyrone took the Carlton up to the embankment end, turned, drove back and stopped about twenty-five yards from the entrance. They would move closer as soon as the van appeared and approached Brand's. It would be conspicuous to lie nearer before that.

Preston felt certain they had secrecy, but his eyes were everywhere, probing all the parked cars and taking in windows and yard entrances and watching anyone walking. This road still felt like a trap to him, and it would feel more like it once they followed the van into the yard past the gatehouse. He thought of Doris for a couple of seconds – of Doris only, neither of the other two, or the child. It seemed mad to have backed her up at the *Annie* show and now, maybe, let her down here by messing up the job. He would have gone to *Annie* and gone again, even if Carol had not been in it. Of course. Carol was just a very nice plus.

On the way up here, they had stopped for a couple of minutes at a quiet spot and put on the trousers of the boiler suits. When the van showed they would pull up the tops and get into the balaclavas. Preston had told the others to keep their faces turned away from the windows while they waited, in case someone saw and remembered. It was advice he could not follow himself, though. All the time, he had to be looking and checking.

Mansel said: 'Everyone's right on top form. I get that feeling. All of us. Great.'

This was Mansel's team talk and you had to be grateful, but Preston replied: 'It's all planned. Stick to it and we can't go wrong.'

'I'm all right,' Dean said.

'Of course you are,' Mansel told him.

'Balaclavas, I hate them. Like the Russian front,' Dean said.

'Just wear it,' Preston replied. 'Forget the fucking geography.'

'Never seen this road looking better,' Mansel said. 'Enough stuff parked to hide us, but not congested.'

'Shooting – it shouldn't be necessary, not at all,' Preston told them. 'Guns are beautiful and they do their own talking, just by being there. This will all be worked by pressure, known as fright.'

Mansel lifted a wrench from the floor of the Carlton: 'I show them this and my teeth and they collapse.'

'They better,' Hoppy said.

Tyrone stared at the car clock. 'They should be here.'

'Most probably traffic,' Mansel said.

'They'll be here,' Preston told them. Now, he wanted it to go ahead. There had been a time when he hoped something would happen to stop it. That had changed. This was a job, with its own life. It took over. It had taken him over. That needed to happen with every job eventually, or it would not work – leadership again, known also as commitment.

'They're late,' Tyrone said.

'We heard,' Preston replied. He would never understand what Grace saw in him, the glasses and bloody denim, like some kid viscount into drugs. Not a plant from another team, like Hoppy suggested, just feeble. Dean might turn out better after all, even with the tattoos. Grace trusted this Tyrone? Hawaii for two? Oh, sure. But he could drive. Well, drivers were cheap. He would get paid all right, but nothing too elastic, not unless he really did stick with Grace. Then he could do better out of the next one. 'So here we go.'

The van turned into Acre Street. Preston could pick out the three faces in the front, the old, white-haired regular driver, looking as pleased as a pissed vicar. Wilf Rudd had done a bit of research on him and found he and his wife were big in one of the churches as a matter of fact, and that he had a quite passable-looking girlfriend who called at bingo, and a stack of lovely grandchildren. Preston had liked the sound of it because it seemed enough to make him content and want to go on living. It was the bingo girl Preston had been most happy to hear about. If it was only a wife and grandchildren he would not have felt so satisfied, but the girl proved this old character still wanted flavour.

You would have thought he might look worried with all that extra load of cash, but perhaps they all came in for a rise because of the bigger risk. He might be thinking about Hawaii, too.

Preston pulled up the top of the boiler suit and put the balaclava on. The others followed. Tyrone started the engine and, a couple of minutes after the van had checked in at the gatehouse, pulled out from the kerb side very fast and screamed the bit of distance to bring them into the yard. The timing now needed to be so right. They had to enter the yard at the moment just after the van had stopped at the wages office and all the crew were at the rear of the vehicle, doors open and ready to carry the cash in. If they were too early the van would still be locked, and if they were late some of the money would have disappeared into the building and the take would be down. Preston wanted every bit of it done in the yard. He had never seen inside the wages office, and he always needed to know the ground he worked on.

Again they had it exact. The doors were open and the old driver had climbed into the back to start handing out the bags of money to the other two. Preston was first out of the Carlton, the Beretta in his hand, and he heard the car's rear doors shoved open behind him and Mansel yell, 'Pushover.' Then Dean went past, on his way back to silence the gatehouse and make sure nothing was shoved across the exit. He was running hard, his legs fine.

Preston shouted: 'Stand still, the three of you. Just stand still. You'll be all right.'

The old one glared out at him from the back. He should have looked terrified, but his face was full of rage and his eyes full of fight. He was gazing at Preston and the Beretta and Hoppy just behind and Mansel, but this fucking grandfather, standing crouched over the green sacks, just stared out, like he was wondering how he would handle this trouble and put everything right again, like John Wayne. The other two, the younger ones, standing in the yard at the doors of the van, turned and faced Preston and the others and put their hands in the air right off. One of them had a sack in his hand and kept it up there, as if trying to save a kitten from dogs.

And then the old one straightened up and moved at the same time towards the doors. It was a kind of stagger and a kind of leap, his arms spread out like a classy dive off the high board. He was trying to reach the doors and slam them shut and locked. Nobody could have done anything cleverer or better. He still had a brain, as well as guts and grey hair. You would think the money was his, he tried so hard.

But he would not make it. They would reach the van before he could finish the move. Preston had planned in case something like this happened, which was another reason timing had to be spot on, and the car brought up close so there would be no distance to run. This job was over the pavement, but not far over the pavement. He reached the back of the van as the old lad got his hands to one of the doors. There was still that cold shine of hate in his eyes, like he was in charge of law and order for the whole world and had instructions to see off all villains.

'Get back you hero,' Preston shouted and waved with the Beretta, to tell him to move to the front end of the van, out of the way. He had done his bit. The driver did not go. 'Shift,' Preston yelled. Then, out of the corner of his eye he saw Hoppy coming up close behind him on his right and pointing the Bulldog stiff-armed at the old guy and howling curses. Suddenly, Preston had the idea Hoppy thought the guard could fuck it all up and was going to fire to knock him clear of the doors. That was Hoppy. Maybe the driver thought so, too. Preston saw his eyes change and the hatred give way all at once to dread. Christ, it was not the way for an old character like this to go. Preston turned his head and yelled at Hoppy, 'No,' and at the same time brought the Beretta down on his pistol wrist, so the Bulldog fell from his hand, skidded on the ground and went underneath the van.

'Fuck you,' Hoppy screamed.

'Get it,' Preston shouted at him. He was pushing one of the doors back, holding it open against the old man's weight.

'Fuck you,' Hoppy said.

Mansel ducked under and picked up the Bulldog and seemed about to return it to Hoppy, but then decided against. He pushed the wrench he was carrying into Hoppy's hand and then Preston and Hoppy both jumped up into the van and Mansel stayed outside with the other two guards. Preston caught hold of the old man's shoulder with his free hand and dragged him away from the doors, then threw him to the front of the van. He stumbled and fell but was going to get up.

'Don't,' Preston said and pointed the Beretta down at him.

'You've had some luck. Make the most of it. We want you to stay alive.'

He gazed up at Preston, all that same hatred and contempt back there now, but did not move. Preston pulled the carrier bags from the pockets of his boiler suit and threw them to Hoppy. It was a reversal of how things were supposed to go. Mansel should have been keeping the driver quiet, while Hoppy looked after the two outside. Any job, you had to be able to adapt though, and if you took someone like Hoppy you should expect flexibility.

'Hurry,' Preston said.

'Christ, you've done my wrist.'

But he was managing, dropping the small sacks of cash into the carriers and then pushing them towards Mansel at the rear, ready for carrying. If Tyrone had backed the Carlton right up to the van they could have loaded the sacks direct into the boot. But Preston had feared one of the guards might stay in the cabin and reverse ram the car. He had seen that happen on a job. So keep clear.

'Right,' Hoppy said.

Preston backed away from the old man, took three of the carriers and jumped down alongside Mansel. Hoppy followed and he and Mansel carried the other six bags between them. Then Hoppy took a step back and pulled away the sack still held by one of the guards above his head.

'Stay here and you're all right,' Preston shouted to the driver and guards. In the windows of the wages office people were staring out, but nobody came from the building into the yard. It was the way reasonable people behaved when they saw guns. They would all be at 999 calls, though.

'Go,' Preston said, and Hoppy and Mansel ran towards where the Carlton stood with three of its doors open, ready. In a few seconds Preston turned and went after them. He reckoned it had taken four minutes. They would stop at the gatehouse for Dean and be out of the yard in five maximum, even after the bother with Hoppy. That was thirty seconds over what he had planned, but nothing too fatal.

He was almost at the Carlton when he saw a scrap-heap Viva turn into the yard and pull across the access road on the other side of the gatehouse, blocking the way. At once he recognised the driver as Harpur, the big fair head and the body too bulky for the driving seat. It was the kind of vehicle he always used, supposed to be a disguise, but a proclamation.

Tyrone said: 'Jesus, what is it?'

'He's on his own,' Mansel muttered.

Harpur climbed very fast out of the Viva and took cover behind it. He had a pistol in his hand.

'Drive through him,' Hoppy said.

'What?'

'Knock the Viva out of the way.'

'What about Dean?' Tyrone said.

'Fuck Dean,' Hoppy replied. 'You'll need speed. Just go, for Christ's sake. There'll be others with him.'

Tyrone hesitated. The Carlton's engine was running but he seemed dazed. 'Police?' he said. 'They should be in the wrong place.'

Preston heard Harpur shout. 'Planner, Mansel, Hoppy, you're cornered. All of you. Armed police. Throw out your weapons. I repeat, you're cornered.'

'Cornered, yes,' Tyrone said. 'Targets.'

'I still say the bugger's alone,' Mansel muttered.

Preston wanted to believe him. But how could it be? They must have had an alarm.

'Tell Tyrone to go, Planner,' Hoppy yelled.

'No.' Not the way. It might work, but there was a big chance against, and Planner could not operate like that. If they hit the Viva hard enough to shove it clear, both cars could be damaged and useless. The safe exit was to get the Viva for themselves. It meant removing Harpur first. Preston hated shooting, but there could be times when it was the only way. The job took over and set its own rules.

The Carlton was head on to the gatehouse, ready to pick up Dean, and, pushing open the front door, Preston got down behind it and tried for a sight of Harpur around the edge. Lining up the Beretta on the Viva, he waited for a sign of movement.

Harpur shouted again, the same rigmarole. Preston heard Mansel tell Tyrone to open the driver's front door and then Mansel got out from the back and took up the same position on that side. Mansel still had Hoppy's Bulldog. God, how many years was it since Mansel had fired, even in a practice?

Preston saw Harpur move swiftly on his hands and knees

at the front of the Viva, trying for a better view, and Preston immediately fired twice. Perhaps Mansel saw the movement, too, and he opened up as well, all his shots. Or he might just be following Preston, the way he always followed. Harpur seemed to have ignored Preston's volley, but now he fired back at once from the cover of the Viva. There were two shots, and both seemed aimed at Mansel. Preston heard a little shout or a groan from the other side of the car. 'Manse,' he called. 'You all right?' There was no answer. Preston could not look to see what had happened because almost at once, Harpur left the car and dashed for the cover of the gatehouse. That would give him a better angle on the Carlton.

'We're finished,' Tyrone said. 'Tell the copper we're finished. We give up.'

'Get me the Bulldog off the ground,' Hoppy told him. 'Get it from Mansel. He doesn't need it.'

'God, chaos,' Tyrone said.

'Just lean and get it,' Hoppy bellowed. 'We can blast this bugger out of sight. I've got ammo.'

Preston could not spot Harpur any longer. He pushed the door further open to give himself a wider view, and to do it lost some of his cover. And then he suddenly saw movement at the side of the gatehouse and was going to fire again when he made out Dean, backing towards the Carlton. He was backing because he had his Bulldog and another pistol pointed at Harpur, who walked front on, a few steps behind him, his hands in the air. Dean must have surprised him from the gatehouse. Harpur could not have realised there was a man of the team in there. Jesus, Dean could definitely do more than dream. He could capture a cop and take his gun.

'We're all right,' Preston said.

'Kill the sod,' Hoppy shouted.

'No, Dean's got it right. Hostage. There's going to be more here any minute.'

Preston stood and ran to meet the pair. Just as he reached them, he was aware of the noise of other vehicles arriving fast near the entrance to the yard, three, maybe four, and then the sound of people baling out and running. They were here, then. It was disaster. All the signs had been right. He should have steered clear.

When he reached the gatehouse, Dean and Harpur were just about to start crossing the yard to the Carlton. Dean seemed so tied up with managing Harpur that he had not noticed the new crew of police.

'I got the bugger, Ron,' Dean said.

'You've done great. But hang on here a minute.' He made Dean bring Harpur back into the cover of the gatehouse. Through the window, Preston could see the elderly man who had been on duty sitting on the floor in the corner, obviously well scared by Dean. Preston looked around the corner of the gatehouse to discover where the running feet had been going. At first, he made out nobody, but they must have been finding themselves siege positions.

'You can't get out, Planner,' Harpur said. 'Stop now. It's over. Cotton's there, and Synott. You don't want that sort of exit.'

Dean, who was standing alongside him, both the pistols pressed against Harpur's stomach, suddenly raised the Smith and Wesson and hit him across the side of the head with the barrel. 'Keep quiet, bastard face. Keep quiet, you hear.' He screamed it, so if the reinforcements had not known before that some of them were at the gatehouse, they did now.

Preston turned and looked at Harpur. Despite the blow, he had stayed on his feet but blood was running from above his ear down his neck and on to his jacket.

'I thought I'd shot you, Planner,' he said. 'Who was it?'

'Mansel.'

'Mansel?' Harpur sounded bad. 'Mansel doesn't use a gun. I fired at someone who was blasting off all over.'

'Mansel.'

'Jesus.'

'What do you fucking care who it was?' Dean said.

He was going to hit Harpur again with the pistol, but Preston held his arm. 'Go easy. We need him. He's got to be able to walk.'

'It's not like you, Planner, this shambles,' Harpur told him.

'It's not like anything. It's a tragedy. All we can do is run.'

'Run how? Run where?'

'You're letting the bugger destroy you, Ron,' Dean said. 'He talks to you like you're his aunty. Shut up, you sod,' he yelled at Harpur.

This time when the shouting re-started it was with a loud-hailer. 'Preston, you are surrounded by armed police. Put down your weapons, come into the yard and lie down. Armed police. You are surrounded. This is Inspector Chappell. Put down your weapons.'

They all learned from the same instruction book. The voice had come from behind the Viva. Preston could make out a few men there now. There were a Jaguar and a couple of Cavaliers, all unmarked, and he thought he could make out more men behind each. Out near the road stood an empty, long, steel rubbish container waiting for collection, and Preston thought most of the group had cover from that.

Not wanting to give them time to organise, he began to shout: 'We're coming out in two minutes. We've got Harpur. I repeat, we've got Harpur. He'll be with us. He's got two pistols against his skin, so don't provoke. Right? We're going to the Carlton. He's coming into the Carlton with us. We want a clear way out and no pursuit. Move your vehicles. Move the Viva.'

Dean said: 'Great, Ron.'

'Get very close to him,' Preston said. 'These are marksmen we're dealing with.'

When Preston and Dean Tait pressed against him, Harpur said: 'I'm no good to you as a shield, Ron. Robert Cotton would like to hit me, by mistake, but not.'

'What? What you talking about?' Dean asked.

'I've heard a bit about that,' Preston said. 'But we're going.' He shouted again to the siege: 'Right, we're coming now, Harpur first.'

They pushed him out ahead and then placed Harpur between them and the police, Dean still using the two pistols to control him. Preston kept the Beretta pointing up, at the ready. They walked slowly towards the Carlton, very close to each other, like people with their legs tied together in a student stunt race. If Tyrone had been thinking right he might have come to meet them, but Preston could see him, half paralysed with fear behind the wheel. Christ, was he going to be capable of driving out of here and away? And Mansel? Well, Mansel was dead, no question, propped on his knees between the car door and the bodywork. He would be staying on the ground when they moved.

'Good,' Preston said. 'Nice and easy.' He was so close to

Harpur some of the blood from the detective's face had soaked into the arm of the boiler suit and Preston could feel the sticky wetness. Hoppy was leaning out of the Carlton's back window, the Bulldog ready, watching them approach, and clutching two of the carrier bags with his other hand.

Two, maybe three of the police, suddenly changed their position, running from behind the waste bin towards the gatehouse. Preston heard the footsteps and turned to look. Dean turned, too, and must have thought the men were going to come on and try a charge. He yelled something, then raised the Bulldog and fired twice. Preston thought it was too late and the men were probably in cover at the gatehouse, anyway. But immediately came two shots of retaliation from behind the Viva, and he saw Dean go down very fast and helpless and then Harpur grunted and slumped, too, falling hard and heavy against Preston's legs and almost knocking him over. Immediately, Hoppy started firing at the Viva through the Carlton window and there were more shots, from all round – the gatehouse, the Viva, the waste bin. Jesus, they said they never started things, but they certainly liked finishing them. Preston threw down the Beretta and raised his hands.

In a few minutes a couple of police appeared from behind the gatehouse and began walking towards Preston, both of them armed, pistols in front in a two-hand grip. He recognised one of them as Cotton. Preston eased his feet very carefully out from under Harpur's bulk, pushed the balaclava up, and bent down to look at the poor bugger.

'Is he dead?' Cotton shouted.

Chapter 35

Iles said: 'I hear you'll probably get full use of your legs back.'

'Grand.'

'Tell me, Col: any other of your, well, powers affected? I don't know where Cotton was aiming, but I shouldn't think he'd worry if certain impulses fell into a decline.'

'Well, I don't know, sir. It's hard to tell in a hospital bed.'

'Oh? Is it? There's nothing wrong with your hands, is there?'

'But was it Cotton, anyway?'

'Of course. His bullet. Naturally, he says he was firing at Dean Tait. But Tait was already on the way down and Cotton's a marksman. Think of Ditto: two bullets in the same spot.'

'Cotton's had traumatic times, sir. He could have been genuinely a bit off. And, if Tait fell at once, it might have made Cotton miss him and hit me.'

'Generous as ever, Harpur. You were nearer to Cotton, remember? They were using you as a shield. As to trauma, Cotton seemed pretty efficient when we watched him with a gun at the range, didn't he?'

'So, why didn't he kill me?'

'Was he shooting to kill? Preston says Cotton called out, "Is he dead?" about you, but, of course, the tone of voice is infinitely arguable. Regret? Hope? Curiosity? Well, there's an almighty inquiry, naturally. These things have to be looked at. We should be able to shape it as suits, though. I can see you don't want your love life given exposure, and neither do we. Christ, an officer wilfully gunning down another. Not good at all.'

'No, I don't think a lot should be made of it.'

'Out of your hands, Col. Turd Tobin is doing his Trot nut, though not about your wounds, naturally: Tait and Short and

237

Manse Billings. Forensic say you did him. Very tricky shooting, I hear. Only the slightest glimpse around the edge of the door. You knew he had a sick mother, did you?'

'I held back at first. Must have been Preston firing. And then this second, crazy all-out salvo, bullets everywhere. I was afraid for the civilians.'

'None actually in danger, were there? But never mind. It will come out all right, I expect.'

'What about Preston?'

'Fine. Also Grace's boyfriend. Ten years for Preston? Seven for Tyrone? She might wait. We're trying to fix the murdered bird, Debbie, on to Tyrone, as well, so he's well marked early in his career. He says Dean, and so does Preston. They would, since he's dead and can't argue. She was killed for turning talkative and inquisitive. In my heart, I think Hoppy's work. A *jeu d'esprit*.'

'Grace Preston a party to the murder?'

'Almost certainly not. They told her Debbie had to go home.'

'I'm glad she didn't know.'

'As to Tyrone, he probably wouldn't get longer even if we could stick Debbie's death on him, though I'm working at it. Hoppy's down the corridor, not at all well. General ward for him, obviously, not a fucking private room.'

Iles was in uniform, on his way to some official visit. As always when dressed up he looked especially malevolent and self-seeking, his skin seeming to pick up a gleam from the buttons so that it grew iridescent with craftiness.

'Are we nailing Leckwith?' Harpur asked.

'We will. Erogynous is doing the interrogation now.' Iles stood and went to look through the window of Harpur's room at the hospital car park. 'Cotton's keen to visit, Col.'

'Christ, no.'

'What I said. But Lane's in favour. He argues that anyone can make a mistake and should be allowed to proffer due apologies. Well, you know the kind of benign shit that seeps from the Chief. Will Ruth Cotton get in to see you?'

'It's awkward.'

'Well, it is. Megan might be here, too. It confuses the nurses.'

'There's a phone, though,' Harpur said.

Iles was asking, in his way, whether it could go on now, Harpur and Ruth Cotton. Would whatever they had survive a shooting? Lying here, in and out of consciousness and clarity, Harpur had wondered himself. When he was at his clearest, he thought it would. He badly needed to see her. Phones did not do. 'How's Sarah, sir?'

'Wonderful. Do you know, we had neighbours in for Monopoly and subsequent drinks? I mean, Sarah actually stayed for it. She's a home bird now, Col. Aston is finished. And we're talking. Interchange. Not just crossword clues.'

'Great.'

'We might even be able to put Aston away.'

'Great.'

'You don't believe it?'

'Accessory? It's possible.'

'No. That it's over between Sarah and him.'

'I'm sure it is, sir.'

He came away from the window and bending over the bed put his face close to the bandage on Harpur's head: 'You think it's not? Oh, you superior git,' he snarled. 'You'd like to believe you can see everything. You really consider you know women and human nature, don't you? So, why are you laid out there with a drip, lucky to retain your genitalia, and only a detective chief super, if you've got second bloody sight? Have you thought of that at all?' After a while, he quietened, as he usually did. 'Col, I need her, you know.'

'I understand, sir.'

After another pause, his voice rose again. 'I went up to the park again a few times, but never saw that girl with the sandwiches and legs. Something's happened there? Had you got in first?' He strolled back to the window. 'Where is she, Harpur?'

'Try amateur dramatics, sir. I hear from my kids they're doing *West Side Story* next.'

'Yes? Sondheim slop, but I like it. There's a place for us.'

'Sir?'

Iles began to sing. 'It was seminal, *West Side Story*. The musical came of age. Tynan said so.'

'I made a few promises to Wilf Rudd,' Harper told him

'The one who briefed them originally? Lane's very down on him – betrayal of his employers.'

'He put us in the right place, though he didn't know it.'

'Put you.'

239

'I'd have taken you, sir. But you were hotting after the Prince Albert girl at the time.'

'That so? Yes, could be. Oh, I suppose I might be able to put in a word for Rudd.' He raised a hand to shade his eyes, gazing into the car park. 'Here's Megan and the daughters coming, Col. I'll say hello, then move off. I have to go down and see the mother of someone you slaughtered. She's in a state where she doesn't know her arse from her elbow, but there are certain niceties to be observed. I've got a potted plant in the car.'

Megan, Hazel and Jill arrived in Harpur's room a few moments later, the girls obviously unthrilled to see Iles. 'He's greatly better, Megan,' the ACC cried. 'The Chief's talking about a recommendation for some sort of gong. Entirely deserved.'

'How come he almost gets his balls shot off by one of his own people?' Hazel asked. 'Some story behind it. People of dad's age – very dirty habits.'

'There's to be an inquiry,' Iles replied.

Jill said: 'Police shot by police and then an inquiry by police. Family matters.'

'As ever, this will be a fiercely rigorous investigation,' Iles remarked, as he left.